STEALING THE
COUNTESS

STEALING THE COUNTESS

David Housewright

MINOTAUR BOOKS

NEW YORK

STEALING THE COUNTESS. Copyright © 2016 by David Housewright. All rights reserved. Printed in the United States of America. For information, address St. Martin's Press, 175 Fifth Avenue, New York, N.Y. 10010.

www.minotaurbooks.com

The Library of Congress Cataloging-in-Publication Data is available upon request

ISBN 978-1-250-04966-7 (hardcover)
ISBN 978-1-4668-5064-4 (e-book)

Our books may be purchased in bulk for promotional, educational, or business use. Please contact your local bookseller or the Macmillan Corporate and Premium Sales Department at 1-800-221-7945, extension 5442, or by e-mail at MacmillanSpecialMarkets@macmillan.com.

First Edition: May 2016

10 9 8 7 6 5 4 3 2 1

RENÉE, ALWAYS

ACKNOWLEDGMENTS

The author wishes to acknowledge his debt to Hannah Braaten, India Cooper; Pat Donnelly, Former's Insurance; Tammi Fredrickson, Keith Kahla; Bill Peterson, Apostle Island Marina; Alison J. Picard, Dr. James Schlaefer, and Renée Valois.

STEALING THE
COUNTESS

ONE

The Maestro insisted that it wasn't his fault.

"What was I supposed to do?" he asked. "Handcuff her to my wrist? Hire armed guards to escort us to rehearsals, to concert halls? You can't live like that. It's untenable. The fact is, she was essential to me, to my profession. She was an extension of myself. I took her to every major city in the world. It was either that or quit my job. Of course, I was always aware of my surroundings when she was with me. I never let her out of my sight. But if you worried about someone running off with her, if you gave in to paranoia, you'd never leave the house."

"The fact remains," I said. "Someone stole your four-million-dollar Stradivarius violin."

"It wasn't my fault."

"According to the newspaper, it was taken from the room in the bed-and-breakfast you were staying at while you went for a walk."

"Should I have taken her with me?" he asked again. "Walk the streets with her slung over my shoulder? People say I was careless. And clueless, I heard that, too. A policeman claimed I was 'criminally negligent.' I don't think my behavior was unreasonable at all. I even had a GPS transmitter embedded in the violin case, although . . ." His voice became softer. "They found the case in the street. It was supposed to be fun, McKenzie. A concert in the park in my hometown, with all my childhood friends in attendance to see how well I had done since I left for the big city. Fun . . ."

"Why are you telling me all this?"

Paul Duclos leaned back in his chair and stared at me as if he were suddenly aware that he was speaking to a dull and listless child. We were sitting at a window table in the Great Waters Brewing Company, about a stone's throw, if you had a good arm, from where the offices and rehearsal space for the St. Paul Chamber Orchestra were located in the Hamm Building. I was drinking a house ale that was a tad too hoppy for my taste, while the Maestro nursed a coffee, black, the way God intended. I liked him partly because of the way he drank his coffee but mostly because he was a world-renowned concert violinist who was now working as an artistic partner with the SPCO, which meant he also conducted. I've always had a soft spot for hometown musicians.

But then he swung his fist down like a judge's gavel and started pounding the tabletop. Conversation ceased. Customers and waitstaff turned to face him. He spoke at a volume loud enough to be heard by anyone within fifty feet.

"I expect you to get her back," he said.

"What's the magic word?"

The Maestro stared at me some more. A smile tugged at the corners of his mouth, and he began to glance around the tavern. Some customers met his gaze; others looked away as if embarrassed. He lowered his voice.

"I'm sorry," he said. "McKenzie. Please. Please bring her back to me."

"A crime like this—the FBI has a special unit, an Art Crime Team, that's probably already on the case, not to mention investigators from the state and county cops. They won't like it if a civilian gets involved. How did you get my name, anyway?"

"Vincent Donatucci called me."

"Midwest Farmers Insurance Group—are they the ones who insured the violin?"

"Yes."

"Mr. Donatucci is their chief investigator. He's very good at his job. I'm surprised he'd give up my name. He wouldn't want me to meddle, either."

"He *was* their chief investigator. They retired him because of his age."

"I didn't know that. Still . . ."

"He told me that the Stradivarius might never be recovered now because of what the insurance company did, what the foundation did. However, he said someone acting independently might be able to . . ."

"What did the insurance company do?"

"Donatucci said no one steals a Stradivarius worth four million dollars with the idea that they're going to pawn her. She's famous. She even has a name. Countess Borromeo. No art dealer would dare touch her, she's so recognizable. Instead . . . Donatucci said this isn't the first time a Strad has been stolen. After a time, the thieves would usually send in mules—that's the word he used, mules—that would pretend to find the violin and return it to the rightful owners for the reward, no questions asked. Except the insurance company, at the insistence of the foundation, took that option off the table. It's still offering a reward—$250,000—but it specified that it won't release the money unless there's a conviction. Someone needs to be arrested. Someone needs to go to jail. This greatly reduces the profit incentive while increasing the risk, according to Donatucci. He said the thieves are now just as likely to toss the violin into the nearest Dumpster as hang on to her. Cut their losses, he said."

"They could wait until the investigation dies down," I said. "Try to cut a deal on the quiet, although—why would Midwest do that?"

"The foundation—"

"What foundation?"

"Georges and Adrienne Peyroux Foundation for the Arts. What you need to appreciate, McKenzie, is that I don't actually own the Countess. The foundation owns her. It's just lending her to me. Not many musicians, even highly successful ones, can afford to own a really fine violin. That's where wealthy music benefactors step in. An investor or a foundation with an interest in the arts will secure an instrument and entrust it to an artist. That's how Countess Borromeo and I became companions. I was starting to build a reputation for myself, especially in Europe, and representatives from the foundation asked if I would be interested in using their Strad. They chose me because I have a relationship with the community. I grew up in Bayfield, Wisconsin. I attended the University of Minnesota before transferring to Juilliard.

"I leapt at the opportunity, of course. It's been a very satisfying relationship on many levels. It was tough at first, McKenzie, making it work, don't be mistaken about that. The Countess has a way of maximizing your strengths and illuminating your weaknesses. The most difficult part was learning how to relax with her in my hands; stop working so hard, to just let her be herself. In the past twelve years, though, she and I have become such good and loyal friends. In many ways she's a part of me now. She knows my moods so well. And she's ungodly beautiful. It's the wood, McKenzie. Gorgeous maple. So smooth, so sensual . . ."

Is he talking about a violin or a girl? my inner voice asked.

"You call her Countess Borromeo?"

"A Stradivarius nearly always goes by the name of a previous owner. This one belonged to Count Borromeo of Milan, Italy, who presented it to his wife, Celia Grillo Borromeo, the famous mathematician and scientist, somewhere around 1760."

"What does the Peyroux Foundation get out of the deal?"

"There's the financial investment of owning the Strad, of course—it'll never go down in value, that's for certain. It also benefits from the private parties and fund-raisers I play for them. That's how I met my wife, you know."

"Your wife?"

I wonder if her wood is smooth and sensual.

"Renée, Renée Marie Peyroux," the Maestro said. "She runs the foundation now. She took control when her father passed. She's adamant, too. Nothing I can say will change her mind. Renée simply will not reward the thieves for stealing from her—that's the way she looks at it. But McKenzie, I will."

"You will what?"

"I'll pay $250,000 for the safe return of the Countess. No questions asked. Donatucci said it's the only way."

"When did you speak to him?" I asked.

"Saturday afternoon. He called right after he heard what Renée and the insurance company were going to do. He was just as upset as I was. It was he who suggested that I offer a reward of my own. He told me to call you. He said you were dependable."

"Opinions differ."

"McKenzie . . ."

"Mr. Donatucci wants you to pay off the thieves?"

"It happens every day, that's what Donatucci said."

"What would your wife say?"

"I don't care. Actually, I care a great deal, but that's for later. I'll think of something, later. Right now, all I want, all I need, is to have the violin returned to me. Will you help?"

"Help you what? Be specific."

"Take the money to Bayfield, find out who stole the Strad, and buy it back."

Hell no, my inner voice shouted.

"Let me think about it," I said aloud.

What's to think about?

"I'm going to need some legal advice before I decide."

"Please, McKenzie," the Maestro said. "I'll do anything to bring the Countess Borromeo home safely."

"Yeah, well, it's the 'I'll do anything' part that makes me nervous."

I said good-bye to Duclos outside the Hamm Building, crossed the square to Wabasha Street, and walked north toward the Fitzgerald Theater, where Garrison Keillor holds forth on *A Prairie Home Companion*—or so I've been told. I've never actually listened to the program myself. As I approached my car, I pulled out a cell phone, tapped CONTACTS, and scrolled down until I found the icon for G. K. Bonalay. Her admin answered on the third ring.

"McKenzie, is that you?" she asked.

"Caller ID never lies."

"Is this an emergency? Are you in custody?"

"Ahh, no and no."

The way she exhaled suggested that she had been holding her breath.

"You haven't been arrested," she said. "That's good."

"Why would you think—"

"Let's face it; the only time you call G. K. is when you're in trouble."

"The only time anyone calls a lawyer is when they're in trouble."

"There's trouble and then there's trouble."

"May I please speak to Genevieve?"

"She's meeting with a client."

"Is the client in trouble?"

"No one's accused him of murder like the last time you called, if that's what you mean."

"That was a simple misunderstanding."

"I'll have G. K. return your call as soon as she's done—wait.

I think the meeting's breaking up. Let me put you on hold for a sec."

It was closer to three minutes. I was unlocking my car when G. K. Bonalay came on the line.

"McKenzie, how are you?" she said.

"Very well, thank you. How 'bout yourself?"

"Overworked and underpaid."

"You should complain to the boss."

"That tyrannical bitch? There's no talking to her."

"She seemed so reasonable the first time we met."

"I take it from all this breezy chitchat that you really aren't in trouble for a change."

"No, and I would like to keep it that way."

"That's so responsible of you, I don't know what to say."

"Oh, for God's sake."

"What is it this time?"

I explained in detail, leaving nothing out. It was one of the reasons G. K. and I got along so well. We've trusted each other implicitly ever since I helped prove one of her clients was innocent of murder. She once told me I would be amazed at how often clients lie to their attorneys and how often attorneys lie to their clients. That's why she started her own law firm a few years back, to cut down on the lies.

"Don't do it," G. K. said.

"That's your informed legal advice?"

"What you're planning is against the law. Listen, McKenzie, from what you're telling me, even though Duclos doesn't actually own the violin, he's entitled to possession, so he's cool. You, the middleman, though—it's a felony to knowingly purchase stolen property, to be in possession of stolen property. We're talking about a year and a day in prison. You would lose your license to work as a private investigator, too, if you actually had a license."

"If I was convicted, being an ex-cop and all, wouldn't it be more likely that I would just receive a fine?"

"It's still a felony conviction. Writing a damn check isn't going to make it go away. Another thing—the prosecutor—he's going to ask who sold you the stolen property. Are you going to tell him?"

"Probably not."

"Then they'll not only nail you for possession, they might tack on a charge of aiding an offender after the fact; they'll claim in court that you're just as guilty as if you were involved in the actual theft. They'll be right, too."

"Uh-huh."

"You're not listening."

"I am, I am listening."

"But you're going to do it anyway, aren't you?"

"I haven't decided yet. Right now, I'm thinking no."

"Sure you are."

You're probably wondering what a lifelong St. Paul boy like me is doing living in a high-rise condominium in downtown Minneapolis. My answer is simple and probably not all that original—there's this girl. Woman, actually. Her name is Nina Truhler. She has short black hair, the loveliest pale blue eyes I've ever seen, and a figure that she fights for in gymnasiums and fitness centers at least four times a week. Plus, she owns a jazz joint called Rickie's where I'm allowed to drink expensive alcohol and listen to tunes for free.

I found her sitting on a stool at the island in the kitchen area absentmindedly popping green grapes into her mouth while she read the latest Regency romance novel by Julie Klassen.

"Hey," she said without looking at me.

"Hey," I answered.

"There's mail. Someone sent you an invitation to something."

I found the envelope on the desk in the library area near the door. The way the condo is laid out, we don't have rooms so much as areas—dining area, TV area, a music area where Nina's Steinway stands. The entire north wall is made of tinted floor-to-ceiling glass with a dramatic view of the Mississippi River. If that weren't enough, there is a sliding glass door built into the wall that leads to a balcony. The south wall features floor-to-ceiling bookcases that turn at the east wall and follow it to a large brick fireplace. To the left of the fireplace is a door that leads to a small guest bedroom with its own full bath. Against the west wall and elevated three steps above the living area is the kitchen area. Beyond that is a master bedroom that also features floor-to-ceiling windows, a huge walk-in closet, a bathroom with double sinks, a glass-enclosed shower, and a storage area with enough room to park a car. Be it ever so humble . . .

I carried the envelope across the condo and mounted the kitchen-area steps. Nina set down her book, wiped her fingers on her jeans, and kissed me.

"What did the Maestro want?" she asked.

"What maestro?"

The question came from the entrance to the guest room; or rather, I should say, from the room commandeered by Nina's daughter, who was taking the summer off from Tulane University.

"Paul Duclos," I said.

"Paul Duclos? You know Paul Duclos? The violin master? That is so cool."

By then Erica was standing at the island. She was two inches taller than Nina. Beyond that, they looked remarkably similar. I once compared photographs of Nina and Erica when they were both nineteen. Clothes, hairstyle, and Nina's remarkable eyes were the only way to tell them apart. Scary. Which isn't to say they resembled twins, or even sisters, today. More like a beautiful young lady standing next to her equally beautiful mother.

"How do you know Paul Duclos?" Erica asked.

"A mutual friend wants me to do a favor for him."

"Then you must. You must."

"How do you know this man?" Nina asked.

"Mother," Erica said. She added an eye-roll and a deep sigh. "He's only one of the greatest violinists in the whole world, that's all."

"You listen to classical music?" I asked. "Since when?"

"McKenzie." She gave me an eye-roll and deep sigh, too, but I figured that was just to be polite. "There's more to life than jazz."

"I listen to all kinds of music."

"Like what?"

"Like, ahh . . . opera."

"Oh, yeah? Name a female opera singer."

"Maria Callas."

"Everyone knows Maria Callas. Name three more."

"Dawn Upshaw, Cecilia Bartoli, Kathleen Battle, Renée Fleming, and Audra McDonald."

"I said three."

Nina snickered around a grape while I opened the envelope. She was correct; it was the size and shape of an invitation to a wedding or a charity event, and it contained a folded white card. Only the cover was blank. I opened it and read what was inside.

"What favor are you going to do for the Maestro?" Erica asked.

"I'm not sure I'm going to do it yet."

"What?"

"He wants me to retrieve his stolen Stradivarius."

"Someone swiped the Countess Borromeo?"

"How do you know these things?"

"That's horrible. For a musician like Paul Duclos, that's like losing his, his . . ."

"Lover?"

The heads of both women came up; their eyes snapped on me.

"Just something that popped into my head while I was chatting with him," I said.

"Are you going to do it?" Erica asked. "Help him, I mean?"

"Like I said, I haven't decided. Although . . ."

I handed the card to Nina. She read it silently and then aloud. "If you're wise, you will not join the hunt for the stolen Stradivarius. Consider this your only warning."

"Wait," Erica said. "What?"

"It gets better."

I handed the envelope to Nina. There was a yellow strip with my current address covering the address that was originally written there with the words FORWARD TO stamped across the top.

"It was mailed to your house on Hoyt Avenue in St. Paul," Nina said. "Whoever sent it didn't know we moved here in January."

"The postmark," I said.

"Bayfield, Wisconsin."

"The Stradivarius was stolen four days ago." I held up four fingers in case there was any confusion. "In Bayfield. This was mailed on Saturday and delivered on Monday."

"That doesn't make sense," Erica said. "How could the thieves know you were going after the violin three days before Duclos asked you to?"

"What makes you think the card was sent by the thieves?"

"Someone doesn't want you to chase the Countess."

"On the contrary, sweetie. Whoever sent it knows this is exactly the kind of thing that would convince me to do it."

"It's not a warning," Nina said. She popped another grape into her mouth. "Like I said, it's an invitation."

TWO

I found Vincent Donatucci kneeling on a foam cushion at the edge of his garden, a three-prong tiller in his hand. There was a small plastic bucket next to him. There were a few weeds inside, but not many.

"I never thought of you as a gardener," I said.

He responded as if he knew I was standing behind him all the time, didn't even turn his head.

"A man needs to keep busy," Donatucci said. "Here."

He offered his arm. I moved quickly to his side and helped him to his feet. I was prepared to assist him to a couple of lawn chairs overlooking the garden, but he shoved my arm away.

"I can walk," he said.

Still, I was surprised by how ancient he seemed. I knew he was old when I first met him. That was nearly eight years ago. He had asked many questions, and even though he didn't like my answers, he eventually handed over a check for $3,128,584.50—my compensation for capturing an astonishingly enterprising embezzler and returning the money he stole to the insurance company.

I saw him again when he recruited me to help recover the

Jade Lily, an artifact stolen from a Minneapolis art museum. Both times I thought that he was far too old for the job—the way he grunted and sighed as he moved, his face so deeply wrinkled that I wondered how he shaved. Now he looked as if he had given up shaving altogether.

He shuffled to a lawn chair and sat as if he were afraid of breaking something.

"I take it you've spoken to Paul Duclos," he said. "Else why would you be here?"

"How do you know him?"

"Through Midwest. I'm the one who insisted he put a GPS chip in his violin case. I wanted to attach one to the inside of the violin, but he refused. Something about acoustics. Also gave him some rules about carrying the damn thing that he apparently ignored. So?"

Donatucci looked up at me from the chair and smiled. Both his eyes and voice were clear. I sat in the chair next to him.

"So?" he repeated. "What do you think?"

"About what?"

"Don't make me work for it, McKenzie. It's too damn hot. Besides, you wouldn't be here if you weren't interested."

"I'm told you're not with Midwest anymore."

"Mandatory retirement. Sonsuvbitches look at a man's age, how much time he spends in the restroom, and completely ignore the quality of his mind, the clarity of his thinking. I was the smartest person in the room. Management didn't care. All they do is crunch numbers."

"You say that as if it comes as a surprise. It was an insurance company, for God's sake. What did you expect?"

"I expected better, especially considering the amount of money I've saved them over the years. Tens of millions. I'm gonna save 'em some more, too. Or I should say, you are."

"I am? Why?"

"Cuz it's the right thing to do."

"C'mon."

"What they're doing—I've never wanted to negotiate with criminals. I wanted to see them go to jail. Every mother's son. Believe me."

"Oh, I believe you."

"How much time did Teachwell do for embezzling all that cash?"

"Many years."

"Arrest them all, I say. But first—do you think it's some kind of moral victory to refuse to negotiate with criminals? 'Look at us. Aren't we virtuous?' That's what Midwest was saying when they made the announcement that they wouldn't pay a reward for the Stradivarius unless there was a conviction. Think that'll deter the thieves? Think they'll throw their hands in the air and admit defeat? Give back the violin and go straight? Puhleez.

"The Stradivarius should come first. That's what matters. Dammit, McKenzie, it's irreplaceable. Priceless. You want to see it burned in someone's fireplace? Dammit. They don't even seem to care if they get it back, happy to write a four-million-dollar check to the Peyroux Foundation to cover their loss. In my day that was the last thing we wanted to do. Instead, we did whatever was necessary to recover what was stolen. Sometimes that meant making deals with crooks. I told them, too. Called Midwest when they went public with their refusal to negotiate. Spoke to my replacement. They wouldn't listen. I'm just an old man. Why listen to me? You, though . . ."

"What about me?"

"Millionaire ex-cop philanthropist tryin' to make the world a better place. Isn't that what you do with your time these days? Isn't that why you helped me go after the Jade Lily? You're a do-gooder, McKenzie. Here's your chance to do some more."

"Do what exactly?"

"Duclos didn't say? He's desperate to get the violin back. He thinks of it as a living thing."

"I got that impression."

"He's willing to pay. He's going to match the reward Midwest Farmers is offering, $250,000. Only with him, it'll be no questions asked. All he needs is a go-between. Someone to take the money up to Bayfield, let it be known that he's willing to deal, wait for the thieves to come forward."

"Do you really believe the thieves are still in Bayfield?"

"No, but it's the logical place to start."

"I don't know. Seems to me a guy could get into a lot of trouble doing this sort of thing."

"When did you start worrying about a little trouble?"

"A lot, Mr. Donatucci. I said 'a lot of trouble.' You still haven't explained why you care."

"The youngster they replaced me with, she's . . . she's not ready."

"She?"

"A girl, McKenzie. They replaced me with a girl."

Outrageous, my inner voice said.

"I'm surprised you feel that way," I said aloud.

"You don't get it."

I've known an awful lot of very smart women in my time, including the one I sleep with, so he was right, I didn't get it.

"What bothers me isn't that she's a female," Donatucci said. "It's that she's so damn . . ."

"Young?"

"Exactly."

"You want to show her up."

"No, no, no, McKenzie. I like her. Maryanne Altavilla. I hired her; gave her a job right out of college. Trained her, too. It's the fucking number crunchers who think that I'm too old to do the job but that a young girl can—they're the ones I want to show up."

"Do you think you'll accomplish that by returning the Strad to its rightful owner?"

"They'll look awfully dumb, won't they, standin' there with idiot expressions on their faces when we hand the violin back to Duclos? The world might not hear of it, the media, but the people in the industry, they'll get the word and they'll laugh."

"That'll teach 'em."

"Damn right," Donatucci said.

"Strike a blow for the AARP generation."

"Why not?"

Why not, indeed? my inner voice asked. *You're never going to get old, and neither will Nina, but all your friends will.*

"I need to know more about the theft," I said.

"I should hope so. Here."

Donatucci offered me his arm again, and I helped him up.

I followed him inside his house. Donatucci had been married, but his wife had passed before we met, and whatever housekeeping skills she instilled in him had dissipated over the years for lack of use. Which isn't to suggest the man was sloppy. He merely lived the bachelor life, always asking why he should find a drawer for something when he could pile it near at hand should he need it. Like the tourist handouts he must have acquired in Philadelphia that were strewn across his dining room table; an expired admission ticket told me he took a tour of Independence Hall at 10:00 A.M. nine days ago. He saw me looking at it.

"Wanted to see where it all began," Donatucci said. "Liberty Bell is a lot smaller than I thought it'd be." He dismissed the literature with a gesture. "Shoulda done it years ago. When I was young."

I might have said something consolatory about age and never being too old, only he was gazing at a photograph of his wife at the time, and I let it slide.

Instead of in the dining room, Donatucci sat me at his empty kitchen table. His age and employment status notwithstanding, he must have maintained his contacts, because he was able to carefully stack copies of reports from the Bayfield Police Department, the Bayfield Sheriff's Department, the Wisconsin Division of Criminal Investigation, and even the FBI in a neat pile in front of me. He also had a detailed statement given by Duclos to the investigators at Midwest Farmers. Taken together, they formed the basis of the story he told me . . .

Twelve years ago, Duclos received a curious e-mail. A woman named Renée Peyroux wrote that the foundation she represented—that her family had established decades earlier— was in the process of purchasing a newly discovered Stradivarius violin known as the Countess Borromeo. She asked if he would be interested in playing it.

This was not unusual. Two or three times a year, the Maestro received e-mails from people and organizations about the discovery of a Stradivarius. It was typical of someone who had achieved his status: two degrees from Juilliard, first violin and concertmaster with the National Symphony Orchestra in Washington, D.C., founding member of the Dresden Quartet, and sought-after soloist appearing with symphonies around the world. Most of the e-mails were wishful thinking if not utter nonsense. The exceptional genius and workaholic Antonio Stradivari created 540 violins—that the world has been able to catalog—of such notable and dazzling quality that they're still considered to be the finest musical instruments ever built 280 years following his death. People have been *discovering* them in the dusty corners of attics and at flea markets ever since.

Yet Renée's e-mail was legitimate. The Georges and Adrienne Peyroux Foundation for the Arts did acquire the Countess Borromeo, it did loan her to Duclos with virtually no conditions amid much fanfare, and he did play her on many of the world's greatest stages. He actually won a Grammy for the classical music album *Songs of the Countess*. At the same time, he was busy wooing the fabulously wealthy Renée Marie Peyroux. Two years after they met, Duclos and Renée married.

They were in their early fifties at the time, and it was the first marriage for both of them; she kept her maiden name. When Georges and Adrienne passed within six months of each other, the couple settled in the Twin Cities, where Renée grew up, and she took control of the foundation. A couple of years later, Duclos became a soloist and artistic partner with the St. Paul Chamber Orchestra.

The SPCO was the only full-time professional chamber orchestra in the country, performing 130 concerts a year and enjoying two million weekly radio listeners. It was in the middle of its summer tour when the Maestro received a call. Would Bayfield, Wisconsin's favorite son consider playing in the city's Concert in the Park Series? Duclos happily accepted the invitation. It sounded like fun.

"That's what he told me, too," I said. "That it was supposed to be fun."

Donatucci ignored my interruption and was about to continue reciting his story when I stopped him again.

"When was the call made?" I asked.

"Two weeks before the concert. The scheduled act had to cancel, and someone said, 'Hey, why don't we call the great Maestro? What could it hurt?'"

The Bayfield appearance had fit neatly into Duclos's calendar. The SPCO had a performance scheduled at the Marcus Center for the Performing Arts in Milwaukee on Tuesday night. He would drive to Bayfield, arriving on Wednesday afternoon, play the concert Thursday evening, and drive the two hours to Duluth, Minnesota, Friday morning, arriving with plenty of time to rejoin the SPCO and rehearse for that evening's performance at Symphony Hall.

The Maestro arrived early Wednesday afternoon as scheduled, stopping at City Hall as requested, where he was welcomed as a conquering hero. "Those were his words, not mine," Donatucci said.

The mayor was there to greet him, as were members of the common council, the chamber of commerce, and the visitors' bureau that had arranged the concert. He was led to the New Queen Anne Victorian Mansion Bed and Breakfast, where he was installed in the Queen Anne Suite on the third floor, the best room in the house, with a splendid view of the city. Afterward, he was treated to dinner at the Hill House Restaurant, where he was reacquainted with several old friends.

"Where was the violin during all of this?" I asked.

"Locked in his room at the B&B."

Thursday afternoon, Duclos met with Geoff Pascoe, the man who would accompany him during the concert. Pascoe was also a local boy, born and raised in Superior, Wisconsin. Duclos liked him, said he had nice technique. After the rehearsal, Duclos left Bayfield to clear his head. "His words, again."

"The Countess?" I asked.

"He took her with him."

"People never saw him carrying it around on the street, then."

"If they did, it was only briefly."

Eventually, Duclos returned to Bayfield, and without much ado, the concert began. It was played from a large gazebo in the corner of Memorial Park between downtown Bayfield and the marina, with Lake Superior glistening beyond. It began at seven and lasted until after sunset, about nine. Several thousand people were there; there's no way of knowing the exact number. Everyone was convinced, though, that it was the largest turnout ever for a Concert in the Park, and the biggest crowd to hit the city with the exception of its annual Apple Festival.

Afterward, Duclos, Pascoe, and just about everyone who was anyone in Bayfield retired to the Hill House for an after-concert party. Duclos stayed until about eleven. He reminded his guests that he had to get up early the next day and drive to Duluth but thanked one and all for their kindness and generosity.

Duclos and the Countess Borromeo returned to the Queen

Anne. He went to bed. The next morning he rose early. He said he took a walk through the mostly empty streets of Bayfield. He returned to the B&B for breakfast at eight, went to his room, began to pack for his trip, and that's when he discovered that the Stradivarius was missing.

"Was it there *before* he took his walk?" I asked.

"He said he didn't notice."

Duclos panicked. He called Connor Rasmussen, the owner of the Queen Anne, and together they called the police. Unfortunately, the Bayfield police officer who responded to the complaint was unimpressed, as indicated by the questions he asked. "How do you spell Stradivarius? What the fuck is a Stradivarius? How could a violin, I don't care what it's called, be worth four million dollars?"

Fortunately, Rasmussen made a call to the Bayfield County sheriff, a man he knew personally, and explained what happened. The sheriff called the Bayfield chief of police. The Bayfield chief of police—his name was Jeremy Neville—called the officer on his cell phone. The conversation went something like this:

"Officer, this is Chief Neville. What do you have?"

"Got a guy here says someone stole his fiddle."

"Listen to me very carefully. This is not a fiddle. This is a fucking multimillion-dollar musical instrument. Secure the crime scene; don't touch anything."

The investigation gained a little momentum after that. Within twenty minutes both the chief and the Bayfield County sheriff were at the scene. Ninety minutes later, investigators from the Wisconsin DCI arrived, and the FBI was notified. A bulletin was issued, searches were made, guests were interviewed, the crime scene was processed.

"What did they come up with?" I asked.

Donatucci tapped the reports in front of me.

"A lot of paper," he said.

"I'd be approaching the case four days late, five if I start to-morrow. Do you honestly believe I'll find anything that they missed?"

"It's possible. Fresh eyes. People in town settling down, not as cautious. Besides, the cops carry badges. Most people are nervous if not downright afraid to talk to them, including the innocent. You'll be carrying something that'll make them much more willing to cooperate."

"What's that?"

"Two hundred and fifty thousand dollars."

Except you'd be an idiot to actually carry it around with you, my inner voice said. *Not unlike leaving a priceless violin in your bedroom while you take a stroll.*

"So?" Donatucci said. "Are you in?"

It was my turn to tap the reports.

"I'm going to take these with me," I said.

"I'd be disappointed if you didn't."

"I'll leave tomorrow morning."

"Have a safe trip. Keep in touch."

"Why don't you come with me?"

The idea seemed to appeal to him at first, but after a brief hesitation Donatucci began shaking his head.

"It'll be fun," I said. "I've been to Bayfield before. There's this bar with a verandah on the lakeshore. We can lounge there in between interviews. Drink craft beers. Catch some rays. Watch the girls."

"I know the place"—he hesitated for a moment before continuing—"I haven't been there for years, but I know the place you're talking about."

Uh-huh.

"You know, Mr. Donatucci, you didn't need to send a formal invitation, trying to use reverse psychology to get me to take the job," I said. "All you had to do was pick up a phone."

"I have no idea what you're talking about."

Of course not.

"I mean it," I said. "Come with me."

"I'd just slow you down."

"I'm not asking you to jog down the beach. Just hang out. I could always use some good advice."

"My advice? Don't ever get old."

I dropped the files on the front seat of my car and made a call before driving off. I was a little surprised when Genevieve answered her own phone, reciting, "Bonalay and Associates, Attorneys at Law."

"G. K.," I said, "it's me."

"I knew it, McKenzie. You're going to ignore my advice and go after the violin."

"What if I had a letter stating that I was acting on the Maestro's behalf?"

"Duclos doesn't own the violin."

"Yes, but you said he's entitled to possession, so . . ."

"A letter won't help if the county attorney decides to prosecute."

"That's the thing, though. If I do recover the violin, I doubt either the foundation or the insurance company will press charges."

"It doesn't work that way. The way the state looks at it, the crime wasn't committed against the foundation; it was committed against its citizens. If the prosecutor wants the case to go forward, it's going forward."

"Yeah, but if the foundation refuses to cooperate . . ."

"That makes it tougher. On the other hand, if the prosecutor calls out the foundation in the media for dealing with criminals—tell me, do you think they'll stand up to all the bad publicity just to protect you?"

I didn't know what to say to that. G. K. filled the silence that followed.

"Honest to God, McKenzie, there's no talking to you sometimes. Just remember—what's the first rule?"

"Never lie to the police."

"Never. Ever. You don't have to talk. The Fifth Amendment protects you. But if you do talk . . ."

"Don't lie."

"They'll nail your ass for obstruction."

"Always a pleasure chatting with you, Genevieve."

"Why do I get the feeling I'll be hearing from you again real soon?"

The Maestro answered his phone on the second ring.

"I'm going after the Countess," I told him.

"Thank you, McKenzie," Duclos said. "Thank you."

"What I need is a letter signed by you and notarized stating that I am acting on your behalf in case this all goes sideways."

"Certainly. Of course. Anything I can do."

"I'd like it early tomorrow morning before I drive to Bayfield."

"Swing by the house. It'll be waiting."

The Maestro gave me the address.

"Tell me about the money," I said.

"Do you think it'll be enough—$250,000?"

"It is what it is. But you'll need cash. The thieves aren't going to take a check, they're not gonna go through PayPal. The question—how long will it take you to get it together?"

"I've already spoken to some people. It'll be tough doing it without Renée finding out, but they said . . . three days, does that work?"

Experience had taught me that three days was about right.

Most people think you can simply walk into a branch office, make a withdrawal, and walk out again with a million bucks stashed in an attaché case—that's what TV and the movies have taught us. In reality, no bank has that kind of cash lying around, and it takes time to negotiate the bureaucracy. What's more, a quarter of a million dollars in twenties and fifties weighs twenty-three pounds and will fill an airline carry-on bag, the kind with wheels and an extended handle. I explained it to the Maestro.

"Once you get it together, keep it in a safe place until I contact you," I said. I nearly added *a safer place than you kept the Countess Borromeo,* yet kept the dig to myself.

"Aren't you going to take it with you?" he asked.

"Hell no."

THREE

I drive a Ford Mustang GT with a 435-horsepower V-8 engine and manual gearbox. And no, I'm not having a midlife crisis, although . . .

I used to drive an Audi S5 until it was smashed beyond repair on the freeway during a blizzard. I had been planning to replace it, test driving a couple of other Audis, a few BMWs, a Mercedes. The day before my birthday, though—I won't tell you which one—Nina called me down from the condo. I found the Mustang at a parking meter on the street adjacent to the building, the sun reflecting off the black paint; I had to bring my hand up to shield my eyes. Nina was leaning against it and dangling the key fob from her finger.

"I hope you don't mind that I drove it first," she said.

I reacted pretty much the same way as I had when I was sixteen and my father brought home a used 1965 Mustang—with unabashed glee. The car was over twenty years old at the time, light blue with a 170-cubic-inch straight-six engine, 101 horsepower, three-speed transmission on the floor, AM radio—not even FM—and I thought it was the most beautiful thing I had ever seen. My father taught me how to drive a stick in that car; I knocked out three transmissions before I finally caught on. Once I did, he gave it to me, tossed the keys nearly the same way that Nina had, and said, "Drive carefully"—exactly as Nina had.

"I hope you have better luck with it than the last Mustang you owned," she said.

Nina meant that she hoped I didn't spin it out on Mississippi Boulevard near the Lake Street Bridge and bust the A-frame like I had with Betsy. Yes, I called my first car Betsy.

"I don't know what to say," I told her.

"And you thought I didn't listen to all those stories you told about when you were a kid."

So, to repeat—if Nina wants to live in a high-rise condominium in Minneapolis, we're going to live in a high-rise condominium in Minneapolis.

I was thinking about Betsy the next morning as I drove along Mississippi Boulevard well south of Lake Street to the address Duclos had recited to me. It was located near a large white house with Greek columns and a breathtaking view of the river that had once sheltered the Hollyhocks Casino, where St. Paul's finest dressed in tuxedos and gowns and mingled with the most notorious gangsters of the Jazz Age.

I parked at the top of the horseshoe driveway and walked to the front door. I rang the bell and waited. I was about to try the bell again when the door was yanked open.

"Good morning, McKenzie," Duclos said. "Come in."

I followed the Maestro inside. It was a very nice house and well furnished, yet I felt somewhat disappointed. Where were the servants? Where was the fountain in the foyer?

He led me to the kitchen. It was large, and I noticed an oversized stove with two ovens, two dishwashers, and a refrigerator big enough to chill a live cow. Still . . .

"May I offer you a cup of coffee?" Duclos asked.

"Yes, thank you."

"Cream? Sugar?"

"No, thank you."

He filled a mug and slid it across the counter toward me, and I thought, Where's the cook?

I guess I was expecting more extravagance in the home of one of the world's foremost concert violinists and his spectacularly wealthy wife. 'Course, this was Minnesota, where conspicuous consumption has never been in fashion. We have world-class museums, the most theaters per capita outside of New York, so many arts organizations that no one has ever been able to pull together a definitive list, and top-shelf performance venues like the Ordway Center for the Performing Arts and Orchestra Hall—most, if not all, made possible by the state's well-to-do. Yet we're the world leaders in thrift, guilt, and luxury shame. Which isn't to say Minnesota's wealthy don't like to spend their money. After all, I once bought Nina a $60,000 piano, and she bought me a $35,000 sports car. It's just that, for the most part, we do it quietly.

The Maestro chatted about the weather. It was surprisingly pleasant for mid-July in Minnesota, with temperatures hovering in the high seventies to low eighties. He felt we deserved a break after the brutal winter we had just survived. I reminded him why I had come.

"Of course," Duclos said. "Just a moment."

He set his coffee mug on the counter and left the kitchen, leaving me to casually study the expensive china stacked behind the glass doors of the cabinets.

"Excuse me," a voice called. It belonged to a handsome woman with hair the color of maple syrup. I knew that she was in her late fifties, early sixties, the same age as Duclos, but she sure didn't look it. She was standing beneath the arch that separated the kitchen from the rest of the house.

"Excuse me," I said.

"Who are you?"

She had a young voice. If I had met her over the phone, I would have said she was twenty.

"My name is McKenzie. I hope I didn't startle you. I'm waiting for the Maestro."

"Let me guess, you're a fan-boy."

"Truth is, I've never heard him play. I'm more of a jazz guy."

She thought that was funny.

"Truth is," she said, "I'm a little bit rock and roll."

She entered the kitchen, brushing past me on her way to the coffeemaker. I watched as she took a white china cup and matching saucer from the cabinet—no mug for her—filled the cup with coffee, added cream and sugar, and stirred it with a small spoon.

"I'm Renée Peyroux." She took a sip of the coffee and returned the cup to the saucer. "Technically, the Countess Borromeo belongs to me."

"Yes, ma'am," I said just to prove I was listening.

"I know why you're here."

"Ma'am?"

"You're here to sell the property you stole back to my husband. And don't call me ma'am."

"No, Ms. Peyroux, I am not."

"Then he hired you to buy the violin back from those who did steal it."

"Is that such a terrible thing?"

"I will not reward the people who robbed me."

"Let's hope it doesn't come to that."

She took another sip of coffee and stared at me over the rim of her upraised cup. She was about to speak when Duclos returned to the kitchen.

"Oh," he said. "Renée. Sweetheart. I thought you went to the office an hour ago."

"I did," Peyroux said. "The first call I received was from our banker informing me that immediately after my husband deposited $250,000 into our checking account, he wrote out a withdrawal slip for the same amount in cash, so I came home."

Duclos gazed at me as if he couldn't believe he got caught.

"This is why my girl and I keep our finances separate," I said.

"Why would you do that, Paul?" Peyroux asked. "Behind my back. And don't you dare lie to me."

"You made it clear that you didn't want to negotiate for the return of the Countess," the Maestro said.

"Oh, and you do, is that it? Tell me—where did the money come from? Paul? Where did it come from?"

"I make money. A great deal of money, even by your standards."

"And it all rolls into our joint accounts. Doesn't it? Paul?"

"Ms. Peyroux," I said, "it's an irreplaceable work of art."

Peyroux pointed her tiny spoon at me.

"This is none of your business," she said.

"Yes, ma'am."

"Well? I'm waiting."

"I love her," the Maestro said. "I need her. I don't know if I can go on without her."

"It's a goddamn violin."

"She's more than that and you know it."

"You—McKenzie. Why are you involved in this?"

"I told you. The Countess is an irreplaceable work of art."

"Yeah, you look like an art lover."

"Ma'am—"

"I told you, don't call me ma'am. And don't pretend that you're anything but a mercenary."

"Since I'm not earning a nickel for this, I must beg to differ."

"You're telling me you're doing this for free?"

"Yes, Ms. Peyroux. That's what I'm telling you."

She didn't know how to respond to that. Instead, she set the china cup and saucer on the counter and strode out of the kitchen.

"That went well," Duclos said.

He might have said more, except he was interrupted when Peyroux returned. She stood under the arch, her fists pressed against her hips. She spoke between clenched teeth.

"Goddammit. Do what you think is best, but if this blows back on my family's foundation, there will be hell to pay."

She left again.

"I like her," I said.

"Yes, but . . ."

"What?"

"She cursed. Three times. She never does that unless she is very, very upset."

I smiled.

"You think that's funny, McKenzie?"

"My girl is the same way. She starts swearing, it's best to duck and cover."

"Easy for you to say. You're going to Bayfield. I'm staying here."

Duclos handed to me a white number 10 envelope. I opened it, read the letter, returned it to the envelope, and put it into the inside pocket of my sports coat.

"If someone does offer me the Stradivarius, how can I tell if it's authentic?" I asked.

"There will be a label inside the violin that reads *Antonius Stradiuarius Cremonensis Faciebat Anno 1727*. You can tell if it's a fake if the cursive *u* in 'Stradiuarius' reads as a *v*. The Roman *v* didn't replace the *u* until after 1730."

"Forgers who know their business will probably know that, too. That's not the point, though. How can I tell if it's the Countess Borromeo at a glance, because that might be all I get—a glance."

Duclos considered the question for a moment. His gaze went

to the arch that his wife had disappeared under while he reached for his back pocket. He had photographs of the violin in his wallet. He showed one to me, a close-up. I didn't notice any photographs of Renée Peyroux in there, but let it slide without comment.

"If you look closely, here, between the F-hole and the corner, you'll see a tiny nick in the wood that's shaped like the lightning bolt on Harry Potter's forehead," Duclos said.

"Harry Potter?" I said.

"Haven't you read the books?"

"No."

"There's a lot of dead time traveling from concert to concert."

"Okay."

"Do you want to keep the photograph?"

"Yes, thank you."

Duclos slipped it out of the plastic sleeve and gave it to me.

"Bring her home safe," he said.

"I'll do my best."

"Please, for both our sakes, don't screw up. My wife has never made an idle threat in her life."

It took two hours to drive I-35 north to Duluth, located at the far western tip of Lake Superior. I stopped for a couple of "Medieval" gyros at the Duluth Grill and proceeded on U.S. Highway 53 across the bridge into Wisconsin. For another two hours, I headed east along U.S. 2 and Wisconsin Highway 13, hugging the south shore of the big lake. Along the way, I used my Mustang's SYNC System to make a hands-free phone call.

"Hi," Nina said.

"Hi, yourself."

"Are you on the road?"

"I am. Are you sure you don't want to come with? I could always turn around and get you."

"I'd love to, but I told you last night—with both my assistant manager and head chef on vacation, someone needs to keep an eye on things."

"Besides, you love the work."

"I do. I do indeed. I always have."

"What's your daughter up to?"

"Hanging with her friends. Did you hear—she wants me to change the name of the club?"

"To what?"

"Erica's."

"What's wrong with Rickie's?"

"She says no one calls her that anymore."

"How many people besides us even know you named the place after her?"

"I explain it on the Web site. Anyway, I told her that when she inherits the club she can call it whatever she wants."

"Here I thought you were going to leave it to me."

"The only thing you're getting is the stool at the bar where you usually sit."

"It does have a lot of sentimental value."

"This is assuming I go first, so do me a favor—be careful in Bayfield."

Bayfield is a tourist town, and a highly successful one at that; people often use the words "picture postcard" and "quaint" to describe it. It has a population of 530, yet there are usually three times that number of people or more roaming its streets on any given day, especially in the summer. Part of the attraction is Lake Superior itself. Last time I was there, Nina and I rented kayaks and explored the many water-sculpted caves along the shoreline. In the winter, you could actually walk across the ice to see the caves, but I had never done that. I have cruised around the twenty-one Apostle Islands, though, checking out the historic lighthouses, hiking the old-growth forests, and lying out on the windswept beaches. There is a large marina where you can rent a boat or book a charter, perches on high hills where you can bird-watch, bike trails, hiking trails, twelve art galleries and antique stores—I think Nina dragged me into each and every one—numerous restaurants and bars, some with live music, and a casino just down the road. Nina had also wanted me to roam the area's many berry farms and apple orchards where, she assured me, we could pick our own fruit, but a guy's gotta draw a line somewhere.

I pulled into town at about 2:00 P.M. A couple of right turns later, I found what I was looking for—the New Queen Anne Victorian Mansion Bed and Breakfast, the place where Duclos had been staying when someone stole his four-million-dollar Stradivarius.

The front door was locked. I examined it carefully. Solid oak and very old. Yet the lock was new, a dead bolt. I bet myself a nickel that the owner had swapped out the old lock after the theft.

I pressed the bell and waited. From the covered wraparound porch I could see much of downtown Bayfield, the ferry to Madeline Island, the marina, and Lake Superior beyond. I gave it another half minute and pressed the bell again. The door opened, and a young man smiled at me—at least he was younger than I was.

"Welcome to the Queen Anne," he said. "How may I help you?"

"I'd like to stay in one of your rooms if possible," I said. "I'm afraid I don't have a reservation."

"Fortunately, we have a vacancy. Please come in."

I followed him inside; he was careful to close and lock the door behind us.

"The Queen Anne was built in 1882," he said. It looked it, with damask walls, floor tiles, elevated ceilings, theatrical wooden staircase, and hardwood floors; both the architecture and furniture featured Renaissance and Gothic themes.

The young man led me to an ornately carved desk, where he proceeded to check me in. There was a registration book on top of the desk that he asked me to sign. I did, adding my name and address to those already listed there.

"You'll be on the second floor in the Peacock Chamber," he said.

Peacock Chamber, my inner voice repeated. *That fits your personality.*

"By the way, I'm Connor Rasmussen," he said.

He extended his hand and I shook it.

"Are you the owner?" I asked.

"I am. I took over the mansion a couple of years ago. It wasn't in very good shape then, but we managed to restore it to its original design while adding a few twenty-first-century amenities."

I was studying the intricately carved woodwork, massive fireplace, spacious parlor, and sparkling chandeliers when I said, "Helluva job."

"Thank you."

"I heard you had a little trouble here a few days ago."

The smile froze on Connor's face; he managed to speak without moving his lips.

"If you're concerned about your safety . . ."

"Not at all," I said.

"The locks have been changed, and we will have a security camera in place by the end of the week."

"I am not concerned."

"If it's me you're worried about . . ."

"No."

"I am not a thief."

"I didn't say you were."

"Others have."

"I apologize," I said. "I didn't mean to upset you."

"Yet, it is very upsetting. People talk, don't they? They've been talking ever since it happened, the robbery. It's all they talk about. Some say I'm responsible for the theft. Others have actually accused me of stealing the Stradivarius myself. I've already lost bookings over this. That's why I have a vacant room. I was booked solid all the way through the holidays; now . . ."

"I'm sorry."

"Do you know how long it took me to get the Queen Anne in order, how much it cost?" Connor asked. "I thought having Paul Duclos stay here would be good publicity. I took his photo; I was going to upload it on the Web site. Now this."

"For what it's worth, Duclos doesn't hold you responsible."

"That's not what he said when he was here."

"He's had time to cool down, to reevaluate."

I had no idea if that was true or not, but I needed the young man's cooperation.

"Do you know him?" Connor asked.

"The Maestro sent me."

"Why?"

"To retrieve the Stradivarius. He's offering a reward for its return."

"I heard the insurance company—"

"Not the insurance company. Just Duclos, $250,000. No questions asked."

"He doesn't care if the thief is arrested?"

"He does not. All the Maestro wants is the violin safe and sound."

Connor gave it a few moments' thought before he asked, "Why are you telling me this?"

"I was hoping you might help me out."

"I didn't steal the damn violin. The police searched my house. They searched it twice. I didn't take it."

"I know that."

You do? my inner voice asked.

"I read the police reports," I added. "You were the victim of a professional burglar; just as much a victim as Duclos."

"Then why is Brian Pilhofer telling everyone that I'm a thief?"

I recognized the name. According to the reports, Pilhofer was the Bayfield cop who was first summoned to the scene, the one who called the Countess Borromeo a fiddle.

"I can't speak for some dip-shit local yokel," I said. "The FBI, though, the Wisconsin DCI, they don't consider you to be a suspect."

I didn't know if that was true or not, either. Yet the way Connor smiled made me think the lie had been well received—and that he would repeat it every chance he got. I decided to give him more; make him my bestie for life.

"If you want, I know the name of a good attorney," I said. "You could sue these guys; at least make them cease and desist with the accusations."

"That would be—no, I don't want to do that."

"Okay."

"But you said . . . you said you were hoping that I might help you," Connor said. "What can I do?"

Tell everyone near and far there's a man with money who's willing to make a deal, my inner voice said.

"How do your locks work?" I said. "Not the new one that you just installed"—I gestured toward the front door—"the old ones."

Connor smiled again. I think he liked the idea that I might actually know what I was doing.

"It's not terribly different than the old one," he said. "Maybe a little better quality. I give each guest a key to the front door." He set one in the palm of my hand. "The door locks automatically when you come in or go out. If you don't have a key, you'll need to ring the bell." He gave me a second key. "Each room has its own key, of course. There are eight rooms. Yours is on the second floor facing the lake."

"Where is the Queen Anne Suite?"

"Top floor."

"May I see it?"

"There's a young woman staying there, so, no, I really can't let you in. I need to respect her privacy while she's here. I hope that's not a problem."

"Not at all. Maybe later."

"If there's anything else I can do . . ."

"I'll let you know."

I don't know why Connor named it the Peacock Chamber. There was nothing even remotely flamboyant about the room. It was, in fact, quite serene, with two bookcases filled with impressive titles, king-sized bed, armoire, desk, matching chair and love seat, stone-top table and nightstand, and gas fireplace. The step-down washroom featured a porcelain soaking tub with rain shower, subway tiles on the wall, hexagonal tiles on the floor, and built-in linen cabinets. There were large windows with a nice view of the edge of downtown Bayfield and the Madeline ferry.

I quickly unpacked and dumped my files on top of the desk. I went through them again as I considered my next moves. The plan, of course, was simple and straightforward: Tell people who I was; tell them why I was there; wait for someone to say, "Psst, buddy, you wanna buy a hot violin?"

What could possibly go wrong?

FOUR

There was a perfect blue sky reflecting in a calm lake, and the temperature was in the low seventies, yet I threw on a light blue sports jacket over my polo shirt and jeans because I knew it would get cool along the shore when the sun left the sky. It made me look less like a tourist, but I didn't mind. I left the Peacock Chamber, making sure the door was locked behind me, and descended the staircase. I looked for Connor and couldn't find him, and then I did. He was working in the garden that surrounded the Queen Anne.

It didn't seem as if he was coming inside anytime soon, so I went to the registration desk and opened the guest book. I very carefully transcribed the names and addresses of every guest who had stayed there in the past two weeks into a notebook that I nearly always carried. I could have gone back further, except I remembered that Bayfield had contacted Duclos only two weeks before he actually played his concert. That narrowed the amount of time an outsider would have had to plan the heist. As it was, I wrote down fifty-nine names. A quarter had stayed only one evening, the others for two nights or more. Connor had done very good business before the burglary.

Afterward, I went to the Mustang, parked in the Queen Anne's lot. I made myself comfortable before speaking to the onboard computer. I could have used my smartphone, of course, or even my laptop, but did I tell you—Nina bought me a new car with all the gadgets.

"Computer, dial Schroeder Private Investigations," I said.

A few moments later, a woman answered.

"I would like to speak to Greg Schroeder," I said.

"I'm sorry," she told me. "Mr. Schroeder is unavailable. May one of our associates assist you?"

"Tell him that it's McKenzie."

"I'm sorry—"

"Yes, I know. Tell him it's McKenzie. I promise he'll take my call."

A half minute later, I heard his voice.

"Damn, McKenzie. How are you? To what do I owe the pleasure?"

Schroeder was a trench-coat detective, one of those guys who carried his gun in a shoulder holster beneath a rumbled suit jacket and chain-smoked Marlboros. When I first met him nearly five years ago, he was just another ex-cop leading a one-man band. Now he ran one of the bigger PI agencies in town.

"I need a favor," I said.

"A favor for which you will gladly pay our going rate?"

"Of course."

"Those are my favorite kind of favors. What do you need?"

"I'm going to give you a list of names and addresses. I want you to find out which one of them is most likely to steal a four-million-dollar Stradivarius."

"You couldn't have given the names to one of my detectives? You have to bother—wait. Four-million-dollar Stradivarius?"

"Yep."

"Are you talking about the violin that was snatched in Wisconsin the other day?"

"I am."

"My, my, look at you. Getting a little ambitious, aren't you, son?"

"Could be. But listen—if you can't be bothered . . ."

"C'mon now."

"I'll talk to one of your employees. How many detectives do you have working for you now?"

"Seventeen."

"Transfer me to—"

"They're all working other cases, and you know me, as busy as I am, I always have time for an old friend."

"Especially if the old friend is willing to pay the going rate."

"I have a pencil, I have paper."

I recited the names and addresses.

"Are we on the clock?" Schroeder asked.

"Not particularly."

"Give me a day or two."

"Okay."

"So, McKenzie. Four-million-dollar Stradivarius, huh? Who's your client?"

"I'll talk to you soon, Greg."

Most of Bayfield was built on a hill, with the downtown area at the bottom, where it touched Lake Superior. Given its size, it was easier to walk through the town than drive, and besides, I could use the exercise. So I left the Mustang and drifted from the top of the hill, where most of the residential area was located, down toward the shoreline.

I found over a dozen vehicles idling in two neat lines in a sprawling asphalt parking lot where Washington Avenue dead-ended. Most of them were waiting for the ferry to shuttle them across the lake to Madeline Island with its beaches, camping areas, restaurants, art galleries, studios, and craft schools.

From there I headed east, following Front Street. I paused when I reached the gazebo overlooking Memorial Park where the Maestro had played his concert. The park was smaller than I would have guessed, with the Pier Plaza Restaurant on the right and the Bayfield Inn with its restaurant and rooftop terrace just behind it. A few thousand people squeezed into this space must have been quite a sight, standing room only.

I crossed the park, following the sidewalk that separated the city from the marina until I reached Manypenny Avenue. Keep going straight and I would come across City Hall and Bayfield's four-man police department, but I was determined to avoid official involvement for as long as possible. Instead, I went south along the avenue until I reached Broad Street and the gray and rose-colored home of the Bayfield Chamber of Commerce and Visitor Bureau. The high school girl behind the desk was more than happy to assist me but was confused by my request—the names and addresses of all the members of the chamber plus a map.

"Why?" she asked.

"So I don't need to search through the police reports to find them."

"What police reports?"

"The ones concerning the theft of the Stradivarius last week."

"What has that to do with the chamber?"

"The chamber brought Paul Duclos here to play."

"So?"

"That makes them suspects."

That's when the girl decided she needed help. Neither the executive director, the office manager, nor the marketing and events manager was available, but the marketing and events assistant was. Her name was Amy, and she looked as if she had graduated from college last week. She asked what I wanted, and I told her. She also asked why. Instead of messing with her, I told the truth—sorta.

"I was hired by Paul Duclos to retrieve his stolen violin." I gave her a quick glance at the letter the Maestro had given me to prove it. "I was hoping that members of the chamber could help."

"I don't know how," she said.

"Are the names secret?"

"No. I mean, if you go to the Web site . . ."

"Ahh."

She printed out the list and gave me a map of the city. I thanked her and announced, "By the way, my name is McKenzie, and I'll be here all week." Amy had no idea what to make of that, which was okay with me, just as long as she repeated it.

There were thirteen names on the list, along with the businesses they owned, nearly all of them tourist related. The president of the chamber operated an inn located on Highway 13 at the edge of town. I decided it was too far to walk, and I didn't want to get the Mustang, so I skipped him and went to the vice president. Lauren Ternes owned an art gallery on Third Street near the Farmers Market. It was only a block and a half away according to my map.

Ternes Studio and Gallery sold watercolors, oil paintings, and original photographs, as well as some pottery and wood carvings—most of it Bayfield related, all of it provided by local artists, including the owner. I didn't see anything I liked, but then I know very little about art. I ended up standing near the door while the plump, brightly dressed woman working the cash register dealt with a steady stream of customers. At first, she probably thought I had accompanied one of the women browsing the merchandise. Yet as customers came and went without me moving, her expression changed to one of overt curiosity.

Eventually, she handed off the cash register to an associate and approached me.

"Can I help you?" she asked.

"Lauren Ternes?"

"Yes."

"Vice president of the Bayfield Chamber of Commerce?"

"Yes."

I offered my hand and she shook it.

"I'm McKenzie," I said.

"What can I do for you, Mr. McKenzie?"

"You can help me find Paul Duclos's four-million-dollar Stradivarius."

"I'm sorry . . ."

"The Stradivarius violin that was stolen—"

"Yes, yes, I know all about it."

"Well, then."

"Well, what? Do you think I had something to do with the theft?"

"You did help bring the Maestro to town."

"I did not. We have a person who plans and manages events for that."

"She wasn't in the office, so . . ."

"Who are you?"

"McKenzie, I told you."

"Are you police?"

"No."

"Because the police have been all over town asking questions. The FBI, too."

"I was hired by Duclos to arrange for the safe return of his violin. He's even offering a reward, $250,000. No questions asked. I have a letter . . ."

"What does that have to do with me?"

"Since you're the vice president, I thought you might be interested."

"We have a quote on the city's Web site—*Making Bayfield the way we like has been the slow and loving task of 150 years. To destroy the Bayfield that we know can take but the careless act of a single day.* Last Friday was that day. It's been just awful for Bayfield; awful for any town that depends as much on tourism as we do."

"Who are you kidding? This isn't food poisoning on a Carnival Cruise or a rash of drive-by shootings from rival drug cartels. It's a high-profile art theft. It's given the city more publicity than it's ever had. I bet your historical society is already planning an exhibit."

"You're crazy."

"There's a town in Minnesota called Northfield. Every September thousands of people flock there to celebrate the day Jesse James tried to rob the place."

"It's not the same thing."

"Sure it is. All your story needs is a happy ending."

"What kind of happy ending?"

"How 'bout the violin is recovered intact and restored to Paul Duclos, who promptly returns to his hometown to play a benefit concert? Do you think that might polish Bayfield's apple?"

Lauren's expressive face held no secrets. I knew what she was going to say before she said it.

"That would certainly help, but I don't know what I can do about it," she said.

"Just spread the word."

"The word? You think whoever stole the violin lives in Bayfield?"

"Not necessarily."

"You think he'll sell it back for the reward money?"

"It's been done before."

Lauren stared at me some more.

"Get out," she said.

I knew she was going to say that, too.

I made two more stops along the avenue. The owner of an antique store seemed to be a fan of detective fiction and had a lot of questions to ask. The manager of the place that sold scented candles and potpourri ordered me to leave thirty seconds after I opened my mouth. Oh well.

Once outside, I scanned my list for another prominent citizen to annoy. The chamber's treasurer lived on Madeline Island, and I thought a twenty-minute ferry ride might be fun. On the other hand, the name just below his owned a joint called the Lakeside Tavern that was three minutes away if I walked slowly.

I found a seat at a small sidewalk table just as the place began to fill for happy hour. I ordered a half-price South Shore Pale Ale, a beer brewed in Ashland just down the road that I had never seen in the Cities, and an order of fried onion rings. The young woman who served them was pleasant and talkative. She and her roommates were students at the University of Wisconsin–Madison working summer jobs in Bayfield to help pay their tuition, although she figured to have at least forty thousand dollars' worth of outstanding student loans by the time she graduated. I asked her what she thought about the theft of the Countess Borromeo.

"I was there," she said. "Not there when the violin was stolen, I mean is that crazy or what? I was at the concert, though. Duclos played Vivaldi's Concerto no. 2 in G Minor. You know, 'Summer,' from *The Four Seasons,* which is like the greatest violin piece of all time. So cool."

I suggested that a smart girl, working in a bar, might hear things.

She said I'd be surprised.

"What have you heard?" I asked.

"About the theft? I don't know. Some people think Connor Rasmussen, the guy who owns the Queen Anne, some people think he did it, but I don't believe them. I met Connor, and he seems like a real nice guy, and besides, you don't steal stuff from people in your own house. That's just crazy. Some other people, they think it was international criminals, you know? But that seems silly, too."

"What do you think?"

"I saw this movie once, an old black-and-white, I don't know who was in it, where the bad guys were like following around the victim for like days before they struck. I think that's what happened. Someone was following the Maestro around waiting for the chance to steal his violin, and then he comes up here and like wham, there you go."

"As good a theory as any. Listen, is Philip Speegle here?"

"I just saw him behind the bar."

"Would you ask, if he has a moment, if I might speak to him?"

"Sure. Should I tell him . . ."

"My name is McKenzie."

"Okeydoke."

Despite its name, the Lakeside Tavern wasn't actually located on Lake Superior. Instead, it was two blocks up the hill. Yet from where I was on the sidewalk, I was able to see straight down the avenue to where the lake slapped against the breakers. The ferry was making its return run from Madeline Island with boats of all shapes and kinds bobbing around it. On shore, tourists flitted from shop to shop and restaurant to restaurant; the colors of their summer attire gave the place a festive atmosphere. Bicyclists pedaled up, down, and around with only a casual regard for the existing traffic laws, and, unlike where I came from, the drivers who shared the streets with them didn't seem to mind at all. It was all very nice; yet I knew from experience that after three days, the place would bore me out of my mind.

I had nearly finished the South Shore, thinking there must be something wrong with me to prefer the noise, crowds, and pollution of the big city, when Speegle appeared at the table.

"Mr. McKenzie," he said. "Is there something I can do for you?"

He was a pleasant-looking fellow—everything in Bayfield seemed pleasant—with the physique of a man who was starting to wonder if all the exercise he had done over the years had been worth it.

"Mr. Speegle," I said, "I was sent here by Paul Duclos."

"The pompous, self-important jerk who left a four-million-dollar violin lying around like it was a coupon for fifty cents off at the grocery store? That Paul Duclos?"

Whoa, my inner voice said.

"Wow," I said aloud.

"Let me guess—you think he walks on fucking water, too."

"I only met him yesterday."

"Yeah?"

"I think he's a guy who desperately wants to get his Stradivarius back."

"Isn't that the way? Man treats his property like crap until he loses it and then suddenly it's the most important thing in his life. What do you expect me to do about it?"

I decided Speegle was a man I wanted on my side—at least for now.

"You, sir," I said, "are a breath of fresh air because you're right, everyone I've spoken to *does* think Duclos walks on water. Truth is, he was careless as hell; one of those guys who thinks he can wander through life without anything bad ever happening to him."

"The people who come into my place, my customers, most of them are having a good time; they're on vacation, right? Around closing time, though, you start hearing stories about how shitty their lives are back home, and the reason—because they fucked up. Oh, they'll tell you it's because of this or that or the other thing. I am so tired of people blaming their problems on the fucking economy or the president or the Democrats or the Republicans or the Jews or the Muslims or whomever else they're pissed off at. In the end, people are their own worst enemies."

"Sir, let me buy you a beer."

"You know what, let me buy you one."

Speegle caught the attention of the waitress, pointed at my pale ale, and held up two fingers. He sat across from me at the small table, cutting off my view of the lake. A few moments later, the waitress set a bottle of South Shore in front of each of us. She left without speaking a word.

"I gather you're not a tourist," Speegle said.

"Not this trip, although, I've been here before. I like it."

"Yeah, Bayfield's a nice town. Good neighbors for the most part. It's like any place you've ever been, though; people have issues, most of them centered on money. Getting money, spending money, keeping what they can."

"The way of the world."

"Tell me—McKenzie, right? What exactly did that violin-playing fool hire you to do?"

I nearly told Speegle that I had volunteered; yet I decided it would be better to let him think I was just a working stiff.

"He wants me to get his Stradivarius back," I said.

"How?"

"With money."

"How much money?"

"Two hundred and fifty thousand dollars."

"That's not much considering what the damn thing is worth."

"Depends on how you look at it. The thieves can't sell it on the open market, and the insurance company refuses to buy it back. This is the only offer on the table."

"If I was the thief, I'd be long gone by now."

"I bet they're paying attention, though."

"We should never have brought that asshole back to town."

"The Maestro isn't Bayfield's favorite son?"

Speegle snorted at the idea.

"I grew up with the little prick," he said. "I went to school with him. Even when he was a kid he thought his shit didn't stink. He went away and became a big success. Whoop-de-do. A lot of us stayed home, and we became successes, too." Speegle waved at his bar. "Just no one applauding us in some fancy concert hall, is all. You gotta ask, too—how much of that success is because he married a boatload of money?"

"Whose idea was it to ask Duclos to play the concert?"

"That's a good question. I have no idea. Could have been Heather Voight. She and Duclos were an item back in the day. King and queen of the prom. You know how it is, though. He leaves, she stays; he becomes famous, she marries the local schnook—typical small-town cliché. It's not like she spent all her time pining for him, though. Heather owns half of Bayfield. If it wasn't her who called that asshole—you should ask the girl who plans our events at the visitors' bureau. She would know."

"I've already made myself unpopular down at the visitors' bureau and over at the Queen Anne. I all but accused Lauren Ternes of helping to plan the burglary."

"That dyke?"

"I didn't mean anything by it. I'm just trying to get the word out that I'm willing to make a deal for the violin."

"I wouldn't worry about it. News travels pretty fast in this town."

Speegle stood. He called, "Ellis," and the young woman who had served us earlier spun away from the table she was bussing to look at him. He pointed at our table.

"I got this," he said.

"Thank you for the beer," I said.

"Come back later tonight and I'll buy you another one. We've got some kids going onstage who think they can play the blues."

"I'll be here."

Speegle moved back inside the tavern. I was about to leave myself when a dark blue police cruiser with the name BAYFIELD stenciled on the door pulled up; the front high-grade push bumper was about five yards away from where I sat on the sidewalk. The car was parked illegally. The driver stepped out. He was an older man and bigger than I was, wearing a police uniform and sunglasses. He stepped around the cruiser. Tourists strolling the sidewalk gave him plenty of room; those sitting at tables like mine watched while pretending not to.

Speegle was right, my inner voice said. *News does travel fast here.*

"You're McKenzie," the police office said.

It wasn't a question, yet I answered anyway.

"I am," I said.

"Come with me."

"Where?"

"We're going to the hall. Now get up."

"No."

My eyes followed his hand as it slowly moved to the butt of his holstered Glock.

"What did you say?" he asked.

"I said no."

My response seemed to catch him by surprise. The officer whipped off his sunglasses with a dramatic flourish and took a step toward me. He pointed his glasses at my face, his other hand still resting on the Glock.

"We can do this the easy way or we can do it the hard way," he said.

He was close enough now that I could read the name tag over his left pocket.

"Chief Neville," I said. "Am I under arrest?"

"I should arrest you."

"I didn't ask what you should do."

"No, you're not under arrest."

"Good, cuz if I was under arrest, I'd lawyer up and not speak to you at all. On the other hand, if you were to remove your hand from your gun and sit down, we could have a friendly conversation about any damn thing that you want. What do you say?" I gestured at the chair across from me. "Sit. Relax. Can I get you anything?"

The chief put his sunglasses back on and reluctantly pulled out a chair. I raised my hand and waved at the waitress, who had been watching the scene intently. She hurried over.

"Chief," she said.

"Iced tea," he said. "Thank you, Ellis."

Ellis, my inner voice repeated. *Another small town where everyone knows everybody. That could be useful.*

Ellis glanced at me, and I pointed at the empty South Shore bottle.

"One more," I said.

She hurried away.

"So, Chief Neville," I said. "What would you like to talk about? The weather? It's just perfect."

"The reason you're in Bayfield."

"What have you heard?"

"Are you trying to be funny?"

"Honestly, sir, I am not."

"You're here to buy stolen property, specifically, the Countess Borromeo. You're willing to pay a quarter of a mil for her."

I was thinking about G. K. Bonalay's warning, the one about lying to the police, when I answered.

"I have been spreading that rumor, it's true," I said. "However, it could be mere subterfuge, a lie spoken to draw out the thieves and see that swift and merciless justice is meted out. Who knows?"

The chief chuckled at that.

"Yeah, okay," he said. "You've done this before."

Ellis returned with our drinks. We both thanked her by name, and she moved away.

"Sir, I mean to cause you and your department the barest minimum of inconvenience," I said.

"I like the 'sir.'"

"And I apologize for flouting your authority in public, only I wanted to talk to you as much as you want to talk to me, and I don't think we could do that at the hall."

"Why not?"

"Too official. Too much public record. I used to be a police officer myself, in St. Paul, Minnesota."

"I did twenty years in Houghton, Michigan, before coming here to do eight more."

"So, we understand each other."

"I was hired to serve and protect the citizens of Bayfield. You're not from Bayfield. Do you understand that?"

"I do. Just out of curiosity"—I glanced at my watch; I had been in Bayfield for just over three hours—"who told you I was here?"

"You're staying at the Queen Anne, am I right?"

Good answer, my inner voice said. *A cop's answer, giving me information without giving it.*

"I am at the Queen Anne," I said aloud.

"Is that where you're keeping the $250,000?"

"Only a moron would carry around that kind of cash."

"You can get it in a hurry, though, isn't that the correct answer?"

"Tell me, Chief. Of the five hundred and thirty people living in Bayfield, who do you think was the most likely to steal the Stradivarius?"

He took a long sip of his iced tea before he answered.

"These violins have been stolen before from dressing rooms and apartments; a café outside a train station in London that I read about . . ."

"Or B&Bs," I added.

"Usually it was done quietly. The thieves—and the owners—always wanted to create as little noise as possible, which would make recovery that much easier. Yet this particular theft created nothing but noise that got louder and louder. There's also the issue of who would buy a four-million-dollar Stradivarius after it was stolen. No dealer in the world would touch it. The FBI's art crime guys told me that a collector might want it even if he could never show it to anyone. But all the collectors I know— and I don't care what it is that they're collecting, cars, comic books, autographs, whatever—they live to show off their stuff."

"What's your theory?"

"You can't discount the nitwit factor."

Another cop answer. He's telling you that the crime was either unplanned or planned by amateurs.

"I have copies of reports," I said. "The FBI's; yours, too."

"Is that right?"

"They tell me that the violin was removed from its case and the case was dumped in the street."

"The case had a GPS tracker."

"Which makes me think the thief wasn't a complete nitwit."

The chief took another pull of his tea; nothing in his expression or demeanor gave away what he was thinking.

"Where exactly was the violin case found?" I asked.

"Didn't the reports say?"

I pulled the map from my pocket and unfolded it. I was going to search for the location noted in his police report, yet before I could, the chief reached across the table and tapped a spot on the map—the intersection of Eleventh Street and Wilson Avenue.

"Thanks," I said.

"You're not carrying a gun in my town, are you, McKenzie?"

"I'm not licensed to carry in Wisconsin."

"That's not what I asked you."

"No, I am not carrying a gun in Bayfield."

"Keep it that way."

The chief stood and stretched; a lot of the tourists standing on the sidewalk and sitting at the tables watched him do it.

"If you're looking for a good restaurant, I recommend Hill House," he said. "I know the owner; a woman named Heather Voight. Say hi for me."

"I will."

"We'll talk again real soon; shoot the shit like old pals. You can tell me what you think of my city after you've had a chance to look around a bit, meet a few citizens."

"Sure."

I watched as the chief climbed into his cruiser and drove away, leaving me to ask myself—did he really just invite me to investigate the theft of the Countess Borromeo and report back to him?

Why would he do that?

I paid for the pale ale and iced tea in cash, leaving Ellis an obscenely generous tip. Using the map for directions, I made my way south through the city. Most of the restaurants and galleries were in the center of downtown, so it didn't take long to escape the tourists. Soon I found myself alone on Manypenny. I walked up the steep hill across Highway 13 into the heart of Bayfield's residential area, past the Lutheran church to Eleventh Street, and then east to Wilson Avenue. I stood in the middle of the T-intersection. There were a few small houses nearby and one mansion large enough to have a carriage house on its property.

"Why here?" I asked myself aloud.

It seemed like such an unlikely spot. Taking Highway 13 east or west was the quickest way to get out of Bayfield by car. Or the thieves could have escaped by boat across Lake Superior. There were many places to ditch the violin case along both possible routes. Yet the intersection was several blocks from the highway, a mile from the lake, and maybe twice as far from the Queen Anne.

"So why dump the violin case here?"

Maybe the neighbors would know, I told myself.

I recorded the addresses of all the houses in the immediate vicinity into my notebook and began hiking back toward the B&B. The quickest way to reach it was to walk down the hill and cut through Bayfield's downtown, and soon I was approaching the Lakeside Tavern again. That's when I noticed a second man dressed in a police uniform. This one was younger, not more than twenty-five. He was standing among the sidewalk tables and talking to Ellis. She shrugged her shoulders at whatever he had to say and moved past him in a hurry as if she wanted to put as much distance between her and the officer as possible. He barked words at her. She spun around abruptly to face him. Tourists sitting at nearby tables looked up. He said something, and they quickly averted their eyes. He spoke to Ellis. She shook her head and waved her arms, then noticed me watching the scene from up the street. She pointed. The officer followed her finger to where I was standing. He stared at me. I folded my arms over my chest and stared back. He moved in my direction. Ellis stepped in close and said something. He shoved her away.

The officer walked toward me with the swagger of a D-I college football player; big man on campus taking up much of the sidewalk, forcing tourists to walk around him instead of giving up space for them to pass. He tried to appear menacing as he approached; think Lee Van Cleef in all those spaghetti Westerns that you've seen late night on TCM.

"You're McKenzie," he said. "I've been looking for you."

My eyes found his name tag—Brian Pilhofer. I recognized it instantly.

"You're the guy who thought a four-million-dollar Stradivarius was a fiddle," I said.

"Who told you that?"

"The Federal Bureau of Investigation"—which wasn't true, but still . . . "You're also the guy who's going around calling Connor Rasmussen a thief, which leaves you, the police department, and the City of Bayfield open to a lawsuit that you would almost certainly lose."

"Wait a minute."

"I already met Chief Neville, so I'm going to guess that you're the bad cop. What do you want?"

"The missing Stradivarius . . ."

"What about it?"

"You're looking for it."

"Yes, I am. Aren't you?"

Pilhofer obviously enjoyed the authority his badge gave him, yet he used it poorly. He expected people to back down when he spoke, and when I didn't he took it as a personal affront. He leaned in, purposely violating my personal space in an effort to make me feel uncomfortable.

"I want you to get the fuck outta my town," he said.

"You realize that people are watching, right? That they can see and hear you threatening an innocent tourist, right?"

Pilhofer backed away immediately. He began turning his head this way and that. There were people watching, not many, but enough. He seemed surprised. I didn't know why. A uniformed police officer confronting a man on the sidewalk, the world the way it is these days, you might be tempted to pay attention yourself.

"Why do you want me to leave town, Officer?" I asked. "How am I a threat to you?"

"You, McKenzie—I know you're here to buy stolen property. That's against the law."

"So I have been told. But that's not why you want to get rid of me—I just spoke with Chief Neville, like I said. No, this is something personal. What is it? The money?"

"What money?"

"If it's about the reward—if you want me to leave so you can recover the violin on your own and collect the $250,000, I'm fine with that. Believe me."

"I don't care about the damn reward."

"Then what's your motivation? Why are you threatening me on a street corner less than an hour after your boss told me to have a nice day?"

"He doesn't know anything about being a good cop."

"He has twenty-eight years. What do you have? A week?"

"I'm warning you, McKenzie."

"Warn away. I'm not going anywhere."

"You're interfering with an ongoing police investigation."

"Then you should slap the cuffs on me."

"What?"

"I'm either guilty of obstruction of justice or you're guilty of police harassment."

"Next time I see you, I will arrest you. I bet you'll resist, too. In fact, I can guarantee it."

"Then I'm free to go about my business?"

Pilhofer didn't say if I was or wasn't.

"Does Chief Neville know what a lousy cop you are?" I asked. "Maybe I should tell him."

It was a foolish thing to do, I know, calling him out like that. Pilhofer could have been a decent cop for all I know, just a little too full of himself—I was accused of the same thing when I started out. Now he was going to react in one of two ways. He was either going to leave me alone, or he was going to make it his mission in life to mess me up.

Philip Speegle was right, I decided—we're our own worst enemies.

FIVE

I found four couples in the parlor, along with Connor Rasmussen, when I returned to the Queen Anne. They were drinking wine from long-stem glasses made of crystal that matched the decanters on the sideboard. Connor called to me.

"Everyone," he said, "here's McKenzie, another of our guests."

Connor beckoned me into the parlor, poured me a glass of wine, and proceeded to introduce the others. One couple was in their sixties, another in their fifties. The other two were in their early twenties and seemed to know one another.

"What do you do, Mr. McKenzie?" asked the fifty-something woman, whose name I had already forgotten.

I've never liked the question because I don't have a ready reply. How should I answer? Unlicensed private investigator? Self-employed do-gooder? Easily bored jazz-loving baseball fan? Rich dick?

"I suppose you could call me a freelance troubleshooter," I said.

"Mr. McKenzie is here to help catch the thieves who stole the Stradivarius violin," Connor said.

The remark surprised the hell out of me; I had thought the man was trying to downplay any news of the theft.

"That is so exciting," said one of the younger women. "Chasing a cat burglar. I can imagine him climbing through a bedroom window, the burglar I mean, all dressed in black, and stealing a famous diamond while we sleep. It gives me shivers."

Her boyfriend grinned as if he also wanted to give her shivers; the fifty-something woman looked like she wanted to slap her upside the head.

"I don't think there's anything exciting about a robbery," she said.

"Actually, the young lady is correct," I said. "It was a burglary. They call it a robbery when someone steals using force or intimidation; you need to be present for that. A burglary occurs when someone gains entry to a house or business, or a garage, and steals without you being aware of it."

Now the woman looked like I was the one she wanted to slap. Her husband, though, began telling a story about how his daughter and son-in-law were not only robbed in their sleep, they weren't even made aware of it until the police knocked on their door and told them. This launched the youngsters into a series of stories of their own. It seemed everyone had been a victim of a crime or knew personally someone who was; such is the world we live in. The couple in their sixties, however, didn't speak a word. They remained planted on a love seat and held hands while they sipped their wine. Their expression suggested to me that they were waiting for a lull in the conversation so they could excuse themselves and sneak upstairs.

Good for them, my inner voice said.

"How are you going to catch the cat burglar?" the young woman asked me.

"Alice," her boyfriend said.

"I'm just asking."

"I'm going to use bait," I said.

"A woman?" Alice was acting all giggly now, as if this was the first time she had been on vacation without Mom or Dad. "She has a famous diamond and she's going to keep it on her nightstand and when the burglar sneaks in late at night to steal it, you're going to leap out of the closet and catch him. Or her. Maybe the cat burglar is a woman. Has anyone thought of that?"

I glanced at the couple on the love seat. They couldn't believe Alice had said that, either.

"No," I said. "No diamonds. All I have is cash. And no woman. Sorry."

"You're going to catch him when he tries to steal the money," Alice said.

"Something like that."

"Can I help?" Alice waved at her friends. "Can we help?"

"It might be dangerous."

"It sounds like so much fun."

"I'll let you know. Now, if you'll excuse me, I have some work to do."

The fifty-something woman spoke in the most derisive voice she could manage.

"Burglar-catching work?" she asked.

"In a manner of speaking," I said.

I set my empty wineglass on the sideboard and drifted toward the doorway. That was enough to launch the other guests toward their evening activities as well. "Good nights" were exchanged, and a couple "see you at breakfasts." The sixty-something couple brushed past me and climbed the wooden staircase in a hurry. I managed to catch Connor's attention.

"I thought you wanted to keep it quiet, the theft of the Countess Borromeo," I said.

"I'm not going to promote it, but if someone brings it up— you can't hide from the truth, can you? Besides, I'm starting to wonder if it might not turn out to be good for business after all. There are some B&Bs that hold mystery nights during which customers try to solve murders. There are some that advertise that they're haunted."

"Well," I said. I didn't know what else to say. "Well."

I returned to the Peacock Chamber and fired up my PC. The Queen Anne provided free Wi-Fi, and I used it to access the Bayfield County Web site. I found a link for property tax information and one by one typed in the addresses of all the homes in the immediate vicinity of Eleventh Street and Wilson Avenue that I had listed in my notebook. A list of parcels popped up with the names of their owners. Only one stood out—Herb and Heather Voight. Immediately, all manner of theories concerning the missing Stradivarius began ricocheting inside my head that had not been there before.

I glanced at my watch. The fried onion rings had taken the edge off my appetite, yet I decided I would take Chief Neville's advice and have dinner at the Hill House after all.

The restaurant was located on the far side of Bayfield, but I didn't even consider taking the Mustang. I hadn't jogged that morning, and I felt all the walking I was getting in was making up for it. Besides, I had already consumed three beers and a glass of wine with the promise of even more alcohol, and Chief Neville struck me as a guy who would just love to write up a DUI. It would probably make Officer Pilhofer's week.

Even though the art galleries, antique stores, and boutiques were closed, there was still plenty of foot traffic. Some of it was heading in the same direction as I was, to Manypenny and Fourth Street. There was a small line waiting outside Hill House, yet it moved quickly. When my turn came, I requested a table for one. The hostess asked if I would mind eating in the bar.

"Not at all," I told her.

The menu offered a typical tourist-town mix—plenty of whitefish from the lake, pasta, burgers, and pizza. I ordered something called Poop Deck Charlie's Garlic Chicken Penne and a glass of wine recommended by the bartender, Ravishing Red from Bayfield's own All Sisters' Winery. They were both very good.

While I was eating, I asked the bartender if Heather Voight was available. He said he'd check. A few moments later, I heard a voice behind me.

"Mr. McKenzie," it said. "I was wondering when you'd get around to me." I spun on my stool. "My, but you've been making an awful nuisance of yourself."

I knew the woman was old enough to have been in the same high school class as the Maestro, yet she didn't look it. Everything about her appearance—from her well-kept hair and trim figure to her fashionable clothes and knowing smile—made me feel both old and shabby.

"Ms. Voight," I said.

"Mrs. I'm an old-fashioned girl. You're welcome to call me Heather, if you like."

"Your food is very good."

"You say that like you're surprised."

"I've eaten in tourist towns before. I'm sure you have, too."

"I'll take it as a compliment, then, and not just sucking up." She gestured at the empty bar stool next to mine. "May I?"

"Please."

Heather sat as if she practiced it the way Steve McQueen practiced getting out of his car when making the movie *Bullitt*—so she'd look cool.

"Mr. McKenzie, did you come here to accuse me of nefarious deeds like you did Lauren?" she asked.

"Just McKenzie. I hear 'Mr.' and I turn around to see if my father is standing there."

I had hoped to elicit a smile, and I received one, only it reminded me of someone's aunt amused by a child's attempt at telling a joke and not the joke itself.

Heather didn't speak, so I did.

"I work for Paul Duclos," I said.

To prove it, I pulled his letter from my inside jacket pocket and handed it to her. Most people, if you gave them such a document, they would merely glance at it. Heather read every word before handing it back.

"I know Paul is quite anxious about recovering the Countess," she said. "I know he was quite disappointed when his wife refused to pay the ransom for her safe return."

"Have you been in contact with him?"

"We have spoken twice since the theft. He didn't mention you."

"You could say that I'm a new development in the case."

"Is Renée aware of what you are attempting to accomplish?"

"Ms. Peyroux is aware, although she does not approve."

"I do not understand her position, do you?"

"Yes. If more victims behaved as she did, there would be far fewer violins stolen, I think."

"Perhaps. However, I would expect a woman to take her husband's side no matter what. If I were married to Paul, I would take his side no matter what. Renée wouldn't even take his name."

"You grew up with Duclos. Philip Speegle told me that you two were king and queen of the prom."

"It was a small prom."

"Have you seen him since?"

"If you're asking if Paul and I still have a relationship, the answer is yes. We've exchanged Christmas cards. I had dinner with him when he performed at Symphony Center in Chicago a couple of years ago. He surprised me by attending the grand opening of a restaurant I opened in Red Cliff last year. If you're asking if our relationship has extended beyond that, the answer is no. To suggest otherwise would be base gossip."

"Understood."

"Did Philip suggest otherwise?"

"No."

"Philip and I don't always get along."

"Is that because you own half the town?"

"I own only three restaurants, an art gallery, and a motel out on Highway 13. Oh, and a full-service gas station."

"So just a third of the town, then."

Heather flung back her head and laughed out loud.

"No, probably not quite that much, either," she said. "I've done well, though. Not only here, but in Washburn and Red Cliff, too."

"Has your husband helped?"

Heather's smile softened with her answer.

"No. Herb likes playing with his boats."

I wanted to ask more about her marriage, yet decided a different time and place would be more appropriate.

"Who thought to invite the Maestro to play in Bayfield?" I asked instead. "Was it you?"

"No, although I was very pleased when he accepted. Ask Zo, our marketing and events planning guru. I believe the idea originated with her. I could be mistaken, however. Why? Is it important?"

"Not necessarily."

"Is it your intention to merely buy back the Countess Borromeo for Paul or are you also hoping to punish the thieves?"

"The violin comes first."

"So you're willing to reward the thieves for stealing the Stradivarius—the very thing Renée is loath to do."

"I tend to deal with the world as I find it, not as I wish it were."

"That's an exceedingly practical attitude."

"Look up the word in the dictionary and you'll find my photo next to it."

"What kind of woman is she?"

"Who? Ms. Peyroux? I spoke to her only for a few moments."

"What is your impression?"

"Button-down, I think."

"Does she strike you as someone who likes to have fun?"

"Define fun."

"What would she give up for love?"

"Nothing. She would want it all."

Heather grew quiet; her eyes focused on something on the wall that I couldn't see.

"Why are you here, McKenzie?" she asked.

"I thought the letter made it clear."

"No, why are you here speaking to me?"

"I'm looking for help."

"Do you want me to tape an announcement on the front door next to the poster promoting the city's annual fish fry? Wanted, one used Stradivarius?"

"Not that kind of help."

"What, then?"

"Heather, why did they find the Countess Borromeo's empty violin case on the street where you live?"

She got that faraway look in her eyes again, although it didn't last very long.

"I don't know," she said.

"You must have a theory."

"Why must I?"

"Human nature. Most people like a world that's neat and orderly and easily explained."

"Mr. McKenzie, I have no explanation as to how the violin case ended up in front of my home, and I do not care to speculate. It has nothing to do with me."

In the next fifteen seconds, Heather slid off the stool, patted my arm, wished me well in my endeavors, and disappeared into the kitchen of her restaurant. She didn't offer to pick up the tab as Speegle had done at his place, but then I hadn't expected her to.

I paid the bill, left the Hill House, and walked the two blocks to Lakeside Tavern. The music started early in Bayfield and lasted only until 11:00 P.M. I heard it through the bar's open door from fifty yards away, a four-piece band trying hard to channel Stevie Ray Vaughan with mixed results. I stepped inside. The place was crowded mostly with younger tourists, although there were a few thirty- and forty-somethings sitting toward the back. Ellis saw me standing in the doorway and waved me to a small table that I presumed was in her section.

"Long shift," I said.

"I don't mind. If I weren't working I'd probably be sitting at the bar. Oh, and I want to thank you. That was the best tip I've received all month."

"I remember what it was like to be a struggling college kid."

"Would you like another South Shore?"

"Sure."

I settled in while Ellis fetched my pale ale. From where I sat, I could watch both the stage and the front door. There was no bouncer at the door, and I noticed some of the younger customers wandering in and out while carrying their drinks, something you never see in the Cities. A man stepped across the threshold. He and I might have been the only two men in all of Bayfield County who were wearing a sports coat. In fact, except for the color of his Dockers and shirt, he was dressed just like me. I tried not to hold that against him

He stood still while his eyes adjusted to the tavern lights. A kid brushed up against him, nearly spilling a beer on his jacket, yet he barely noticed.

That's because he's looking for someone.

The kids on the stage were finishing up another selection from the Stevie Ray Vaughan catalog. Three of them played drums, bass, and lead guitar exclusively, while the fourth alternated between guitar, harmonica, and electric piano. When the applause subsided, they introduced a fifth member of the band from the audience, a young woman who mounted the stage in a dress that covered only a third of her land mass. I didn't catch her name because Ellis reappeared with my ale. She set the bottle on the table and leaned in so I could hear her.

"I heard some guys talking about the Stradivarius, but I can't tell you about it right now," she said. "I'll tell you later. Okay?"

"Sure."

Ellis left again just as the woman began singing "Angel from Montgomery." She did a nice job of it except her voice was young, strong, and crystal clear and conveyed none of the pain the song was meant to communicate.

Only Bonnie Raitt should be allowed to sing this song, my inner voice announced.

Still, the lady received a nice ovation when she finished.

I had finally changed my ringtone, swapping Ella Fitzgerald's timeless cover of "Summertime" for Louis Armstrong's famous syncopated opening to "West End Blues," a fifteen-second cadenza that literally changed American music. It played to me in the brief lull that followed. I glanced at the cell's caller ID before answering.

"Hey," I said.

"How are you?" Nina asked. "Staying out of trouble?"

"Just barely. How 'bout you?"

"Typical Tuesday. Nice crowd, not huge."

"Who's in the big room?"

"The Willie August Project."

"Are they going all epic tonight with flutes and vibraphones?"

"No, it's just the trio."

"Tell them to play 'Chilly and the Mustangs' for me."

"Do you expect me to hold the phone up so you can listen?"

"Now that you mention it."

"I hear music. Where are you?"

For some reason, the question nudged me into looking around the bar as if my subconscious needed to confirm my location. The man in the sports coat was now sitting on a stool near the door and drinking from a white coffee mug.

"I'm at the Lakeside Tavern listening to some kids play the blues," I said.

"Anyone I should hear?"

"Not yet. Maybe in a couple of years after they learn their craft."

"What's the name of the band?"

I told her, and she paused long enough to write it down. Nina liked to keep track of talent and over the years had managed to give a boost to several unknown acts that hadn't stayed unknown for long. Esperanza Spalding came to mind.

"When are you coming home?" Nina asked.

"In a couple of days. If I haven't heard anything by then . . . It's a bit of a long shot, anyway. People keep telling me that the thieves who stole the Stradivarius are probably long gone, and they're probably right." I glanced at the man in the sports coat again. "There are a couple of things that don't quite jibe, though."

"There are always a couple of things that don't quite jibe."

"True. Very true."

I noticed Philip Speegle standing at the side of the stage. He was attempting to catch my eye without catching the eyes of everyone else. I gave him a head nod.

"I have to go," I said. "The club owner wants to speak to me."

"Is she as pretty as I am?"

"*He* most certainly is not, but then who is?"

"Good answer. Call me tomorrow."

"I will."

I slipped past Ellis, telling her I'd be right back, and made my way to the side of the stage. Speegle took my arm and led me down a short corridor to a small office. He shut the door behind us, effectively muffling most of the noise.

"Do you like this music?" he asked.

"If aliens invade the Earth, it won't be for our technology. They'll be coming for the blues."

Speegle wagged his finger at me.

"I like that answer. I don't believe it, but I like it."

Are you going to tell him that you stole the line from Wynton Marsalis? my inner voice asked. *I didn't think so.*

Speegle moved to a credenza that was shoved against the wall behind his desk. A bottle of Booker's and a stack of glasses were on top of it. He filled two glasses and handed one to me without asking. I said, "Thank you," and took a sip of the bourbon because I'm nothing if not polite.

"Any progress?" Speegle asked.

"I expect major developments at any moment."

"That's what the cops said. I didn't believe them, either."

"Give me time, I've only been here seven hours."

"Have you spoken to Heather? What did the Great Lady have to say?"

"I take it you don't like her much."

"Truth is, I like her very much. Don't tell her I said that."

"You've had your ups and downs, though."

"What did she tell you?"

"That you've had your ups and downs."

"We were born six hours apart on the same day in the same hospital, God's truth—the same doctor and nurses delivered us. Did she tell you that?"

"No."

"You'd think that would have created a bond between us."

Speegle finished his drink with one giant gulp, turned his back on me, and reached for the Booker's. A moment later, he spun back and let me see him drink half of the bourbon he had poured into his glass.

"I've been thinking how I can help you," Speegle said.

"I appreciate that."

"I think you should speak to Zofia McLean. She works for the chamber; handles our marketing and events."

"You told me that already, although not her name."

"I did? Huh. Must've forgotten."

Speegle took another pull on his bourbon.

"Tell me about the Great Lady," I said.

"Heather . . ." He drew the name out as if it were a lyric to a song. "You know who you should talk to, really talk to? Herb. Herb Voight. He can tell you a thing or two."

"Was he here when the theft took place?"

"No, he wasn't here, I don't think. That's cuz he was out on his goddamn boat like usual. But Herb, he sees things. He's the nicest guy in the world, but he sees things."

"What does he see?"

"Things. Things. They say the husband is always the last to know. That's not true. He's always the first to know, just the last one to admit it."

"Are you saying that Heather is cheating on him?"

"I didn't say that. I never said that. Don't be putting words in my mouth, McKenzie. I didn't say that about Heather."

"My mistake."

"Goddamn right. But McKenzie. You should talk to him."

"Thank you, Mr. Speegle. It's kind of you to help." I finished the Booker's and set the empty glass on his desk. "Thanks for the drink, too."

Speegle slumped in the chair behind the desk and balanced his glass on the arm.

" 'Sokay," he said.

I left the office, being sure to tightly close the door behind me.

Ellis caught my arm as I was heading back to the table.

"What I said before, about some guys talking about the Stradivarius?" she said. "One of them came back. There were three of them, and they left before the band came on. Now one of them is back, and he asked me, did I know McKenzie?"

"What did you say?"

"I said yes but that you weren't here."

"Is he still around?"

Ellis turned and looked down the length of the bar.

"Yes," she said.

"Do you know his name?"

"Curtis Shanklin. He works summers as a guide for Apostle Island Adventures outside town; gives kayak tours of the caves. This is his third year. Otherwise, he's at a school somewhere in Southern California."

"He goes there?"

"No, he teaches."

"Ellis, you are worth your weight in gold."

She actually patted her stomach as if she were wondering if she should put on a few pounds.

"Give me a minute to get back to my table," I said. "Then tell him who I am, okay?"

"Okay."

"Bring me another South Shore, too, will you?"

"Yes, sir."

I returned to my table. The band was on a break. A couple of the musicians were leaning on the stick and drinking bottled beer. A half-dozen guys were vying for the attention of the singer. I didn't blame them. If I had been twenty years younger, the dress she almost wore would have seized my attention as well.

Only a couple of moments passed before a young man approached my table. He looked as if he had been out of college for about three years; his hair was sandy and his face windswept like he spent a lot of time on the water.

"McKenzie," he said. "I wanna talk to you. Outside. Now."

Shanklin moved toward the door. He stopped when he realized that I wasn't following him. He quickly returned to the table.

"Didn't you hear me?" he asked.

"Manners," I said, "is how we show respect to one another."

"Huh?"

Ellis appeared with my ale. She dropped a napkin with the bar's name and logo in front of me and set the bottle of South Shore on top of it before removing the empty. Not once did she look at Shanklin or me.

I pointed at an empty chair.

"Sit," I said.

I deliberately refrained from using his name or what little else I knew about him. Knowledge really was power, and I wanted to hit him with it when it would do the most good.

"I said outside," Shanklin said.

"I said sit."

He set one hand on the back of my chair and the other on the tabletop. He leaned in close. His breath was scented with nachos and beer.

"If you ever want to see the violin again, you'll do exactly as I say," he said.

"Yes, but then I'd be an idiot. Look here . . ."

I removed the bottle from the napkin and pulled a pen from a pocket. I carefully wrote my e-mail address on the napkin and slid it across the table toward him.

"Take a photo of the violin and send it to me. If it looks like the real thing, maybe then I'll go with you."

"You can come see it now. It's outside."

"I don't believe you."

Shanklin's expression suggested that I had genuinely hurt his feelings. He stuffed the napkin in his pocket.

"Do you have the money?" he asked. "The $250,000?"

I made a show of patting my pockets.

"Not on me," I said. "You can tell that to your two friends outside in case they decide to jump me when I leave."

Shanklin flinched when I mentioned his friends.

"Where is the money?" he asked.

"You haven't done this sort of thing before, have you? The money's not in Bayfield. I can get it, though, in a reasonable amount of time, half in twenties and half in fifties, if you actually have the Stradivarius."

"I have it."

"Then I'll be delighted to conduct business with you. Now, off you go. Oh, and in the future—behave like a professional and not a thug, okay?"

Shanklin didn't like that at all. Any other time he would have made it a test of strength between us. He might have tried it anyway except for the way I smiled at him.

"You're one fucked-up old man," he said.

Old man?

He left. I watched him go, but only so I could search for the man in the sports coat while pretending not to. He was still sitting on the stool near the door, except now he was playing with his smartphone. I wondered if he took a pic of the kid. I had no doubt he already had mine.

The band came on for its final set, only by then I had already heard enough. I paid cash for the ale, once again leaving a hefty tip for Ellis, and headed for the door. The man in the sports coat did a nice job of not noticing.

I stepped outside and stretched while taking in a lungful of cool, clean air. Bayfield had quieted down considerably by then. I saw only a handful of people on the street and only a few vehicles, all of them on the main drag.

I headed west toward the Queen Anne. I walked only a couple of blocks, yet downtown had already become a blur of lights in the distance. Lamps still burned in some of the homes I passed, and occasionally I saw the flickering blue-gray hue of a TV, but most of the houses were dark. Early to bed, early to rise, I thought. I already missed the city.

The farther I moved away from downtown, the darker and quieter it became. My shoes on the pavement made the only sound I heard until— Tap. Tap. Tap. The noise startled me. I stopped walking and listened.

Tap. Tap. Tap. It reminded me of the dripping of a faucet. I pivoted slowly to determine where the sound was coming from and failed.

Huh.

I continued walking. The sound became louder; it reverberated almost like an echo. I stopped again.

Tap. Tap. Tap.

What the hell?

Granted, I was feeling a little light-headed by then—after all, I had consumed five beers, two glasses of wine, and a shot of bourbon since late afternoon. Still . . . My first thought was that Shanklin and his pals were stalking me, yet there was no sign of them.

The man in the sports coat? Officer Pilhofer?

I couldn't see them, either.

My hand went to my hip where I would have holstered my gun, but what I had told Chief Neville earlier was the truth—I wasn't carrying in Bayfield. Instead, my nine-millimeter SIG Sauer was nestled against the spare tire in the trunk of the Mustang. I kept walking.

Tap. Tap. Tap.

Up ahead I spied a dim light. It disappeared, reappeared, disappeared, and then I saw it again. I slowed my pace. The light seemed to be attached to a shadow. The shadow moved beneath a yellow streetlamp. It was a figure of a woman. She was wearing a dark cloak with the hood pulled over her head and carrying a lantern. In her hand was a walking stick—no, a staff with some kind of crystal fixed to the top. I called to her even as I sped up.

"Miss? Excuse me. Miss?"

The shadow passed through the streetlamp's circle of light and disappeared into darkness.

I started jogging. I reached the streetlamp and kept going in the direction of the shadow. I could no longer see the lantern. I stopped.

Tap. Tap. Tap.

I moved forward again. I thought I saw the light up ahead, yet when I reached the spot, it was gone.

"Miss?"

I seemed to be alone at the edge of a park; there was an iron bridge spanning a deep gorge and plenty of trees.

Tap. Tap . . .

The noise stopped.

I waited for it to continue; heard only silence.

Minutes passed.

This is what comes from mixing your drinks, my inner voice told me.

———

It was 11:00 P.M. when I returned to the Queen Anne. I saw no one and heard nothing as I climbed the wooden steps and went to my room. I was more than half in the bag, but at least I knew it. I set my alarm and lay down fully clothed on the bed. It took me about two minutes to fall asleep.

The alarm went off at exactly 3:00 A.M.—the "witching hour," although I'd be damned if I knew why demons would prefer that time of night; the shadow I had encountered earlier was wandering the streets closer to ten thirty. I silenced the alarm as quickly as I could for fear of waking my neighbors. Afterward, I stepped into the washroom and threw water on my face. I dried off and moved to the door. I put my ear against it. Heard nothing. I opened the door and stepped through it. I wasn't singing bar songs, yet I wasn't being particularly quiet either. Instead, I walked down the stairs and out the front door as if I owned the place.

The streets of Bayfield were empty; there was no pedestrian traffic and no vehicles of any kind. I walked slowly around the block. No one asked who I was or where I was going, no dogs barked, and I heard no tap, tap, tapping, only the sound of leaves trembling in the light breeze.

I reentered the Queen Anne. This time I moved slowly and carefully, as a thief might. I mounted the wooden stairs, transferring my weight from foot to foot in search of a creak. There was none. I walked all the way up to the third floor. The door to the Queen Anne Suite was at the far end of the corridor. It was closed, as I would have expected. I carefully gripped the doorknob and tried to turn it. It was locked. I rested the flat of my hand against the wood and counted slowly to ten. No one shouted, no one screamed, no one demanded to know who was out there. I stepped back and slowly made my way to my own room. I had heard no one, and apparently no one had heard me.

It could have been done like that, my inner voice told me.

Assuming Paul Duclos wasn't a light sleeper, the Countess Borromeo could have been taken just that way.

So why didn't I believe it?

My alarm went off again. This time it was 6:00 A.M. I opened my door and stepped into the corridor. There was movement in the room occupied by the sixty-something couple. I liked the idea that they were getting some early morning delight; I thought it spoke well for my future.

I took the staircase up. There was a morning news program playing softly from a TV behind the door of Victoria's Room, yet nothing from the Queen Anne Suite.

I took the staircase all the way down. This time I heard noises emanating from the kitchen and a woman's voice singing that she was all about the bass, the bass, no treble. Not Connor, I decided. Probably a cook he hired to prepare breakfast. I would have to learn when she arrived in the morning and what her routine was.

I returned to my room. True, I didn't see anyone, and no one saw me, yet the likelihood of encountering traffic made breaking into Duclos's room and stealing the Stradivarius while he was on his morning walk less viable. 'Course, I never cared for that theory anyway.

SIX

The four couples I had met the previous evening, plus one more, were all sitting at the dining room table and chatting amiably among themselves when I came down the stairs again at eight o'clock. A woman, standing at the buffet with her back to me, was pouring coffee from a silver pot into a china cup. There were murmurs of recognition as I entered the room. Alice said, "Good morning, McKenzie"—and the woman turned abruptly, an expression of shock on her face that quickly turned to pleasure.

She was wonderfully wholesome-looking, a twenty-eight-year-old Nordic princess with perfect teeth in a perfect mouth formed into a perfect smile, eyes glittering like liquid azurite, hair as lustrous as spun gold, skin that reminded me of fresh buttermilk. She was wearing khaki shorts that revealed long, sculptured legs, and a short-sleeve scoop-neck T-shirt made from stretch-fabric that clung to her athletic body like damp cloth. She was the most beautiful woman I had ever met in person, although I would never admit that to Nina, and easily the most treacherous.

"Heavenly," I said.

Connor chose that moment to emerge from the kitchen with

a tray of mimosas that he doled out to the other guests. He heard the word and from the grin on his face obviously thought I was referring to the woman's appearance instead of her name—Heavenly Elizabeth Petryk.

"McKenzie," he said. "Have you met Caroline? Caroline, this is McKenzie."

Heavenly crossed the dining room with the coffee cup in her left hand. She extended her right.

"Caroline Kaminsky," she said. "A pleasure to meet you."

Her eyes sparkled with humor.

"Ms. Kaminsky," I said. "The pleasure is mine."

She exhaled softly—apparently relieved that I hadn't given her up.

"Caroline is with the Wisconsin Department of Natural Resources," Alice said. "She's investigating the Lake Superior shoreline for . . . what was it again?"

Heavenly paused at an empty spot at the dining room table. She looked at me with that beatific grin of hers. I stepped over and pulled out the chair. She answered as she sat.

"I was sent to conduct an inventory of aquatic invasive species in coastal wetlands," she said.

"To what purpose?" I asked.

Heavenly knew I was testing her.

"To determine which of the region's canals and waterways are most susceptible to invasion by AIS such as Asian carp," she said. "And to prioritize those areas for invasive species management and control."

"What have you discovered so far?"

"My research remains inconclusive. I'll need to remain here for a few days more."

"We're delighted to have you, Caroline," Connor said.

I bet, my inner voice said.

"I don't know if you know it, but McKenzie, he's also some kind of an investigator," Alice said.

"Is that what he is?" Heavenly said.

"He's trying to recover the Stradivarius violin that was stolen last week, but he won't let us help."

"I'd be too frightened to get involved with something like that," Heavenly said.

Yeah, right.

By then I was sitting comfortably at the table, a scone on my plate.

"May I trouble you for the marmalade?" I said aloud.

The fifty-something woman whose name I had forgotten passed it to me without comment.

Conversation picked up after that, none of it about the Countess Borromeo, I was happy to hear. Mostly, it dealt with the adventures the vacationing couples had already enjoyed in Bayfield and the ones that they were hoping to embark on. Meanwhile, Connor deftly served our breakfast. It consisted of poached pear with yogurt sauce, raspberry-stuffed French toast, baked eggs with tomatoes and basil, red new potatoes with dill, hickory smoked bacon, lemon-iced buttermilk scones, and orange and cranberry-raspberry juice. What I enjoyed most— the bacon. You can't take me anywhere.

Connor had returned to the kitchen by the time I asked, "Have any of you seen a woman dressed in a black cloak and carrying a lantern and a long staff with a crystal on top?"

"Oh, yes, yes," said the fifty-something woman. "The Ghost Lady."

"Ghost Lady?"

"She conducts ghost tours of the city, pointing out those places that are supposed to be haunted. Tells stories—she's wonderful."

"She's a real flesh-and-blood woman, then."

"Oh, yes. What did you think?"

"I saw her walking late last night and I didn't know what to think."

"Did she frighten you, McKenzie?" Heavenly asked. "Were you sure you were seeing a ghost?"

"I was just curious," I said.

"She claims that a man was murdered in the Queen Anne," the fifty-something woman said.

"Don't say that, Cassie," her husband said.

Cassie, my inner voice said. *I remember now. Her name's Cassie. And her husband's name is . . . arrrg.*

Cassie leaned forward and lowered her voice.

"The man who originally built this house was very rich," she said. "He owned a sawmill, fishing boats, a brownstone quarry, a hotel—a lot of things. Only he died without leaving a will—or at least no one found a will—so everything went to his eldest son, which started a family war that lasted over a hundred years."

Cassie edged even closer to the table; we all leaned with her.

"People were murdered," she said. "They say—the Ghost Lady says that some of their spirits still haunt Bayfield."

She doesn't care for a high-profile burglary, my inner voice said. *But cold-blooded murder and ghosts—that's something she can get behind?*

We were so intent on what Cassie had to say that we didn't notice when Connor reentered the dining room.

"Oh, no," he said. "You've been on one of Maggie's ghost tours."

Cassie sat back in her chair. She seemed embarrassed.

"Is any of it true?" Alice asked.

"Not very much," Connor said. "But Mags was never one to let the facts get in the way of a good story. I'll give her credit for one thing, though—she knows more about what's going on in Bayfield than anyone."

"Perhaps she knows what happened to McKenzie's violin," Heavenly said.

———

I was a little surprised that Heavenly was the first to leave the dining room. Soon the remaining guests followed suit, leaving me alone. When Connor retired to the foyer to help the sixty-something couple check out, I made my way into the kitchen. I found a woman cleaning pots and pans while she hummed to herself.

"Breakfast was wonderful," I said.

"Thank you. But . . ." She wagged a finger at me. "No recipes."

Her smile made me smile.

"I wouldn't dream of trying to re-create your meal," I said. "I don't handle failure very well."

"Oh, it's not that hard."

"Have you been working here long?"

"A couple of months. I cook Wednesday through Saturday in the mornings here and then at Hill House in the evenings."

"Long days."

"No, no," she said. "I'm here starting at about six and done by nine-ish. I'm at the restaurant from four through ten at night, when we stop serving, so it's only a nine-hour day with a six-hour lunch break, and I get Sunday, Monday, and Tuesday off."

"Were you responsible for the garlic chicken penne I had last night?"

"I wasn't cooking, but . . . it is my recipe."

"Delicious."

"We're going to be real good friends, I can tell."

"My name is McKenzie."

"Connor mentioned you. You're investigating the violin thing."

"I am."

"What can I do for you?"

"You said you arrive here at six?"

"Usually. Sometimes earlier, sometimes later, depending on how complex the menu is that day."

"You were here at six when the Stradivarius was stolen?"

"The cops asked me that. So did the FBI. I was here at six, well, more like a quarter to. I didn't see anything, though; I didn't hear anything, either. Sorry. I was too busy battering pots and pans. Besides, I almost never leave the kitchen."

"Did you see any strangers lurking about? Perhaps when you arrived that morning?"

The cook spread her hands wide.

"Sorry," she said again.

"About the chicken penne recipe."

She laughed heartily.

"Nice try," she said.

I returned to the Peacock Chamber and reviewed the police reports that Mr. Donatucci had given me, just to be thorough. Everything the cook said coincided with what she had told the authorities.

I was deciding on what to do next when I heard a knock on my door.

"Who is it?" I asked.

"Caroline Kaminsky."

"Come in."

The door opened and Heavenly swept into the room—it was the correct word, swept. She closed the door and leaned her back against it. Damn, she was a fetching lass.

"Good morning, Caroline," I said. "What can I do for you?"

"McKenzie," she said.

Heavenly opened her arms wide and came toward me. She hugged me and I hugged her back because, well, like I said earlier, I'm nothing if not polite.

"It is so good to see you again," she said.

"I wish I could say the same."

"McKenzie!"

She pulled away. The shocked and outraged expression on her face lasted about two seconds before it was replaced by a smile.

"What are you doing here, Heavenly?" I asked.

"The same thing you are. I'm after the Countess Borromeo."

"You mean you didn't steal it already?"

"What kind of question is that?"

"Based on past experience . . ."

"I'm hurt, McKenzie. Hurt by your insinuation."

"Paul Duclos is offering $250,000 for its safe return."

"I heard. I bet the thieves were expecting more."

"How about you?"

"I'd be more than satisfied with a quarter of a million."

"Sure you would."

"Just as long as I come out ahead, that's the main thing."

"Heavenly—"

"I don't have the violin, McKenzie. Honestly, I don't. If I did, I'd make a deal right now and invite you to dinner. At least I'd buy dinner after you came up with the money. You do have the money, don't you?"

She moved closer to me.

"It's in the Cities," I said.

"Oh? Is Nina holding it?"

"No, she's not."

"How is Nina these days?"

Heavenly ran the tips of her fingers under the collar of my shirt.

"Do you care?" I asked her.

"I do. I've always liked her, even if she doesn't like me. What did she call me last time? A thug?"

"Actually, I called you a thug. In any case, Nina doesn't object to your profession so much as the fact that you're always hitting on her boyfriend."

Heavenly kissed me hard on the mouth and smiled her irresistible smile.

"Stop teasing," I said.

She thought that was funny.

I gave her a gentle shove. Heavenly found a comfortable spot on the corner of my bed. I sat in a chair far enough away that it would take an effort for her to attack me again.

"Seriously," she said. "I really am happy to see you."

"If you don't have the Countess already, what are you doing in Bayfield?"

"Looking for it."

"For whom?"

"Does there have to be a for whom?"

"You checked into a bed-and-breakfast under an assumed name."

"There could be a lot of reasons for that."

"Only one. You don't want anybody to know that you're here. Why? You're not wanted, are you, Heavenly?"

"People have been wanting me since I was fourteen years old—except for you, of course. Maybe that's why I like you so much."

"I meant by the police."

"No, I'm not wanted by the police."

"I could check."

"What are you going to do? Call your friend Bobby? How is Commander Dunston these days? He's still a commander, right? They haven't made him chief of police or anything, have they?"

"Not yet."

"There's no paper on me, McKenzie. As far as I know."

"Well, then . . ."

"There you go again, being all accusatory."

"When did you get here?"

"I'm going to answer that question. Do you know why?"

"Why?"

"Because I know you're going to check anyway. I arrived Saturday morning."

By then the theft was national news, I reminded myself, but the Peyroux Foundation—and Midwest Insurance—had not yet posted the conditions for the $250,000 reward they were offering. That would come later in the afternoon.

"Do you think the Stradivarius is still in Bayfield?" I asked.

"Yes."

"Who do you think took it?"

"Connor Rasmussen." Something in my expression must have given me away, because Heavenly quickly added, "You don't believe it."

"I walked the Queen Anne last night and again this morning—"

"So that was you outside my door at three A.M."

"I don't think Connor could have taken the Countess while Duclos was sleeping in the room. I don't think he would have dared try it while Duclos went for his walk for fear of bumping into one of the other guests or the cook."

"I agree."

"So . . ."

"He did it while everyone was at breakfast. He dashed up the stairs, took the violin, came down the stairs. Ninety-three seconds flat. I timed it."

"How did Connor get the violin out of the house before the authorities searched it?"

"He had an accomplice."

"Who?"

Heavenly waved a finger at me.

"I don't know," she said. "What do you know about a kid named Curtis Shanklin?"

"Teacher from Oceanside, California, works summers as a guide for Apostle Island Adventures. Fancies himself to be an extreme sports athlete. He's not a kid, either. He's only a year younger than I am."

"Look at it from my side of forty. What does he teach?"

"Junior high English. Why do you ask?"

"Last night he offered to sell me the Countess Borromeo. All I needed to do was step outside with him."

"Did you?"

"I might have if I knew where his two friends were."

"I met Shanklin's friends; don't remember their names. How did you leave it?"

"I told him to e-mail me a photo of the Strad, and if I liked it, we'd talk."

"I take it you haven't heard from him."

"Not yet."

Heavenly glanced at the gold watch around her wrist.

"He's probably on the lake with a tour," she said. "Won't be back until midafternoon."

"You know his schedule, too? I'll be damned."

"McKenzie, I've been here five days. Every heterosexual male within a twenty-mile radius has hit on me, and a few non-heterosexual females as well."

"Still."

"Shanklin likes to talk about himself. Most men do."

"Did you attempt to recruit him; get him to do your heavy lifting?"

"Why do you ask?"

"He reminds me a little of your last boyfriend."

"The one you threw in front of a speeding car?"

"That was an unavoidable accident."

"I'm on my own this time."

"Does Shanklin have any kind of relationship with Connor?"

"I don't think he's Connor's accomplice, if that's what you're asking. I don't think he has the Countess, either. Do you?"

"No. I've been spreading word that I'm willing to buy back the violin. He thought I was carrying the $250,000 in my pocket."

"That's what you get for painting a target on your forehead. What are you going to do now?"

"I have a few ideas."

"Want some company?"

"No."

"We've worked well together in the past. The gold hidden by Jelly Nash. The lily—"

"We've never worked together, Heavenly. Or should I call you Caroline? It was always you on one side and me on the other and somehow, some way, we'd meet in the middle."

"Think about it."

I did. What is it they say about keeping your enemies close? Of course, Heavenly wasn't really my enemy. More like an unscrupulous rival.

"What's your cell number?" I asked.

I inputted the digits into my smartphone as she recited them to me.

"I'll give you a call if something comes up," I said.

Heavenly rose from the bed and moved to the door.

"Be sure to give Nina my love," she said.

"If I do, she might come up here and give you hers."

SEVEN

Bayfield Superior Marina practically glistened the way sunlight reflected off the water and the boats riding in their slips. I studied it from a metal bench in Memorial Park. The benches were all angled to look out at Lake Superior and Madeline Island beyond. Anyone watching Paul Duclos play from the gazebo on the corner would have had to sit sideways. 'Course, there had been so many people in the park that night, even those who had arrived early enough to secure seats probably ended up standing to see anyway.

The marina was tucked behind imposing breakers. Children and their parents crawled over the rocks and concrete, but there were no tourists walking the docks. The man who operated the marina explained to me that permission was required to gain access to the boats.

"Many of our guests, at least during the season, this is their home," he said. "You'd be amazed how many people live on their boats."

I asked if Herb Voight was on his boat. He didn't know, but he allowed me to take a look. I walked along the docks until

I reached slip number 77; the marina boasted 135 slips, and the man said 110 were rented for the season. I discovered a thirty-footer there with the name *Heather II* printed across the transom. I knew enough about boats to know that you don't hop on board without asking permission first; that would be like walking into someone's house without knocking.

"Ahoy," I called. "Anyone aboard?"

There was no answer.

"Mr. Voight?"

"He'p ya, son?"

The question came from a man standing on the deck of another thirty-foot boat that provided full accommodations in the slip next to *Heather II*. He was much older than me with white hair, and so thin I was sure a heavy wind could pick him up and carry him across the lake at any moment.

"Yes, sir," I said. "I was looking for Mr. Voight."

"Not here."

"I guess not. Maybe I'll find him at his mansion on Wilson."

I tossed in that last bit so the old man would think I knew Voight personally.

"More likely he's out getting himself some breakfast," the old man said. "Buy ya a beer while ya wait?"

"I haven't turned down a free beer in my life."

"Come aboard."

I did.

"Name's Jack," the old man said. "Jack Westlund."

His way of shaking hands was to hand me a Leinenkugel.

"McKenzie," I said.

I took the beer and drank.

"Good morning, Bayfield," I said.

"Attaboy. So, whaddya want wit' Voight? Can I ask?"

"I'm looking into the theft of the Stradivarius."

"Yeah, yeah, yeah. Isn't that somethin'? No crime in Bayfield t' speak of for God knows how long, and then this. 'Mazing."

"Are you from Bayfield?"

"Me? Nah. From Fitchburg down by Madison. Retired a few years back and now come up here t' stay durin' the summer. Some people have lake homes. This is my home. Superior is my lake."

"That is so cool," I said. I meant it, too.

"I like it," Jack said.

"May I ask how all this works?"

"Whaddya mean?"

"You rent a slip in the marina for the summer, am I right?"

"You are correct, sir."

"Do you just come and go as you please?"

"Yeah, man. That's what makes it fun. Go across t' Isle Royale or Grand Marais, up to Houghton, whatever. Sometimes, I'll just scoot over t' the Apostles, find a protected anchorage, drop anchor, lower the dingy, barbecue on the beach, catch some rays. You'd be surprised. Some nights you'd see a hundred boats out there from all over Superior. Just one big party."

"You don't inform the marina when you leave?"

"Oh, oh, I see what you're askin'. Well, yeah, sometimes. See, what you do, if you're gonna be gone overnight or for maybe a couple of nights, you might pass the word. That way they can rent out your slip t' some other boat while you're gone; get yourself a few bucks rebate on your rent, you know? I do it all the time. Fixed income, what can I say?"

"How about Voight?"

"Doubt he bothers. Man has more money than God. At least the old lady does."

"When you travel, do you file . . . what's the seagoing equivalent of a flight plan?"

"Float plan."

"No kidding?"

"Yeah, yeah, yeah. Go over t' the Coast Guard station across the way and let 'em know what's going on. Leastways I do. On long trips, I mean. Let 'em know if I'm crossing over t' Canada or what. Most people don't bother, though. It's not required by law or nuthin'. I don't do it myself if I'm just takin' a short trip, huggin' the shoreline to Duluth or someplace like that. Why bother?"

"Were you here for the big concert?"

"Yeah, I was. Sittin' right where you are now, sippin' Leinie's, the music comin' across the water, oh man, it was beautiful. I'm not what you'd call a classical music fan. Give me Hank or Johnny, any day. The way that boy was playin'—it made me reconsider, you know?"

"Was Voight here, too?"

"That was the damnedest thing. He wasn't here. Then he was. Then he wasn't. What I mean—he wasn't here for the concert. Or the big after-party, neither. Him or his boat. He didn't tie up till—I was asleep until like close to one o'clock. That's when I hear 'im. I peek outta the porthole. He's got a woman wit' him, Heather, I figure, so I roll over, go back to sleep. Next mornin', Voight and the boat is gone. I don't see him again till Friday afternoon. Now, they done that many times before, him and Heather just takin' off in the boat. But after midnight? What's that about?"

"Are you sure it was Heather?"

"Who else?"

We chatted some more, although I changed the subject—I didn't want Jack to wonder why I was asking so many questions about Voight. He offered me a second Leinie's. I declined, telling him that I needed to get back to it, without actually explaining what that meant. He told me to drop by anytime.

A few minutes later, I was back on shore and walking along First Street. Tourists interested in kayaking to the sea caves, boating, fishing, hiking, and other physical activities were already up and at it. Those planning a day of leisurely sightseeing and shopping, though, were mostly still at breakfast; the galleries and stores had not yet opened to greet them. Which meant the streets of Bayfield were virtually empty. Which made it ridiculously easy for me to spot the man I saw at the Lakeside Tavern the previous evening.

He was sitting on a bench outside the Bayfield Maritime Museum, and since I had switched to shirtsleeves, I could say with confidence that he was now the only man in Bayfield County wearing a sports coat. It was already seventy-three degrees with the weatherman's promise of another ten later in the day, so I was pretty sure the jacket was meant to hide a gun. That was just a guess, though.

He buried his face in a tourist newspaper as I walked past. I pretended not to notice him. I didn't want him to start working harder at conducting his surveillance; I found it far more comforting to know exactly where he was at all times.

Still, I had to wonder—who the hell was this guy?

The high school girl sitting behind the desk at the Bayfield Chamber of Commerce–slash–Visitor Bureau viewed my presence with alarm. She didn't even wait until I told her what I wanted before she was on her feet and seeking assistance in the offices behind her. A woman appeared that I had not seen during my previous visit. She was tall and slim, and her brown eyes watched me as if she were afraid she might miss something important if she looked away.

"May I help you?" she asked.

"Yes. I'd like to speak with Zofia McLean."

"I'm Zofia."

"Zo." I smiled brightly and offered my hand like we were old friends who hadn't seen each other for a while. "It's a pleasure to meet you. I'm McKenzie."

She shook my hand reluctantly. People in Wisconsin were nearly as polite as those living in Minnesota, but not quite.

"I'm told that you're the marketing and events manager for Bayfield," I said.

"Yes."

"Both Heather Voight and Philip Speegle suggested that I speak to you."

"They did?"

"Is now convenient?"

"If it doesn't take too long."

"How 'bout outside? It's such a beautiful day."

"I guess that would be all right."

I went to the front door and held it open for her. She stepped past cautiously. I didn't know what others had told her about me, but it seemed to have made her nervous.

There was a garden outside the gray and rose-colored building with a bench in the middle of it—there were benches everywhere you looked in Bayfield. I glanced around as we sat yet didn't see the man in the sports coat, which didn't mean he couldn't see me.

"I want to apologize first of all," I said. "I certainly didn't mean to agitate you or your colleagues when I arrived yesterday."

"Oh, McKenzie, of course you did."

"I'm here to help recover the stolen Stradivarius—"

"I know. I suppose everyone in Bayfield knows by now."

"I have a letter from Paul Duclos."

"I know that, too."

So much for being nervous, my inner voice said.

"You seem to think that the theft of the violin is a good thing for Bayfield," Zofia said. "You are so wrong."

"It wouldn't be the first time. However"—I held up a finger to emphasize my point—"recovering it could only be to your advantage, am I right?"

"What is it that you want?"

"I'm told that you're the one who invited the Maestro to play in your Concert in the Park series."

"Yes—regrettably."

"How did that come about?"

"I contacted the St. Paul Chamber Orchestra, and they put me in touch with a man who put me in touch with another man who put me in touch with Duclos."

"Yes, but whose idea was it?"

"Mine."

"You knew that Duclos was a Bayfield native?"

"Certainly."

"Are you from Bayfield?"

"No. I'm originally from Milwaukee. I attended Marquette University. When I graduated, I moved up here and took the assistant's job that Amy has now. When my boss—the woman who was the city's marketing director before me—when she moved on I was promoted into her spot. That was three years ago. Since then I've often been told that the great Maestro grew up in Bayfield and that I should arrange to have him return for a concert, only he's a world-class violinist and I have a limited budget."

"Who told you?"

"About Duclos? Heather Voight, for one. The mayor, Lauren Ternes, dozens of people."

"Did you know that Heather and Duclos were high school sweethearts?"

"It's no secret. There's a photograph of the two of them in Egg-Ceptional."

"Egg-Ceptional?"

"Egg-Ceptional Breakfast and Bakery. It's one of Heather's restaurants. Just up the street. I'm surprised you haven't been there. It's probably the most popular spot in Bayfield."

"How did the concert come about?"

"It was the result of pure desperation. Have you ever heard of Big Top Chautauqua?"

"No."

"How do I explain those guys? Big Top Chautauqua is a kind of weekly down-home variety show performed mostly in an eight-hundred-seat circus tent on top of Mount Ashwabay some miles south of here. I say mostly because Big Top also tours. Excerpts of their performances are broadcast across the country in an hour-long radio program called *Tent Show Radio,* usually on public stations. It's very popular. They've had artists like Johnny Cash, B. B. King, Lyle Lovett, and Willie Nelson sitting in.

"For our concerts, we try to book a variety of acts—folk, bluegrass, country-western, jazz, whatever—mostly from around the region, mostly lesser-known artists who meet our budget. Sometimes, though, we're able to lure the better-known artists who come up here to do Big Top Chautauqua. They're going to be in the area anyway, and if they can fit us into their schedule, some figure why not? They're entertainers, after all. They like to entertain. We play up the venue, too—the open-air park, the gazebo, the lake. A lot of musicians seem to really like that. One group actually recorded their performance for a live album, although I never did hear what happened about that.

"Two weeks ago, well, closer to three now, the group that we had scheduled, who was also scheduled to play Big Top, canceled on both of us. Something about a car accident. Big Top had the resources to deal with that; all they needed to do was pick up a phone. Only there was no guarantee that their replacement act would have had the time to play Bayfield, or even that it would want to. So I needed to find someone else who was going to be in the area and who had an empty date on their calendar. That's when I thought—why not give Duclos a try? I knew he was going to be in Duluth with the St. Paul Chamber Orchestra; WHWA-FM, the local public radio station, had been promoting the concert. I made my calls, and damn if he didn't agree. For free, even.

"The people at Big Top were very jealous, but everyone else was excited as can be. And everyone did what I wanted; I hardly needed to ask. The local radio stations, even Real Rock J96, played up the concert. Flyers went up everywhere. Heather agreed to host both a welcome-home dinner and the postconcert reception at Hill House. Connor Rasmussen agreed to put up the Maestro at the Queen Anne on Wednesday and Thursday nights at no charge. I was a hero. Then the Stradivarius was stolen and now I'm not."

"What about Geoff Pascoe?"

"That was the one condition from Duclos. He wanted someone to play piano with him. Someone really good, although he didn't specify what that meant. I knew Pascoe because he had played for us once before; he had a master's in music from UMD and played with the Duluth Superior Orchestra. I gave him a call, and he jumped at the chance to accompany the great man. I didn't learn until later that he actually canceled a job so he could do it. He said he'd perform for free, too, but I gave him a stipend anyway."

"Where can I find him?"

"He lives in Superior. Do you want his phone number and address?"

"Yes, please."

Zofia went into the building. While she was gone I wandered the garden and pretended to look at the flowers while searching for the man in the sports coat. I couldn't find him. I was surprised by how apprehensive that made me feel. Zofia returned with a square of paper that she thrust into my hand. I think she was anxious to be rid of me. I moved her back to the bench just the same.

"Did you spend much time with Duclos?" I asked her.

"I didn't let him out of my sight from the moment he arrived. I escorted him to and from the Queen Anne, to the dinner, sightseeing around Bayfield the next day, to the park for rehearsals, to the reception. I did everything but tuck him in at night, and I might have done that, too, if he had asked."

My, my, my, my inner voice chanted.

"Are you telling me he was never alone?" I asked aloud.

"Not before the concert, anyway. After the reception, he said he was going to bed early, and when I offered to drive him to the Queen Anne he told me to stay and enjoy myself, and, yeah, I wasn't there when he went for his walk the next morning, either. I should have been. People say I should have been."

"That's because they're looking for someone to blame. It isn't you, Zofia. From what I've heard, you were fabulous."

"That might not help. My contract comes up for renewal at the end of summer."

"Who did Duclos see while he was here?"

"Everybody."

"Everybody?"

"Ev-er-ry-bod-y. The mayor shook his hand, the common council members, most of the chamber; old friends from when he used to live here; neighbors who knew his family before they moved away—I never saw so many selfies being taken in my life. I thought the Maestro would get annoyed after a while, but if he did, he didn't show it. He was lovely to everyone he met."

"Was he more lovely to anyone in particular?"

"You mean besides Heather? I don't think he was ever more than a dozen feet away from her either at the welcome-home dinner or the postconcert reception the next evening. I told you about the prom picture—it must have been a helluva night, because it's almost forty-five years later and they were still all touchy-feely. My date to prom, I hope he falls off a mountain."

"Did anyone show particular interest in the violin?"

"Not that I noticed. You know what, though? I knew it was a Stradivarius. I knew it was worth a fortune. Yet I didn't pay a moment's attention to it from the time he arrived. I don't remember anyone else asking about it, either. It was just a violin; something he carried, you know?"

"I know."

"Don't you think that's odd?"

"Not as odd as I thought a couple days ago."

"McKenzie, some people—at least people in the chamber—they're upset that you're here. They want all this business to just go away. If you actually do find the violin, though, it might save my job."

"I'll do my best."

Now that I was armed with Zofia's note, my first thought was to give Geoff Pascoe a call and arrange a meeting. Yet when I moved from the bench to the sidewalk in front of the tourist bureau, I was able to read a sign just up the street—EGG-CEPTIONAL BREAKFAST AND BAKERY—and two facts collided in the back of my head, causing me to change my mind. The first was Jack Westlund telling me that he thought Herb Voight had gone to get breakfast. The second was Zofia telling me that the Egg-Ceptional was the most popular spot in Bayfield.

I walked the half block. A bell tinkled above my head when I entered, adding to the noise inside. There was a kitchen, a half-dozen glass cases filled with bakery goods, and plenty of tables with picnic-style tablecloths. Most of the tables were occupied. I asked the woman behind the cash register if Voight was around. She pointed behind me. There was a hole in the wall. Apparently, Egg-Ceptional had expanded from that one room to the building next door. There were about a hundred framed photographs on the wall between the two rooms. I found one with Heather Voight dressed in a soft blue shift-dress and wearing a wrist corsage. She was posing with Paul Duclos, who was dressed in a fawn-colored tuxedo with dark brown lapels and a tie that reminded me of the arms on a windmill. They were both smiling happily, and I wondered, Were they ever really that young? Was I?

I stepped through the hole in the wall and found more tables filled with customers and waitresses serving them. No waiters, I noticed.

There was a sixty-something man sitting alone at a small table by the window reading a copy of the *Ashland Daily Press* over the remains of his meal. I took a chance and went up to him.

"Mr. Voight?" I asked. His head came up and he smiled. "I'm McKenzie."

"The troublemaker?"

He said it as if it were the finest compliment he could give a fellow.

" 'Fraid so," I said.

He stood and shook my hand as if he were genuinely happy to meet me.

"Have a seat, have a seat," he said.

I sat.

"Mr. Westlund told me I might find you here," I said.

"Offer you a beer, did he?"

"Yes, sir."

"Did you take it?"

"Of course."

"There you go. He's a good man, Jack. Hates to drink alone. I've often cracked open a cold one early in the morning just to keep him company. Now you tell me, what can I get you?"

"Coffee. Black."

"Darcy." Voight waved at a waitress, who scurried over. "Black coffee for my friend McKenzie. Put it on the boss's tab."

"That's kind of you," I said.

"Don't thank me. Thank my wife. It's her tab."

He laughed like it was a great joke on her.

Darcy returned with the coffee. As I picked up my mug, Voight lifted his.

"My old man used to tell me when I was a kid, find yourself a beautiful rich woman to take care of you," he said.

"Funny, my father used to say the same thing."

"There you go."

Voight tapped my mug with his, and we both drank.

"McKenzie, they say you're looking for Duclos's violin."

"I am."

"Any success so far?"

"None whatsoever."

"Explain something to me."

"If I can."

"When the burglary happened, the police were all over the place asking questions, the police and the county sheriff—where were you, what did you see, what do you know—and then it was the FBI's turn and the insurance company's, and most people were okay with that. We watch TV; we know how it works. But then you come to town and everyone gets discombobulated. My wife, the chamber—McKenzie this, McKenzie that, why's he here, when's he leaving. What's that about?"

"My presence suggests that the crime was committed by someone in Bayfield and that the violin is still here. It makes people anxious. It makes them wonder if their next-door neighbor might be the culprit."

"Was it committed by someone in Bayfield? Is the violin still here?"

"Damned if I know."

"Basically, then, you're just wandering around shaking cages until someone jumps up and says, 'Yes, I did it and I'm glad, ha, ha, ha, ha, ha,' like in those old Perry Masons."

"Something like that."

"Well, I wish you luck."

"Thank you."

"I gotta say, though, to be honest, I don't care if you ever find the damn thing."

"No?"

"I figure it serves Duclos right."

"Because he was careless?"

"Because he's an asshole. Coming to town like he owned the place and everyone in it, making moves on my wife like he did."

"He hit on Heather?"

"At the so-called welcome-home dinner. I understand my place in the world, McKenzie. I know I was Heather's second choice. Maybe even third or fourth. And maybe our marriage isn't what it should be, but you don't make a play for another man's wife while he's standing there watching, I don't care if you did dance with her at your high school prom. That's just not right."

"No, it isn't."

"Heather and I . . . I moved here fifteen years ago, ran a full-service gas station, the only one within miles, popular with the tourists; she bought it from me. Paid enough that I could spend most of my time on my boat. That's how we met, when she bought me out. Afterward, we spent time together, mainly because I was the most presentable single man in town that was near her age, which makes me sound more special than I really am. Let's face it, the entire population of Bayfield County wouldn't fill Lambeau Field if you multiplied it five times. Yet there was never any talk of us getting married."

"What changed?"

"I don't really know. Just one day she started asking if I ever thought of settling down with a wealthy, mature, fairly attractive woman who she promised would make very few demands on my time—her exact words, so help me. Do you think Heather's beautiful, McKenzie?"

"Yes, sir."

"I think she's beautiful. Even at her age. She has a kind heart, too, although maybe it's not so easy to see sometimes. So I said yes. Hell yes, I said yes. Wouldn't you? Our tenth wedding anniversary is coming up soon."

Tenth, my inner voice said. *Didn't the Maestro marry Renée Peyroux ten years ago?*

"At first we shared everything," Voight said. "Especially our time. All we share now is a house and occasionally a bed. Heather has all of her businesses to occupy her, make her happy. I spend most of my time on the boat. My point, McKenzie"—he raised his coffee mug again—"the old man gave me bad advice."

I raised my own mug in reply.

"There you go," he said, and we both drank.

"Then Duclos gets all touchy-feely with my wife at dinner," Voight said. "Shoulda busted him up. Would have too, except . . ."

"Except?"

"Heather wouldn't have liked it."

"Is that why you left?"

Voight stared as if I had accused him of something.

"What do you mean?" he asked.

"Jack Westlund told me you weren't here for the concert."

"Yeah, that's right. I just took off. Didn't want to hear that idiot play. Went down to Duluth on Thursday instead. Didn't return until Friday afternoon. I found out what happened with Duclos's violin when I tied up at the marina. Gotta tell you, McKenzie—it didn't make me cry."

We left Egg-Ceptional together. Voight walked off in the direction of the marina. I headed back toward the Queen Anne. The streets were more crowded than before, so I didn't see the man in the sports coat again until I was about thirty yards away from him. He was sitting on yet another bench, this one in front of an antiques store, and pretending to read the same tourist newspaper. The sight of him actually made me feel more relaxed, although . . .

C'mon, man, my inner voice said. *You're not even trying.*

As I approached the bench, I retrieved my smartphone from my pocket. I slowed as I inputted the phone number that Zofia had given me, and stopped altogether when Geoff Pascoe answered my call. The man in the sports coat was only a few feet away, so I was probably speaking louder than I needed to when I identified myself and asked Pascoe if he would be kind enough to spare me a few minutes of his time.

"Where are you?" he asked.

"Bayfield."

"I'm in Superior . . ."

"Yes . . ."

"But I'm heading up to Red Cliff in a couple of hours. I'm playing a happy-hour gig at the casino with a vocalist I've only met once, and we're meeting ahead of time to plan the sets and rehearse. If you want to meet then . . ."

"That would be great."

"How 'bout Superior 13 at, say . . . I have a couple of errands to run first. Would two-ish work?"

"Yes, it would. Thank you."

"Superior 13 is right off the highway, in case you're wondering."

I thanked him again before ending the call and turning to the man in the sports coat.

"Did you get all that?" I asked.

"Are you talking to me?"

I stepped closer. He was as tall as I was and about the same age, with eyes that gave nothing away. He deliberately folded his newspaper and set it on the bench next to him. There was tension in his body as if he expected me to attack. I slipped the smartphone into my pocket. He shifted his weight. The sports coat opened slightly to reveal the handgun holstered to his hip.

"I'll be heading to Red Cliff at a little after one thirty to meet a guy, in case you want to plan your afternoon," I said. "I'll be driving a black Ford Mustang GT, so I should be easy to follow. Well, if you can keep up. In the meantime, I'm heading back to the Queen Anne to take a nap. I didn't get much sleep last night, but then you already know that."

He yawned, covering his mouth with the back of his hand.

"I'm sorry," he said. "What were you saying?"

"You're not from around here, are you?"

"What's that supposed to mean?"

"Never mind."

I returned to the Queen Anne. The man in the sports coat did not follow.

I unlocked the front door and went inside. Connor intercepted me as I was about to mount the staircase.

"There's someone waiting for you in the parlor," he said.

He said it like I should be afraid. I didn't know why. When I stepped into the parlor I found a young woman—she couldn't have been more than twenty-six—looking about as scary as a summer cold. She had long black hair and wore a white dress shirt, black knee-length skirt, black hose, and sensible black shoes. My first thought was that she worked as a hostess in one of Heather Voight's restaurants.

I approached the tall wing-back chair where she was sitting.

"Good afternoon," I said. "Are you waiting for me?"

She stood and draped the strap of her large black bag over her shoulder as if she expected to leave in a hurry.

"Are you McKenzie?" she asked.

"Yes."

I offered my hand. She looked at it as if it were germ-laden. I put it in my pocket.

"What can I do for you?" I asked.

"I've come to give you a warning."

She had set a verbal trap, and the question I was expected to ask—warn me about what?—would spring it. Instead, I said, "That's very kind, thank you," and stood there smiling. It threw her off, which was exactly my intention.

"Don't you want to know?" she asked.

"Can I get you something? The Queen Anne has a pot of coffee on at all times, and it's very good. Jamaican, I think."

"No, I don't want . . . McKenzie?"

"Yes, dear."

"I'm not your dear. My name is Maryanne Altavilla. I'm chief investigator for Midwest Farmers Insurance. I've come to tell you that you must cease your activities immediately. If you make any further attempt to recover the Stradivarius violin called the Countess Borromeo, I and my firm are prepared to have you arrested for receiving stolen property and aiding and abetting an offender after the fact, both felonies punishable by considerable prison terms."

"You're kidding?"

"I assure you, Mr. McKenzie, I am not."

"I don't mean about arresting me, I mean—you're the woman who replaced Vincent Donatucci?"

"I am."

"How old are you?"

"What difference does it make?"

"The question isn't about age, it's about experience."

"I assure you, I have a great deal of experience. I have already saved Midwest millions of dollars in bogus claims."

"How?"

"Analytics."

"Insurance companies have always been about crunching numbers," I said. "Yet any kid with a PC and access to Wi-Fi can do that."

"I am not a kid."

"What about field experience—accident and crime scene analysis, gathering witness statements, performing surveillance? Insurance companies still investigate arson and theft, don't they? You still investigate disability claims."

"Field experience is overrated. Much of that work can now be accomplished using computers, although I appreciate how a man of your and Mr. Donatucci's generation might find that difficult to comprehend."

A man of my generation? my inner voice asked. *Wow.*

"In other words, you've never in your life attempted to recover a nickel's worth of stolen property," I said aloud.

"No, I have not. Neither will you if you know what's good for you."

"That sounds less like a warning and more like a threat."

"Take it as you will."

"Why are you being so unpleasant, a pretty girl like you?"

Altavilla leaned in close and hissed at me.

"I'm not a girl," she said. "It would be foolish for you to think so."

"Why should you care what I think about anything, Maryanne? Why come all the way from the Cities to tell me what you're telling me? If I recover the Countess, I'll be saving your company four million bucks without costing you a penny in out-of-pocket expense. If I don't—that's my hard luck, isn't it? Yet you're telling me to not even try. It raises questions that I did not have five minutes ago. It motivates me to discover the answers. Simply put, young lady, you have overplayed your cards. If you had more *field* experience, you would have known not to do that. You would have remained in the Cities and waited to see what happened."

The lecture didn't ruffle Altavilla a bit. Maybe she was expecting it; maybe she had heard it before.

"You must stop involving yourself in matters that are none of your concern," she said. "I assure you, McKenzie, the letter from Mr. Duclos that you are carrying will not protect you if we choose to prosecute."

"I notice you do that a lot—assure people. Sounds slightly insecure to me."

"You've been warned."

"You don't happen to have a man working for you who likes to wear sports coats on warm, sunny days, do you?"

Altavilla brushed past me without answering and made a beeline toward the entrance of the parlor. I called after her.

"Hey, Maryanne," I said. "You know, we can still be friends. If you're in the Lakeside Tavern later tonight, I'd be happy to buy you a drink and talk it over."

"You're a sexist pig."

Who? Me?

Altavilla left the Queen Anne in a hurry, slamming the door behind her.

Connor was waiting for me in the foyer.

"Do you always have this effect on women?" he asked.

"I'd say maybe three out of four. By the way, have you seen Caroline Kaminsky?"

"Not since breakfast. Why? Are you going to insult her, too?"

"You never know."

"She's not who she claims to be, is she? She doesn't work for the DNR."

"I wouldn't know."

"Yes, you do. You're friends. I could tell by the way that you looked at each other, the way you spoke to each other. I've been doing this a long time, McKenzie, running B&Bs, a motel in Door County. I've seen people meet unexpectedly before." He air-quoted the word "unexpectedly" with his fingers. "Except the meetings aren't unexpected, are they? Most of the time they're very carefully arranged by people who want to be together without anyone knowing. You two—you and Caroline were actually surprised to see each other at breakfast; the meeting wasn't arranged. That doesn't change anything, though. You're still friends."

"I don't know what you're talking about."

"Caroline is looking for the Stradivarius, too, isn't she? She thinks I stole it. That's why she's staying here. I didn't do it, McKenzie. Why won't people believe me?"

"I believe you."

The way he turned and walked away, I knew he thought I was lying.

A few minutes later, I was safely ensconced in the Peacock Chamber, my shoes off, and sprawled out on the king-sized bed. My smartphone was pressed against my ear. It rang four times before Vincent Donatucci answered.

"Did you find the violin?" he asked.

"No."

"Then why are you calling?"

"Is there anyone in the insurance business who's pleasant to talk to?"

"I didn't mean it that way. When I saw your name on the caller ID I thought you might have had good news."

"Well, news, anyway. Tell me—Midwest Farmers didn't fire all of its investigators, did it?"

"Of course not. It still has field agents; it still has a special investigative unit."

"Then what is Midwest's chief investigator doing in Bayfield telling me to go away and not come back?"

"Maryanne Altavilla is in Bayfield?"

"She confronted me at the bed-and-breakfast. Threatened to lock me up and throw away the key."

"Maryanne knows better than that. I trained her, for God's sake."

"Nonetheless . . ."

"Besides, she has people who can do that, do the heavy lifting; people who are good at it."

"Exactly."

"Something must have happened. Maryanne is a busy woman. At least she should be. For her to drop everything and go up there personally—what did you do?"

"All I've done so far is make my presence known to the local cops and a couple of Bayfield bigwigs."

I gave him details because I knew he'd want to hear them. He paused long enough before replying that I thought my network might have dropped the call.

"Heavenly Petryk is in Bayfield, too?" he asked.

"I thought you'd remember her."

"Oh, I remember, all right. What does she know about the theft?"

"Probably a lot more than we do, but she's not saying."

"That's our girl."

"She doesn't worry me, though. What worries me is Altavilla. It can't be the money, can it? Midwest can't be concerned that if I recover the Countess *and* corral the thieves, it'll have to pony up the quarter-mil reward?"

"No, hell no. These guys are always concerned about the bottom line, but the reward money, it's insured."

"For the record, I purposely leaned on Altavilla, leaned heavily. She didn't give an inch."

"What's that supposed to mean?"

"Just making an observation."

"She's an amateur. She doesn't know the job."

She'll learn, my inner voice said.

"Something else," Donatucci added. "From what you're telling me, Maryanne is all but saying that Midwest Farmers and the Peyroux Foundation don't actually want to recover the Stradivarius."

"Seems no one cares. Except the Maestro. And you."

"And Heavenly Petryk."

"Yeah, her, too."

EIGHT

At one thirty I hopped into my Mustang and maneuvered out of the parking lot of the Queen Anne. I searched for the man in the sports coat yet did not see him. And then I did. Or at least I saw a Toyota attach itself to my rear bumper when I caught Highway 13 and headed out of town. I couldn't make out the driver's face, but the car slowed when I slowed and accelerated when I accelerated. I considered briefly how much fun it would be to crank the Mustang all the way to eleven and dare him to keep up before deciding against it. Since I had already told Mr. Sports Coat that I was meeting a man in Red Cliff, there was nothing to gain by leaving him in my dust.

Red Cliff was only a few miles north of Bayfield. It wasn't really a town. It was an unincorporated community within the City of Russell—don't ask me how that worked—and it served as the administrative center for the Red Cliff Band of Lake Superior Chippewa. The tribe owned the Legendary Waters Resort and Casino and the adjacent Buffalo Bay Campground and Marina on the north side of Highway 13; the parking lots of both were jammed with vehicles of every kind. Directly across the highway was the Superior 13; its lot was nearly empty.

I used my turn signal to inform the car behind me where I was going and turned into the lot. The Toyota kept driving straight, yet not very far. As I was getting out of the Mustang, I noticed that it had doubled back and was parking in the lot across the highway.

I stepped inside the restaurant. Only five of the thirty tables were occupied, one by a man who was sitting alone. I walked up to it and introduced myself.

"McKenzie," the man said. He stood and shook my hand. "I'm Geoff Pascoe."

"Thank you for meeting me."

"Please, sit."

I sat. A waitress was quick to my side. She seemed disappointed when all I ordered was a South Shore Pale Ale.

"What can I do for you?" Pascoe asked.

I repeated what I had told him over the phone, that I was searching for Duclos's missing Stradivarius.

"I don't know what I can do to help," he said.

"How much time did you spend with Duclos?"

"Hours. We met at Pier Plaza around three, talked about what he had in mind, rehearsed, but not very much, I was surprised by that, did a sound check—I was using an electronic keyboard, the gazebo wasn't big enough for anything else—and then we got out of Dodge."

"What do you mean, got out of Dodge?"

"The Maestro didn't want to hang around waiting for the concert to begin. I think he was nervous, which kind of surprised me, so we took off."

"Where did you go?"

"Here."

"Here? Superior 13?"

"I don't think the Maestro cared where we went just as long as we left Bayfield. We hopped into a car and ended up here."

"Whose car?"

"The Maestro had a rental."

"So he drove—"

"No, no. Zofia McLean was behind the wheel. What happened, the Maestro announced that he wanted to get away for a while. Suggestions were made, but he said, 'Let's just drive.' Apparently, he liked to take little walks before a performance, to clear his head, he said, except in Bayfield, where everyone knew him and would be happy to stop him on the street and beg for a selfie, that wasn't an option, so we decided to take a drive. Zofia's car was parked near the tourism bureau, and traffic the way it was, Bayfield was filling up nicely by then, we decided not to take my car and get stuck later, so we walked up to the Queen Anne Bed and Breakfast and used the Maestro's rental. Zofia drove. She insisted. We left town, just cruising along the highway, and the Maestro said let's stop here for a quick bite. That's when I started getting nervous. I couldn't eat. The Maestro, though, had a cheeseburger topped with coleslaw and hot sauce. I guess I expected him to be different than he was."

"How was he?"

"Like an average guy who just happened to be a great violinist. You know what we talked about? Baseball. He talked about Paul Molitor, who grew up in St. Paul but played eighteen years in Milwaukee and Toronto before finishing his career in Minnesota and later being named manager for the Twins. That appealed to him, the idea of a man going home after making a Hall of Fame career for himself somewhere else. He liked that.

"Zofia, of course, kept staring at her watch. I think if she had her way, she would have chained the Maestro to the gazebo. She nearly freaked out when Heather said—"

"Heather Voight?"

"Yes. She owns the place. This restaurant. Opened it about a year ago. She came out from somewhere and saw the Maestro and said she was just about to drive to Bayfield to listen to him play. Maestro said he'd be happy to ride with her. Zofia wasn't going to let that happen, though. By then she was a nervous wreck. So was I. So was Heather, I think. The only one who was calm was the Maestro. He was having a wonderful time. I think it was the cheeseburger."

"Where was the Stradivarius during all of this?"

"Locked inside the rental."

Jeezus.

"What happened after that?" I asked.

"We went back to Bayfield, parked in the lot at the Queen Anne, which turned out to be a smart move because the city was packed by then, not an empty space anywhere. We walked down to Memorial Park, went into the gazebo, and the Maestro, he didn't say a word, he pulled out the Strad and started playing Locatelli's Caprice in D Major, which is one of the hardest solos ever written, we're talking three minutes of pure hell for a violinist, and he does it perfectly and people applaud, but there's no way they could appreciate what he had just accomplished. I could, though. It was magnificent. After that we just played— Bach's Sonata for Solo Violin no. 1 with Busoni's keyboard arrangement, *The Lark Ascending* by Vaughan Williams, the Violin Concerto by Sibelius, Vivaldi's Concerto no. 2 in G Minor, Johann Pachelbel's Canon in D. Two hours we played without a break, and finally, we just stepped out of the gazebo. The crowd demanded an encore, so the Maestro went back by himself. Do you know what he played? 'Eleanor Rigby,' by the Beatles, at twice the pace of the original composition, and he finished with, are you ready?" Pascoe beat a rhythm on the tabletop. "Shave and a haircut, two bits. The place went wild. It was the most fun I ever had as a professional musician. I learned more in those two hours with the Maestro than I had in six years at the University of Minnesota–Duluth. It was wonderful."

"And then?"

"And then party city. We went to the Hill House. 'Course, it was the Maestro's show, but everyone was congratulating me, too. Zofia was as happy as I had ever seen her. Celebrating way too much."

"What about Duclos?"

"He wasn't drinking. He held a glass in his hand all night, but I don't think he took more than a sip or two. He's a professional, after all, and this kind of party—it was new to me but not to him."

"The Maestro left early," I said.

"Yes, he did. Zofia volunteered to walk him back to the Queen Anne, only he turned her down, which worked out fine for me."

"In what way?"

"I got to take her home. After the Maestro left, the party broke up, and Zofia and I decided that she was too drunk to drive, so . . ."

"Ahh."

"That's when I saw him."

"Saw who?"

"The Maestro."

"Wait. What?"

"When I was taking Zofia home, I saw him in his rental waiting at the light on Highway 13 and Sixth Street."

"Are you sure?"

"Yes, I am."

"When was this?"

"Eleven thirty, eleven forty-five."

"Where was he going?"

"I have no idea. I knew what he was doing, though."

"What?"

"McKenzie, what you need to know, no one gets more pussy than musicians, not even professional athletes."

I searched for the man in the sports coat when I left Superior 13, yet couldn't find him or the Toyota. Eventually, I returned to the Queen Anne. I carefully parked the Mustang and slowly walked inside.

Connor was vacuuming the parlor. I attracted his attention, and he turned off the machine.

"Can you do me a favor?" I asked.

The way he hemmed and hawed, he clearly didn't want to commit without additional information.

"Tell me where can I find the Ghost Lady."

According to the flyer Connor gave me, "Ghost Lady" wasn't just a nickname—it was the title that the woman I knew as Maggie gave herself. She conducted two rotating spirit tours, one on the east side and the other on the west side of the city. You'd think a place that small wouldn't have enough ghosts to go around, but what did I know? The Ghost Lady operated out of the Bayfield Heritage Center on Broad Street across from the Bayfield Carnegie Public Library. Both were only a couple of blocks away. Then again, everything in Bayfield was only a couple of blocks away.

I walked up there. It was near the Heritage Center that I found the park built on the side of the hill where I had last seen the Ghost Lady. It was mostly a heavily wooded ravine with about a mile and a half of hiking trails, yet it had a far-from-civilization vibe to it. A long, high iron bridge spanned what seemed to me like a harmless creek at the bottom of a deep gorge that trickled into Lake Superior. Except a sign told me that during the spring thaw, the creek became a monstrous river that would wash away anything in reach if not for the city's flooding protocols. In July of '42, in fact, eight inches of rain fell during a twenty-four hour period, causing water to crash out of the hills and fill the creek, creating an immense flood that surged through the heart of downtown Bayfield, burying it under tons of sand, rock, mud, and broken buildings. The half-buried car in front of the Heritage Center served as testament to the event.

I was contemplating the black-and-white photographs that made me glad I hadn't been there on the day the rain fell when a car pulled into the small parking lot. Officer Pilhofer hopped out. He was dressed in tight jeans and a T-shirt designed to let everyone know that he worked out. There wasn't a badge in sight.

"What did I tell you?" he asked.

He moved swiftly across the lot; gravel crunched beneath his boots. The scowl on his face betrayed his intentions.

"You're making a mistake, Officer," I said.

He didn't believe me. He came in close and grabbed a fistful of my polo shirt just under my chin. He stabbed a finger at my face.

"I told you what would happen if you didn't leave, didn't I?"

Well, no, my inner voice said. *You didn't.*

I didn't argue the point, though. Instead, I seized his hand with mine and began to push upward on his elbow. I pulled his hand down even as I kept pushing, causing him to arch his spine. He tried to resist; except gravity was working against him. I applied more pressure and flipped him onto his back. I kept pushing his elbow until it was flat against his face. The pain in his shoulder joint made him writhe against the gravel, yet he refused to cry out.

Good for him.

I was contemplating what to do next when I heard a woman's voice behind me.

"Stop it, stop it," she called.

At the same time, a sharp object was jabbed into my side— once, twice, three times in quick succession. The pain wasn't great, but still . . . I released Pilhofer and turned to face the threat. I was hit twice more in the center of my chest. I brought my hands and arms up in self-defense and stepped backward.

"Stop it now, just stop it, do you hear me?" the voice said.

It belonged to a woman dressed in a black cloak, the hood pulled over her head, a lantern standing upright on the ground next to her. She was waving a staff fitted with a large crystal at my face.

My first thought—is that thing loaded?

"Lady . . ." I said.

"You don't talk."

"Ma?" Pilhofer said.

Ma?

"Are you all right?" the Ghost Lady asked.

"Ma, what are you doing here?"

"I was walking to the center. I saw what he did."

"He was assaulting me," I said.

"He's a police officer."

"Not today."

"What's that supposed to mean?"

"Ma, cut it out," Pilhofer said.

He was on his feet now, brushing off the dirt and gravel dust.

"What does he mean you're not a police officer? Of course you are."

"It's a personal matter."

"Lady, could you put the stick down?" I asked.

The Ghost Lady replied by waving it at my face some more.

"You don't talk," she said. "Brian . . . Brian, what's going on here?"

"Nothing, nothing at all," he said.

"It certainly was something."

"He wants me out of the way," I said. "He's protecting someone."

"Who? Who are you protecting? Why?"

"It's none of your business," Pilhofer said.

"It's Heather, isn't it? What did she do?"

"She didn't do anything."

"I told you to stay away from her. She's old enough to be—she's older than I am. And she's married."

"Leave me alone."

"Brian?"

"I need to go to work."

Pilhofer crossed the parking lot to his car. The Ghost Lady called after him.

"Please, be careful," she said.

He started up his car and drove away. The Ghost Lady turned to look at me, the business end of her staff still aimed at my face.

"Nice kid," I said. "You must be very proud."

"Who are you? Talk fast."

"Could you please lower the stick?"

"It's not a stick. It's a staff used for circle casting, summoning, opening portals, and long-range energy magic."

"For whacking people upside the head, too, I guess. Ma'am, please. I know it doesn't look like it, but I'm one of the good guys."

"So is Brian."

"Probably, but he's going about it all wrong. Can we"—I reached out, rested a hand on top of the staff, and gently lowered it until the crystal was pointed at the ground—"talk?"

"Talk about what? Who are you?"

"My name is McKenzie. I was sent here by Paul Duclos to try and find his missing Stradivarius."

"Oh, that. I've been wanting to use the burglary in my tours, except I don't have much of a story to tell yet."

"Maybe we can help each other out. Mrs. Pilhofer? May I call you Maggie?"

The Ghost Lady pulled back the hood, revealing copper hair and green eyes in a round face. She directed me to a bench at the edge of the park next to a locked stone cellar built into the side of the hill. According to a sign, William Knight built the cellar using field stones in 1920 to store the apples that came from his many orchards; it was his large and ancient house that hovered above the park from the top of the hill. It was haunted, the Ghost Lady informed me.

"I don't just talk about ghosts, though," Maggie said. "I like to work in some of the history of Bayfield, too."

"Like with the Queen Anne?"

"Exactly like that. Peter Rasmussen originally built the house over a hundred and thirty-five years ago. He lived there with his wife and eight children; he was one of the people who built Bayfield. When Peter died, the house went to his eldest son, along with everything else, which is how things worked back then. This started a violent feud that lasted more or less until the family's businesses collapsed. The brownstone quarry, commercial fishing, the lumber mill, the hotels—they made a lot of money, but when they went away the family went with them. The Queen Anne had at least a half-dozen owners before Connor finally acquired it. In case he didn't tell you, he's Peter's great-great-grandson. I hope he makes a go of it."

"Why wouldn't he?"

"He spent a lot of money buying the property and restoring it, converting it into a B&B. I heard that even though he's mostly full up the year 'round, he's still having trouble paying his notes."

"That's too bad."

"He's not the only one with money troubles. Take that whore Heather Voight."

"Is Heather a whore?"

"She's married and she's sleeping with a man who's thirty-five years younger than she is. What would you call her?"

"Troubled?"

"Yes, she's troubled all right."

"Why would your son be protecting her?"

"Guess."

"I mean, what is he protecting her from?"

"You, you numbskull."

"Me?"

"You're here to buy the Stradivarius from the thieves. Everyone in town knows that; it's all we're talking about. Well, who do you think has it?"

"You tell me."

"The violin case was found outside Heather's front door."

"That doesn't mean she took it."

"McKenzie, she needs money. She did very well for herself, but then she got greedy. She built a restaurant in Washburn, a town that's four times as big as Bayfield but only half as busy. If that wasn't enough, she also opened one in Red Cliff in direct competition with the casino."

"I was over there earlier."

"Did you see many people?"

"No."

"Now she needs money."

"Do you really think she stole her ex-boyfriend's violin to get it?"

"Who said she stole it? Who said she's Paul's *ex*-girlfriend? Her being here and him being there doesn't make them *ex*-anything. It just means they can't spend as much time together as they would like, that's all."

"But?"

"But what?"

"It doesn't make sense."

"Think about it. She needs money; she calls her longtime lover. Paul arrives outta the blue and arranges for Heather to *steal* his violin. A couple days later he arranges to buy it back from her."

"I am definitely going to take your tour, Maggie. You're a terrific storyteller."

"Is it a story?"

"Unless you have evidence—look. If Heather needed money,

Duclos could have just given it to her. Or at least he could have arranged a low-interest loan."

"Do you think his wife, Renée Peyroux—do you think she would have let him?"

"I met her."

"And?"

"No, I don't think so."

"Okay, then."

"If Heather had the violin, she would have made a deal by now. She's had the perfect opportunity."

"Except then she'd have to admit that she and Paul were in on it, together. That's not going to happen. If they had wanted you to know what they were doing, they would have told you from the very beginning. Wouldn't they? No. The whore'll be using someone as a what-do-you-call-it, a go-between."

"Who would that be, I wonder? Her husband?"

"Herb? That poor man? I doubt it."

"Who, then?"

"Just as long as it isn't Brian I don't care."

As if on cue, my smartphone made the metallic pinging sound associated with navy ships and sonar, alerting me that I had a notification. I excused myself and checked. There was a message in my e-mail from Curtis Shanklin with the subject line URGENT.

Heavenly was with me in the Peacock Chamber, examining the photograph that filled the screen of my laptop.

"What does that look like to you?" I asked.

"It looks like a pic of a violin lying on top of the front page of today's *Ashland Daily Press*."

I used the touchpad to enlarge the photo. Harry Potter's lightning bolt was scratched into the wood exactly where Duclos had told me it would be.

"It's the Countess Borromeo," I said.

"Yes, but is it *the* Countess Borromeo and not just an image he picked up off the Internet and Photoshopped?"

I manipulated the laptop so it would take me back to Shanklin's e-mail message:

Take the 9 PM ferry to Madeline Island. Drive Old Fort Road east until it turns north and becomes Casper Road. You'll find a spur that leads directly to a deserted beach near Grants Point. Stay on the spur until you can't drive any further. It's a short walk to the beach. Bring the money. Come alone. We'll be watching. Any shenanigans and the Countess Borromeo goes into the lake.

"Shenanigans," I said.

"He teaches English."

"Still . . ."

"It's a trap."

"What a suspicious nature you have."

"They don't have the Countess. They're just trying to rip you off."

"On the other hand, if they do have the violin . . . What are you doing later tonight?"

"McKenzie, it's a trap."

"Yes, well, there are traps and then there are traps."

I had dinner alone at Hill House; I even wore a black sports jacket to impress the hostess. This time I started with crostini with smoked salmon and then moved on to grilled whitefish Alfredo over linguini, the whitefish fresh from Lake Superior. It was excellent, yet I have to admit that there was a tightness in my stomach that kept me from fully enjoying it, not to mention the discomfort of the 9 mm SIG Sauer pressed between the small of my back and the chair.

I had hoped to meet Heather Voight, except her waitstaff told me that she hadn't been in all day. Just as well. What was I going to say to her? Please, if you have the Stradivarius, let's make a deal right now; don't make me go to Madeline Island where I might get shot?

After I finished dinner I wandered around town, killing time. I found myself at the marina looking for Jack Westlund's boat. It wasn't in its slip. Neither was the *Heather II*.

At eight twenty by my watch, I drifted back to the Queen Anne. I went to my room. A few moments later, I left the B&B with a small suitcase. I had filled it with books from the Peacock Chamber's collection so it would look like I was carrying twenty-three pounds of cash.

I went to the Mustang. It had Intelligent Access, meaning its sensors could read the key fob I carried from three feet away, allowing me to unlock the door at a touch and start the engine with the push of a button. I opened the door, slid inside, pretended to adjust my rearview mirror, started the car, and left the parking lot. It took all of three minutes to drive to the landing for the Madeline Island ferry, another three to pay my passage, and thirty seconds more to maneuver into line.

The large boat had left its berth on the island and was now making its way across the expanse of water toward Bayfield; I could see the setting sun reflecting off its hull. The damn thing seemed to take forever.

I had music loaded into the Mustang's system and turned it on. The shuffle function selected Sarah Vaughan's cover of "Black Coffee." I switched it off thirty seconds in—something I had never done before, quit Sarah in midsong.

At eight fifty, the ferry arrived. It dropped its massive iron ramp. Two college kids dressed in blue knit polo shirts stood on either side, directing traffic. First the pedestrians were allowed to disembark, followed by a dozen vehicles. Once that was accomplished, tourists who were on foot climbed the ramp and made their way up a gangway to an elevated passenger lounge. Vehicles then entered one at a time, parking bumper-to-bumper on the deck. Finally, the ramp was raised and the ferry pulled away from the dock. It was 9:00 P.M. exactly. The sun was just a sliver of orange light on the horizon.

I left the Mustang and managed to squeeze past the parked vehicles to the gangway. I climbed it to the passenger lounge and leaned against the railing. The lights of Bayfield were slowly receding in the distance while those on Madeline Island were becoming brighter. I spent most of my time, however, studying the people in the lounge and the drivers and passengers who had remained in their vehicles. Shanklin had two accomplices that I knew of, the young men Ellis had mentioned at the Lakeside Tavern the night before. That didn't mean he didn't have others. Like the two young women dressed for clubbing who were sitting near the stern.

Get out of your head, my inner voice said, a task more easily said than done.

There was a white, thirty-inch round ring buoy and safety rope hanging from the wall of the lounge with the name NICHEVO II painted in red block letters.

I caught the attention of one of the college kids dressed in blue.

"What does *Nichevo* mean?" I asked.

He shrugged.

"You don't know?" I said.

"No, that's what it means." He shrugged again. "*Nichevo* is a difficult word to translate into English. Basically, it means okay, pretty well, not too bad. How was your dinner?" He shrugged again. "Meh. *Nichevo.*"

"That's the worst name for a boat I've ever heard."

"It's Russian," he said, as if that explained everything.

At nine twenty, the *Nichevo II* docked on Madeline Island. Mine was the fifth car off the ferry. I switched on my headlights and followed the driveway onto Colonel Woods Avenue, hung a left at Ninth Street, and turned right again on Old Fort Road. The road took me past Captain Bob's Marina, Madeline Island Yacht Club, the golf course, and the Ojibwe National Prayer Pole and Memorial Park. There were very few lights to be seen beyond.

Less than five minutes later, I found the spur off Casper Road that Shanklin had written about. I was alarmed by how quickly the trip went; I thought I would have more time to prepare.

The spur was flanked by trees and shrubs made ominous by the lack of illumination, and I thought, That's where I would be if I were planning an ambush. I followed the spur, yet was forced to stop after only fifty feet. My headlights scanned the sand beach beyond. It was empty.

I prepared the Mustang before turning it off. The windows were down, and I could hear night sounds—crickets, gentle waves lapping the shoreline. Finally, I opened the door. I pulled the suitcase out with my right hand while fondling the key fob in my left. I closed the car door with my hip.

I walked to the center of the beach. Lake Superior was a black void punctuated by tiny lights; they could have been stars except some of them were moving.

"That's far enough."

I recognized Shanklin's voice and turned toward it. He stepped away from the shadow of the trees onto the beach. The moon wasn't yet high in the sky, nor were the stars as bright as they soon would be, yet I could make him out clearly. He was carrying a gun.

"Did you bring the money?" he asked.

"Did you bring the violin?"

"I must have forgotten it."

"Why am I here, then, I wonder?"

"You're here to give me $250,000."

Shanklin raised his gun and pointed it at me. At the same time, his two accomplices stepped out of the woods, one on each side of the Mustang. I couldn't see if they were armed or not.

"Give it to me," Shanklin said.

I heaved the suitcase toward him. It landed with a muffled thud on the sand near his feet. Shanklin's friends were so appreciative of the gesture that they moved forward until they were standing in front of the Mustang.

Shanklin lowered his gun and bent toward the suitcase, yet stopped before his hands reached the handle. He slowly straightened up.

"It's empty, isn't it?" he said.

"Not at all. There's some really fine literature in that suitcase. *Moby-Dick. Pride and Prejudice.*"

He raised his gun.

I pressed the button on my key fob.

A piercing wail was emitted from the Mustang; its lights began flashing.

Shanklin and his friends were clearly visible now; all three pivoted toward the car.

I reached behind my back and pulled the SIG Sauer out from beneath my sports coat.

I went into a Weaver stance, the gun sighted on Shanklin's core.

He turned toward me; his piece was pointed at the sand.

If he raised it I would kill him.

I was about to tell him so when three shots rang out; volcanoes of sand erupted in front of Shanklin's two accomplices.

"Don't anyone move," Heavenly said.

She also walked out of the shadow of the woods. She was wearing a bikini beneath a filmy cover-up that hung open and a floppy hat. Her hands were gripping what looked to me like a small Colt.

"Drop your gun," I told Shanklin.

"Caroline?" he said.

"Drop the damn gun."

Shanklin let it slip from his fingers into the sand.

"Caroline, is that you?" he asked.

Heavenly stepped into the light. She was aiming her Colt more or less at the two accomplices. Neither of them was armed, which seemed inexplicable to me. My SIG was trained on Shanklin. We were standing only feet apart.

"Do you mind?" she said. "The noise."

"Oh, yeah."

I used the key fob to turn off the Mustang's alarm system. The silence that followed seemed almost louder than the siren had been.

"I like your outfit," I said.

"It's my disguise."

"Yeah, nobody will notice you dressed like that."

"I was pretending to be a girl walking on the beach."

"Caroline," Shanklin said. "What are you doing here?"

"Watching you go bad, apparently."

"But . . ."

"But what? You're a junior high school teacher, for God's sake. What were you thinking?"

"On your knees, all three of you," I said. "Hands behind your heads."

All three did exactly what I told them without argument.

"Now what?" Heavenly asked.

"Where's the violin?" I asked.

No one answered.

"Shanklin, where the fuck is the violin?"

"I don't know."

"Don't you have it?"

"No, no—I don't."

"Told you," Heavenly said.

"Who stole it?" I asked.

"I don't know, I don't know, I don't know."

"Then why did you bring me out here?"

"I thought . . . we thought . . ."

"What did you think?"

"We thought it would be easy money. Ellis told us who you were and what you were doing, and we thought—"

"Who's Ellis?" Heavenly asked.

"Waitress at Lakeside Tavern," I said. "Was she in on it? Shanklin. Was she involved?"

"No, no, she just told us, and we thought—"

"It would be easy money—and fun, too, I bet."

"Do you know how much a teacher makes in California?"

"Probably as much as a cop."

"Should we shoot them?" Heavenly asked.

"No, please, please, Caroline."

This time it was one of the accomplices speaking. I didn't know his name and I didn't care to learn it.

"Well?" Heavenly said.

"I'm thinking."

"Please, don't kill us," Shanklin said.

"Why not? That's clearly what you intended to do to me."

"Caroline. Please. Tell him."

"Not my job," Heavenly said.

She spun toward the lake, whipped off her hat, and waved it back and forth. The lights of a boat flicked on, and I heard the low moan of its engine coming to life. Almost immediately, the lights began moving forward across the lake. Soon I discerned the shape of the boat. It drifted gently toward the beach until its bow scraped the sand a few yards out.

"My ride," Heavenly said.

"You kids all right?" Jack Westlund asked.

"Just great, Mr. Westlund," I said. "Thank you."

"Need any help?"

"Stay where you are."

"Are you ready?" Heavenly asked.

"Cover me."

I moved cautiously toward Shanklin. He crawled away from me on his knees as I approached, his heads still behind his head. I picked up his gun and heaved it into Lake Superior. I bent down and retrieved my suitcase. I decided the books were just too damn good to leave behind. Afterward, I carefully maneuvered around the trio until I was behind them and standing next to the Mustang.

"Okay," I said.

Heavenly lowered her Colt and crossed the sand. She was splashing through the water when Shanklin called to her.

"Caroline?"

"Shut up, Curtis."

Westlund lowered a ladder, and Heavenly climbed aboard.

"I'll be buying the drinks later," I said.

"Got that right you will," Westlund said.

He put his engines in reverse, and the boat slid off the sand. A few moments later, it was crossing Lake Superior at high speed toward the lights of Bayfield.

The trio turned on their knees in the sand to face me.

"I have no idea what to say to you guys," I said. "Except, if I see you again, I'll blow your brains out."

Probably that wasn't true, I told myself. They didn't know that, though.

I climbed into the Mustang, backed down the spur, caught Old Fort Road again, and drove back to the landing.

NINE

I had to wait nearly a half hour for the *Nichevo II* to return to Madeline Island and another twenty minutes for it to make the crossing to Bayfield. Westlund and Heavenly were waiting for me when I arrived. Heavenly had changed into boots, jeans, and a soft blue V-neck sweater.

"I begged her not to do it," Westlund said.

I would have liked to see more of the bikini myself, but Heavenly had tucked it and the filmy cover-up into a large wicker bag. After I drove off the ferry's iron ramp, she tossed the bag and the floppy hat into the backseat of my Mustang and climbed in after it. Westlund sat next to me.

"Where to?" I asked.

"Not that many places open late night in Bayfield," Westlund said. "Lakeside?"

"Why not?"

It took me three minutes to reach the Lakeside Tavern and another to park. Stepping inside, we were greeted by a loud saxophone. Alas, its owner wasn't playing jazz. He was part of a rock and roll cover band trying to play "Urgent" note for note. I was sure that both Foreigner and Junior Walker would have been appalled, although the many people dancing in front of the stage didn't seem to mind a bit.

You're a music snob, my inner voice told me.

Which was probably true.

We found a table. Ellis arrived to serve us. I was tempted to tell her what had happened on Madeline Island, except I was afraid that she would blame herself and decided to let it slide. I ordered bourbon, Heavenly had vodka, and Westlund settled for a Leinie's after first making the girl recite the tavern's entire beer menu.

Heavenly scrunched her nose at the band.

"I wonder if these guys even know who Paul Duclos is?" she asked.

Okay, now who's the snob?

I didn't answer Heavenly or my inner voice. I was too busy searching the bar for the man in the sports coat and not finding him

After the drinks were served, Westlund slapped his hands and rubbed them together.

"That was fun," he said. "I wasn't close enough to see their faces, but I bet them boys were real surprised when Heavenly stepped outta them woods with her gun."

"I think it was the bikini, not the gun, that caught their attention," I said.

"I was a little worried about dropping her on the beach all alone like that, gun or no. Lookin' the way she looks and those roughnecks waitin'."

"She is a beauty."

"You know I'm sitting right here," Heavenly said.

"You are a beauty," Westlund said. "Damn if you ain't."

"You're very kind."

"So, how long have you kids been together?"

I damn near choked on my bourbon. Heavenly patted my back.

"You all right, baby?" she asked.

"Fine."

"Want me to kiss it and make it better?"

"Stop it."

Heavenly thought that was funny.

"No, Jack, we're not together," she said. "We've known each other for over three years—"

"Closer to four," I said.

"McKenzie is involved with a woman who's"—I was expecting an insult. Instead, I heard—"very smart, and very kind, and twice as pretty as I am."

"Hard to believe," Westlund said. "That last part, anyway."

"I, on the other hand . . ." Heavenly wrapped her arm around Westlund's arm. "I'm looking for someone with a little more maturity."

"Well, then, you've come to the wrong place, doll. I've got three ex-wives who'll tell ya I have all the maturity of a frat boy on spring break."

"Sometimes that's exactly what a girl's looking for."

"McKenzie."

The voice came from behind me. All three of us turned to look.

"McKenzie, you're here."

Maryanne Altavilla stood several feet away, balancing a double Bailey's Irish Cream on the rocks and not doing a very good job of it. She was wearing the same clothes as when she accosted me at the Queen Anne, the large black bag slung over her shoulder.

"You said you'd be here, only I was beginning to think that was a . . . prevarication."

Prevarication?

"Ms. Altavilla." I stood, although that was less out of courtesy and more because I wanted to be able to catch her should she keel over. "Join us."

I guided her to an empty chair and helped her sit. She spilled some Bailey's on her fingers while setting the bag on the floor.

"Oops," she said and licked it off.

Heavenly gave me a look I've seen before—the one that asked, "What the hell?" Westlund, on the other hand, seemed enthralled.

"Aren't you pretty?" he said. "You don't mind an old man saying that, do you?"

"You don't look so old to me."

"I'm Jack." He offered his hand and Altavilla shook it.

"Maryanne," she said.

"Ms. Altavilla is an investigator for Midwest Farmers Insurance Group," I said.

"Chief investigator. I just got promoted."

"From what?" Heavenly asked.

Altavilla stared at her for a moment; she seemed to have trouble focusing.

"Who are you?" she asked.

"This is Heavenly Petryk," Westlund said.

It occurred to me then that when I introduced them earlier that evening I should have used Heavenly's alias—Caroline Kaminsky. Oh, well . . .

"Heavenly?" Altavilla asked. "Where have I heard that name before? McKenzie, where have I heard that name before?"

"I have no idea."

"Midwest Farmers," Westlund said. "Are you the guys who insured the Stradivarius what's been stolen?"

"We are them."

"Then you should know what happened tonight. We—"

Heavenly and I both raised our voices in a euphonia of confusion, tossing out phrases like "look at the time" and "I remember this song." Westlund realized what we were attempting to do and stopped speaking. Altavilla swiveled her head from him to us and back to him again.

"What happened?" she asked. "McKenzie, what happened? You didn't find it, did you? Did you? No, wait, you couldn't have. Could you?"

"Find what?"

"The violin, dammit. Just because I've been drinking doesn't mean I'm drunk."

"Why are you drinking?"

"Killing time waiting. I've been waiting all night."

"Waiting for whom?"

"For youm."

"Why?" Heavenly said.

"Who are you again?"

"Maryanne—Maryanne, why were you waiting for me?" I asked.

"To apologize. I was quite inconsiderate this afternoon, and I apologize. I have no excuse. My only explanation is that I was speaking for the company and not for myself."

"Think nothing of it. I was rude myself."

"You didn't, did you?"

"Did what?"

"Recover the violin."

I couldn't think of a reason to lie to her.

"Not yet," I said.

"Not yet, not yet. It's a dangerous game you're playing, Mc-Kenzie."

"Why dangerous?"

"Because money is involved. Lots and lots of money. I know you think I came down with yesterday's rain, but I'm not so inexperienced I don't appreciate what happens when lots and lots of money is involved. You two. Are you helping him?"

"Sure am," said Westlund.

"Depends," said Heavenly. "If McKenzie finds the Strad first, I'm helping. If I find it first . . ."

"Oh, oh, oh, now I remember," Altavilla said. "Heavenly Petryk. Mr. Donatucci warned me to keep an eye out for you."

"Before or after he was fired?" I asked.

Altavilla ignored the question.

"Mr. Donatucci said you were one of those people who likes to profit off the misfortune of insurance companies," she said. "You make a business out of finding lost and stolen property and selling it back, collecting rewards."

"Beats working retail," Heavenly said.

"He thinks that sometimes you arrange to steal the property that you later recover and sell back. He says you should be in prison."

"Is that what he says?"

"Heavenly is my friend." I spoke loudly. I spoke firmly. Altavilla's face came around because of the way I spoke. I looked directly into her eyes so there would be no mistaking my meaning.

"I apologize," Altavilla said. "I'm just saying what Mr. Donatucci told me." She turned to look at Heavenly again. "You're the second person I insulted today without meaning to. I assure you, it will not happen again."

"I'm not nearly as offended as McKenzie seems to be."

"Mr. McKenzie is intensely loyal to his friends. Mr. Donatucci told me so."

"I'm not offended at all," Westlund said.

Altavilla patted his hand.

"Thank you," she said. "Mister . . ."

"Westlund. Call me Jack."

"Have we met?"

"Just now."

"Are you from Bayfield?"

"Yep. I'm living on my boat in the marina."

"On a boat? That must be fun."

"Yes, it is."

"I'd like to see it sometime."

"I could show it to you tonight."

Altavilla gave Westlund's shoulder a gentle shove.

"Oh, you," she said.

"You must be awfully smart to be a chief investigator at your age," Westlund said.

"I'm a protégée."

"What does that mean?"

"I scored a thirty-six on my ACT," she said. "Thirty-six. I bet—what did you score, Mr. McKenzie?"

"Thirty-one," I said.

Heavenly held up two fingers.

"Thirty-two," she said.

"Then you're both really smart, too."

"What's ACT?" Westlund asked.

Altavilla shoved his shoulder again.

"Oh, you," she repeated.

Altavilla stood abruptly.

"I have to go now," she said.

She reached for her bag, draping the strap over her shoulder.

"Where are you staying?" I asked.

Altavilla pointed toward the band.

"Bayfield Inn," she said.

Westlund took her arm and aimed it at the door.

"It's that way, Maryanne," he said.

"Oh."

"I'm heading in the same direction. I'll make sure you get there."

"Whoever you are, I have always depended on the kindness of strangers. Tennessee Williams. *A Streetcar Named Desire.* December 1947." Altavilla spread her arms wide. "What? Thirty-six, bitches."

With that, she and Westlund headed for the door; Altavilla swung back.

"I'm sorry, Heavenly, that I called you a crook," she said. "Although . . ."

Altavilla wagged her finger as she walked away. Westlund followed close behind. He was grinning widely. I silently wished him luck, yet I doubted he would get any—luck, I mean.

"What was that about?" Heavenly asked.

I took a sip of the Bailey's Irish Cream Altavilla had left behind and could barely taste the alcohol. I waved Ellis over.

"The woman who was with us, did you serve her?" I asked.

"Yep."

"How much did she have to drink?"

"Just the one."

"When did she get here?"

"She arrived shortly after you did."

"Thank you."

Ellis left, and I turned to Heavenly.

"I think she was telling the truth," I said. "I think Maryanne really did score a thirty-six on the ACT."

We chatted about it at some length. Neither Heavenly nor I could figure out what Altavilla was up to, although we were quite certain it wasn't good for either of us. While we talked, I kept a weary eye on the other customers of the Lakeside Tavern. I wasn't sure what I was looking for until I saw it—the man in the sports coat walking up the short corridor off the stage that led to Philip Speegle's office. Speegle was right behind him.

Enough is enough, my inner voice said.

"Wait here," I told Heavenly.

The man in the sports coat spotted me as I was slowly weaving around tables and past the other customers. He went straight for the door; was through the door before I could reach him. I intended to follow him outside, except I was intercepted.

"McKenzie," Speegle said.

He stood between the doorway and me.

"Excuse me just a second," I said.

It took only a moment to maneuver around Speegle and out the front entrance. Unfortunately, the brief delay gave the man in the sports coat all the time he needed to disappear. I searched up and down the avenue yet couldn't find him anywhere. I went back inside the tavern. Speegle was waiting for me.

"Who was that?" I asked.

"Who was what?"

"The man in the sports coat."

"I didn't notice."

"He came out of your office."

"No he didn't. He must have been using the restroom."

I glanced over Speegle's shoulder. From that angle I could see the names on the two doors just past his office. White type on a black background; they read MEN and WOMEN.

"Listen, about last night," Speegle said. "I might have given you bad advice."

"About what?"

"About talking to Herb Voight. That was uncalled for. Herb is a good man. Whatever I feel about the Great Lady, there was no reason to drag him into it. He doesn't deserve to have people talk about him behind his back. What I'm saying—I was outta line. Guess I was feeling my bourbon."

"I spoke to Voight this morning. He seems like a nice guy."

"He is."

"I also got the impression that he sleeps on his boat more than he does at home."

"So they say. Heather should never have married him. She should've married someone more like her. An entrepreneur."

It didn't take a genius to figure out whom he meant.

"About Voight and his boat," I said. "Does he always sleep alone?"

"See, McKenzie, that's what I mean. Talking behind Herb's back. He doesn't deserve that, and I wish you would leave him alone. Look, I gotta go. I have things to do."

I watched Speegle turn and march to his office.

He didn't answer your question, my inner voice said.

I returned to the table.

The drinking age in Wisconsin is twenty-one, which made me wonder how the young man who was asking Heavenly to dance got into the place. I demanded to see his ID.

"Who are you?" the kid asked.

"Oh, Daddy," Heavenly said. "We were only going to dance. Can't I have any fun?"

"Daddy?" the kid said.

I wagged my finger at Heavenly much the same way Altavilla had.

"You know what the doctors said, honey," I told her. "No touching until we know that you're cured."

"But it's been so long," she said.

The kid left without another word. I sat down.

"You're a bully," Heavenly said.

"Think I'm going to let just anyone dance with my little girl?"

"Now that you brought it up . . ."

Heavenly gestured with her pretty chin at the dance floor.

"No," I said.

"Just as well. Old man like you, I bet it's way past your bedtime."

"Funny."

A few minutes later, though, we were outside the Lakeside Tavern and walking toward my Mustang with plans to retreat to the Queen Anne for the evening. The streets were nearly empty, just a few revelers heading back to wherever they came from, like us. Heavenly wrapped her arm around mine.

"Such a beautiful night." She was looking up at the sky. "You never see stars like this in the city, all that ambient light. Some kids growing up in New York, places like that, they never see the stars at all. Isn't that sad?"

"It is."

"I like what you told Maryanne before—'Heavenly is my friend.' That meant a lot to me, I want you to know."

"Yes, but is it true?"

"What do you mean?"

"I know that I'm your friend. But are you mine?"

"Of course I am."

"Then why are you holding out on me—Caroline?"

"That hurts, McKenzie. It does. Here I thought we were having a moment."

"The time has come to talk of many things," I said.

We reached the passenger side of the Mustang. My hand was resting on the door latch, yet I did not open it.

"Of shoes and ships and sealing wax," Heavenly said. *"Of cabbages and kings."*

And her upper chest exploded.

The bullet hit her high on the left side, just below her collarbone.

The blood splashed her sweater, the Mustang, and me before I registered the shot.

Heavenly didn't seem to notice at first. Her body didn't so much as flinch when the bullet bored into her. But then her head flung backward and her shoulders arched. Her eyes found mine and she seemed to reach her hand out to me as her body twisted hard to her left and she collapsed.

It was like I was watching her in slow motion.

Maybe I was.

I didn't try to catch her. Instead, I slid down the side of my car. I reached behind my back and gripped the butt of the SIG Sauer. I pulled the gun, grasped it with both hands, and turned.

Two more shots were fired. I didn't see where the bullets hit. I saw the muzzle flashes with my peripheral vision, though. They came from behind a parked SUV across the street. I sighted on the car. Something moved, a shadow near the rear bumper.

I fired three times.

And waited.

No one fired back.

I swiveled my head to find Heavenly. She was flat on her back, her right hand pressed against her wound. Blood seeped between her fingers.

God help me, I left her there.

I dashed across the street, holding the SIG low until I reached the SUV. Breathing hard. I brought the gun up and sighted on— nothing. No one was there.

I moved slowly around the bumper. I crouched. I moved to the next car parked up the street. And the next. And the next. I looked up and down the boulevard. Searched doorways. Nothing moved in front of me.

Behind me, people were moving cautiously, aware that something unexpected had happened yet not knowing what.

I ran back to the Mustang. A crowd was gathering there. They seemed frightened by the gun in my hand; someone actually shouted, "He has a gun."

I slid the SIG behind my back. Heavenly had rolled on her side and pressed her arm against the sidewalk as if she were attempting to get up. I pushed her back and told her to keep still.

"I've been shot, McKenzie," she said. "Do you believe that?"

"Don't talk."

I took a handkerchief from my pocket, removed her hand, pulled up her sweater, stuffed the handkerchief into her wound, and replaced her hand.

"Press down hard," I said.

"I thought it would hurt more, getting shot," Heavenly said.

I looked up at the crowd and found a familiar face.

"Ellis," I said. "Ellis, come here."

She knelt next to Heavenly.

"I need your help. Can you help me?"

Ellis nodded.

"Where's the nearest hospital?"

"I'm not—"

"Where's the nearest emergency room?"

"Ashland. Memorial Medical Center in Ashland."

"Where is that?"

"South of here about twenty-five miles."

"That's too far. Can't wait for an ambulance. I'm going to take her. Help me."

"Are you sure—"

"Help me."

I slipped my hand behind Heavenly's shoulder to brace it. There was no exit wound. The bullet was still inside her.

Ellis and I gathered her up and hauled her upward. Heavenly winced; tears filled her eyes.

"Now it hurts," she said.

With Ellis helping to steady her, I was able to remove a hand from Heavenly's shoulder and open the car door. We stuffed her into the seat. I locked the seat belt in place. Blood was still seeping from her wound, yet it wasn't flowing freely. I took that as a sign neither a major artery nor vein had been blown.

"I'm getting blood all over your car," Heavenly said.

"Don't worry about it."

"Is this new?"

I shut the door and circled the Mustang.

"I need you to do two things, Ellis," I said. "Can you do them?"

"What?"

"Tell Memorial Medical that we're coming. Tell them it's a gunshot wound. Do you have a cell phone?"

"I'll call them."

"When you're done with that, tell Chief Neville what happened."

"I don't know what happened."

"I saw it," a man in the crowd said. "I saw everything."

"Tell the chief," I said.

"You're fleeing the scene of a crime," someone else said.

"Tell the chief."

I entered the Mustang, slamming the door behind me. I adjusted the seat belt at the same time that I pressed the start button. The engine roared to life. I pulled away from the curb without bothering to look for traffic, probably a foolish thing to do, but I was in a hurry. I drove straight up the street until I hit Highway 13, hung a left, and accelerated.

"McKenzie, did you see?" Heavenly said. "Someone shot me. Did you see?"

Her face was ghastly pale beneath the few streetlights that we passed, and for some reason I thought of the Ghost Lady.

"I saw," I said.

"Who? Who was it?"

"I don't know."

"Then you didn't see."

"Shhhh, don't talk."

"Why not? Do you think I'll stop bleeding if I keep quiet?"

We were out of the city by then; there was nothing but darkness all around us, punctuated by the occasional light far off in the distance. My headlights were on high. The speed limit called for fifty-five miles per hour. I was pushing the Mustang over seventy-five and would have been going faster if not for the dips and curves.

"I've never been shot before," Heavenly said. "Never been hurt even. You have."

"Shot, knifed, blown up, had my head fractured twice."

"Occupational hazard."

"Something like that."

"Still, I never thought I'd be shot. Never even occurred to me. You should be very happy. You and Jack."

"Why?"

"The last two men who will ever see me in a bikini."

Heavenly chuckled at that. I didn't think it was funny.

"You'll be back on the beach in no time," I said.

She glanced down at her hand pressed against her wound. Her soft blue sweater was now saturated with blood.

"I don't think so," she said. "Still, I can't complain. I've been lucky. Always been pretty. Never needed anyone to tell me; I've always known. Pretty all through school; one of those girls. I took advantage, too. Walked through doors closed to others. Knew it wouldn't last, though. The women in my family, at forty they start going downhill. Genetics."

"Not you."

"Why not me?"

"Diet. Exercise. Stay out of the sun. You take care of yourself."

"I've been shot. How's that for taking care of myself? McKenzie?"

"What?"

"I don't think my wound is life-threatening. Your driving is, though."

"Clearly, you're delirious from the pain."

"Slow down. Please, McKenzie."

I slowed, but not so much that I couldn't pass the vehicle in front of me like it was standing still.

"Now Nina—she's what?" Heavenly asked. "Forty? Forty-five?"

"Somewhere in there."

"She looks thirty. When she's sixty, she'll look forty. When she's dead, she'll be the most beautiful corpse in the cemetery."

"That's something to aspire to."

"I've always been jealous of her. She has such a perfect life."

Heavenly coughed hard into her palm. She looked down into her hand afterward. If there was blood there, she didn't show it.

"How are you doing?" I asked.

"I've been better. McKenzie, I'm sorry."

"For what?"

"For not being better."

Heavenly slumped in the seat.

"Hey," I said. "Sweetie? Talk to me, sweetie."

Heavenly didn't answer.

I downshifted and stomped hard on the accelerator.

According to my odometer, it was seventeen miles to Washburn. The Ghost Lady had told me that it was four times the size of Bayfield, yet it looked to me like it was deserted as I sped through it on Highway 13. From there it was six miles to Ashland, population 8,216 according to the sign. Google Maps said the trip should have taken thirty-two minutes. I managed it in twenty-one.

I followed the highway along the south shore of Lake Superior down along Chequamegon Bay and up again. I became confused when I hit the traffic circle where 13 intersected with U.S. 2, yet I managed to keep going in the right direction until I found Sanborn and went south and then Maple Lane and went east. There were empty fields on both sides of the street, which didn't boost my confidence any. Nor did the flat, dull building on the right.

I turned in and came to a stop in front of the entrance. There was a large sign that read MEMORIAL MEDICAL CENTER next to the sliding glass doors and another in red and white that read EMERGENCY directly above; there were potted plants and benches on both sides of the door. If not for the signs, I'd swear it looked like a bus terminal.

I turned off the engine, slipped out the door, and ran around the car. The sliding glass doors parted. Doctors and nurses approached in a hurry; they all seemed to be pushing the same gurney.

"Are you McKenzie?" someone asked.

"Yes."

"Get out of the way."

One of them pushed me aside—literally.

Another asked, "How long has she been unconscious?"

"Ten minutes," I said.

They slid Heavenly out of the front seat and placed her on the gurney. There was a man wearing his steel gray hair in a ponytail. Except for the white coat over blue scrubs, he looked like a fifty-year-old hippie.

"Everyone knows their job," he said. "No mistakes."

They wheeled Heavenly past me into the hospital. I made to follow her. A nurse pressed her hand against my chest.

"You need to move your car," she said.

TEN

The waiting room was as drab and joyless as the hospital building. I sat alone on a chair, my legs outstretched and crossed at
the ankles, my arms folded, my chin resting on my chest. Heavenly's wicker bag was next to me. I had removed it from the
Mustang after parking in the near-empty lot across the street.
I searched her wallet for a health insurance card and found only
a Wisconsin driver's license and credit card, both in the name
of Caroline Kaminsky. That's the name I gave to the admitting
nurse. I also told her that I would be responsible for all hospital
costs; I signed a paper to prove it.

I had never been in a hospital so quiet. There were no an-
nouncements made over the PA system, no paging of hospital
personnel, no soothing music piped in. I could hear the pages
being turned on the magazine the receptionist was reading.
They sounded to me like pistol shots.

Twice I asked the receptionist for news. Twice she said she'd
tell me when someone told her.

I knew guys who punched walls in moments of frustration—
major league pitchers risking their careers, for God's sake—
guys who would throw cell phones through windows, smash

perfectly innocent HDTVs. Not me. I'm the guy who sits down and carefully runs revenge scenarios through his head, starting with the most violent and ending with the most satisfying, although sometimes they were the same.

That's what I was doing when the doctor with the ponytail rounded the reception desk—and a deputy wearing the uniform of the Bayfield County Sheriff's Department came in through the front door. I stood up. They both reached me at the same time.

"Are you McKenzie?" the deputy asked.

His hand was resting on his Glock.

"Yes," I said.

"I'm Dr. Rockman," the medic said. "Daniel Rockman. Caroline asked me to give you a message. She told me to call her Caroline."

"Are you armed?" the deputy said.

I reached behind my back and pulled the SIG Sauer. I handed it to the deputy butt first. If the doctor was surprised, he didn't show it.

"What did Caroline say?" I asked.

"She said—sorry about making a mess of your car," Dr. Rockman said.

The things women worry about, my inner voice said.

"How is she?" I asked aloud.

"You're coming with me," the deputy said.

I raised my hand, showing him the palm, letting him know that he was second on my list of priorities at the moment.

"How is Caroline, Doctor?" I asked.

"Lucky," he said. "There was no major injury to her subclavian artery or vein, and the hematoma is not expanding. Chest X-rays were negative. There's no fluid building up in her lungs; it's all good."

"It's all good? Doctor, pretend that you're talking to a complete moron."

"All right. The patient was shot in the upper chest, left side. The bullet entered"—he put his finger against his own collar-bone—"and chipped the clavicle, causing a hairline fracture. It continued behind the clavicle, where it transected a branch of the subclavian artery. A CTA indicated that the transected artery had already retracted and clotted; it stopped bleeding on its own. The vessel is, for all practical purposes, starting to heal itself. Basic lab work indicates that the patient's hemoglobin is ten, so we're not giving her blood. We'll continue checking her hemoglobin every six hours to make sure it doesn't start trending downward."

"Wait," I said. "But she lost a lot of blood."

"We estimate a pint, perhaps a pint and a half. But at this level, it's like giving blood at the Red Cross. The body will take care of itself. What else? BUN testing indicates that her kidneys are functioning properly—"

"What about the bullet?"

"We left the bullet where it is."

"What?" the deputy said.

"We rarely go after the bullet if we don't need to. We can cause much more damage, more injury, more bleeding by looking for the bullet. First, do no harm."

"We need it for evidence," the deputy said.

"Tough."

"You're leaving the bullet inside her?" I said.

"Best place for it."

I'll be damned, my inner voice said.

"She was concerned about the scar," I said aloud.

"The bullet left a mark; what can I say?"

"Can I see her?"

"No. She's lost a lot of blood, as you said. I gave her something to help her sleep. You can speak to her in the morning. We'll contact you when she wakes. Where will you be?"

"Bayfield Sheriff's Department," the deputy said.

"Right here," I said.

"It'll be a long night," the doctor said.

Not as long as the last ninety minutes, my inner voice told me.

"You're coming with me," the deputy said.

"Were you instructed to arrest me?" I asked.

He stumbled over his answer.

"I'm not going to answer any questions until Chief Neville arrives anyway," I said. "I'm sitting right here. You can sit over there and watch me sitting right here. There's coffee." I gestured at the setup in the corner. "I don't recommend it."

The doctor said, "Neither do I."

"I'm in your debt," I told him.

"Not at all," he said.

He patted my upper arm and walked back behind the reception desk. I sat down. The deputy stood in the middle of the room looking confused. He spoke into the mic attached to his shirt, seeking instructions. I didn't hear what his superiors told him, but a moment later he sat down across from me. He set the SIG on the chair next to him.

I thought about calling Nina. It was nearly 1:30 A.M., which meant she was probably just getting home from the club. Except I didn't want to make a call in front of the deputy, making him anxious about whom I was talking to and why. Instead, I closed my eyes . . .

"McKenzie."

My eyes snapped open and I saw Chief Neville hovering above me. He didn't look happy.

I stretched myself awake, no sudden movements. A gray light was pouring through the windows. The deputy was still in the chair across from me, his elbow on the armrest, his head propped in his hand. If he had slept, he didn't show it.

"Chief," I said. "What time is it?"

"Why? Do you have a date?"

I glanced at my own watch—5:45 A.M.

"I expected to see you sooner," I said.

"I've been busy. Do you know the last time there was a shooting in Bayfield? Never. It's one of the reasons I decided to retire here."

"It wasn't my fault."

Dammit, my inner voice said. *You sound just like the Maestro.*

"You told me that you weren't carrying a gun," the chief said.

"It was true when I said it."

The chief sat next to me.

"Start talking," he said.

I told him I left the Lakeside Tavern with Caroline . . .

"Her name is Heavenly Petryk," the chief said.

"Who told you that?"

"Keep talking."

I did, finished with driving Heavenly to the hospital.

"No disrespect," I added. "I just couldn't wait for you or an ambulance."

"That's it? You're not going to tell me about Curtis Shanklin and his posse on Madeline Island trying to hold you up? How 'bout the kid in the tavern that you chased off when he hit on Petryk. Did you forget him, too? And the man in the sportcoat?"

"You have been busy."

"I have two eyewitnesses at the scene. They confirm your account of the shooting. They were watching every step you took since you left Lakeside; or rather I should say they were watching Petryk. Something about the way she moved in those tight jeans and boots. They couldn't identify the shooter, unfortunately. Phil Speegle told me about the kid; he was inside the tavern drinking beer with his friends when the shooting took place. Speegle also said you were concerned about some guy in a sportcoat, but he didn't know whom you meant."

"I have no idea who he is, either, but he keeps popping up everywhere I go."

"Uh-huh. Speegle told me you were spending time with Jack Westlund and a blonde. I went to see him on his boat. Westlund told me the story about Madeline Island. I checked. Shanklin and his pals were still on the island when the shooting took place. They missed the last ferry and were staying at a motel near the landing. They denied everything, by the way. Westlund also told me about Maryanne Altavilla; said he walked her to the Bayfield Inn and left her there after she turned down his invite for a nightcap. I interviewed her, too. You like to surround yourself with pretty girls, don't you, McKenzie? Altavilla said that she didn't know anything about the shooting until I told her. She also said that you were not working with her insurance company. She was quite adamant about that."

"I never said I was."

"Something else, which caught me a little by surprise. She seemed genuinely concerned about your welfare."

"My welfare? Not Heavenly's?"

"I think the lady has a crush on you."

"Yeah, that must be it."

"Now it's your turn."

"My turn?"

"You're going to answer my questions. You're not going to give me any Fifth Amendment bullshit. You're not going to lawyer up. You're not going to lie. If you do, I will arrest you for carrying a concealed weapon without a permit, discharging a weapon illegally within the city limits, and felony assault. I won't be able to make the last charge stick. Add that to the others, though, and I can keep you off the street for a few days, and you don't want to be off the street for a few days, do you?"

"You're not going to like it."

"Try me."

I told him about Officer Pilhofer. The chief sat quietly for a few moments.

"Tell me," he said. "What would you have done if Maggie Pilhofer hadn't come along and poked you with her stick?"

"I don't know."

"Do you think Brian is protecting Heather Voight?"

"I'm just telling you what the Ghost Lady told me."

"You're right, McKenzie. I don't like it."

He asked more questions. I answered truthfully. Through it all, though, I could tell there was a question nagging the chief that I couldn't answer—where was his officer when the shooting took place?

Finally, the chief stood and crossed the waiting room to the reception desk. The same woman was sitting there as before; for all I knew she was reading the same magazine. The chief said something, and the receptionist picked up a phone. Apparently, she was willing to give the chief more cooperation than she gave me. A few moments later, a plump woman wearing a white coat over blue scrubs appeared. She was smiling.

When I stood, the deputy got to his feet as well. He didn't interfere, though, when I crossed the room. The chief saw me coming.

"This is McKenzie," he said.

The woman extended her hand.

"I'm Dr. Sauer," she said. "I have relieved Dr. Rockman. You're the one who brought Caroline in, am I right?"

"Yes. May I see her?"

"No. As I was telling the chief here, Caroline is still asleep, and I have no intention of waking her. Once she wakes on her own, then you can see her."

"When will that be?" the chief asked.

"I don't know. Personally, I like to sleep in when I get a chance."

"Candy. It's important."

Candy?

"I never said it wasn't," the doctor said. "I'll call you when she wakes."

The doctor left the room, leaving us standing there. We both glanced at our watches at the same time.

Four hours later, Dr. Candy Sauer returned. By then the receptionist had been switched out and the deputy had been sent on his way. He gave the chief my nine-millimeter before he left. The chief bounced it in his hand for a bit before giving me a spot-on Sean Connery impersonation. *They pull a knife, you pull a gun. They send one of yours to the hospital, you send one of his to the morgue. That's the Chicago way.*

"Nice," I said.

"Are you from Chicago, McKenzie?"

I flashed on a few of the revenge scenarios I had run through my head earlier.

"No," I said.

"I'm going to keep your gun anyway."

You can always get another, my inner voice told me.

When the doctor arrived, Chief Neville slipped the nine into his pocket.

"You can see her now," she said.

We stood together. The chief placed a hand on my chest.

"Where are you going?" he asked.

"To see Heavenly."

"When I'm done questioning her."

I might have argued, except I knew there was no way to win.

Chief Neville was twenty minutes with her. When he emerged from Heavenly's room, he had an odd sort of grin on his face.

"Interesting woman," he said. "I can see why you like her so much."

"Who said I liked her?"

"How long have you been sitting in the waiting room? We'll talk again, McKenzie. Soon."

The chief left, and I walked down the wide corridor to Heavenly's room—the hospital had only one floor. She was sitting up, dressed in an off-white hospital gown, her left arm in a sling, and eating breakfast. She wasn't wearing makeup, yet her golden hair had been brushed. I was shocked by how healthy she appeared.

"They serve Jell-O here." Heavenly pointed at a slot on her tray with a plastic utensil that combined a spoon with a fork. "I haven't had Jell-O in years."

"You seem awfully chipper for a woman who was shot less than twelve hours ago."

"What can I say? Another day in the life . . ."

I set her wicker bag on the bed next to her, and she began rummaging through it with her right hand.

"Heavenly, is there anyone I should call? Family?"

She pulled a smartphone from the bag that was twice the size of mine.

"No," she said. "I've got it. My God, McKenzie. You look like hell. Were you here all night? You were, weren't you? That is so sweet."

Dr. Sauer entered talking. "Let's take another look beneath that bandage . . . Oh, I'm sorry, you have a visitor."

"This is my good and true friend McKenzie," Heavenly said. "McKenzie, have you met Dr. Sauer?"

"Yes," I said.

Dr. Sauer came toward me anyway to shake my hand. The smile on her face suggested that her opinion of me had improved exponentially based on Heavenly's endorsement.

"If you care to step out of the room for a few minutes," she said.

"No, it's okay," Heavenly said. "I want him to stay."

The smile never left the doctor's face as she spun toward her patient. She pushed away the cart that held Heavenly's breakfast tray above the bed. Heavenly leaned forward; her face tightened with pain. The doctor untied the thin cords behind her neck and back that kept Heavenly's hospital gown closed. I turned and stared out the window. The sun was climbing in the sky, and I had a good view of the empty fields that surrounded the hospital.

"This is going to hurt," Dr. Sauer said.

Heavenly hissed. "It did," she said.

"That doesn't look too bad at all. Dr. Rockman does nice work."

"It's going to leave an awful scar."

"Plastic surgery will help. I know a doctor; he helps patients that have undergone mastectomies. He's very good."

"When can I leave?"

"First, we need to make sure your hemoglobin is stable. During the night it dropped to nine. We want to make sure it was caused by the IV fluids that we gave you and not because you're bleeding internally. We'll give you another chest X-ray—make sure blood isn't going somewhere we can't see, into the chest cavity, for example. We need to transition you to oral pain medication, too; make sure you're okay with that before we send you home."

"None of what you just said answers my question."

"Tomorrow. You can leave tomorrow. You can turn around now, Mr. McKenzie."

I did, just in time to see Dr. Sauer finish retying Heavenly's gown.

"Thank you for your concern, Doctor," Heavenly said. "I'm leaving today."

To prove it, she attempted to swing her legs off the bed. She stopped abruptly; a sudden inhale followed by a slow exhale hinted at the distress the movement caused her. Heavenly's eyes became wet and shiny.

"Also, you need to be fitted with the correct sling," Dr. Sauer said. "Something that'll restrict your movements, prevent you from moving your arm in a way that'll cause you pain—like right now. We can't put a cast on a fractured collarbone. The best we can do is stabilize it. You're going to experience a great deal of discomfort for several weeks, young lady."

"Give me some pills and I'll be on my way," Heavenly said.

"What are you going to wear?" I asked. "Your sweater and jeans have been destroyed, haven't they, Doctor?"

" 'Fraid so," Dr. Sauer said.

I gestured at the wicker bag.

"Your bikini?"

Heavenly's eyes narrowed and her nostrils flared. If she'd had a gun, I would have been in fear for my life.

Wait, she does have a gun.

"Do what the doctor tells you," I said. "I'll bring your clothes tomorrow. I'll take you wherever you want to go."

Dr. Sauer patted Heavenly's knee.

"See you before my shift ends," she said. She nodded her head in my direction. "Mr. McKenzie."

The door closed silently behind her.

"Daniel Rockman and Candy Sauer," I said. "Sounds like a couple of porn stars. The doctors will see you now."

"Don't try to make me smile. I'm angry."

"Okay."

I stared at her. She stared at me. She smiled.

"Dammit, McKenzie," Heavenly said. "I'd thank you for saving my life, but I'm not sure you did. The chief seems to think that you were the target last night and that I just got in the way."

"We both know that's not true."

"We do?"

"I'm the one with the money. You never shoot the guy with the money. Besides, *Caroline*, you're the one who's on the lam."

"On the lam? Who talks like that? You watch way too many black-and-white movies."

"Heavenly, why won't you tell me the truth? What's the problem?"

"I don't have a problem except that I sometimes stand too close to you. You can be detrimental to a girl's health."

"Swear to God, sometimes looking at you is like looking at a reflection in a fun-house mirror, so many levels of deception."

"That's a terrible thing to say to someone on her sickbed."

Heavenly brought her fist to her mouth and fake-coughed into it. I pointed at the wicker bag.

"Your Colt .380 auto is beneath your bikini," I said. "If I'm not mistaken, you only have three rounds left."

"You should take it. You're the one people are shooting at."

"You're very good at keeping your secrets, but you have to know—eventually I'll figure it out. I always do. And if you don't have an exceptional reason for holding out on me, I'm going to kick your ass."

"Promises, promises."

ELEVEN

The blood had dried to a thick paste by the time I returned to my Mustang, and it gave off a sour-sweet odor that made me nauseous even with the windows down. I decided to clean it up later, except later lasted only until I reached Washburn. I pulled into a gas station that also had a car wash and sold groceries. I bought cleaning supplies and went to work in the parking lot. It took a while before I was able to replace the smell of dried blood with industrial disinfectant—much better, I decided. I gassed up, ran the Mustang through the hands-off car wash, and was on my way.

It was well past noon by the time I reached town, far too late for breakfast at the Queen Anne. Connor met me at the door with a couple of dozen questions about Caroline; news really did travel fast in Bayfield. I waded through most of them until he asked, "What should I do with Caroline's belongings?"

"Why should you do anything with them?"

"Caroline had planned to check out, today."

Dammit, Heavenly, my inner voice said. *You couldn't tell me even that much?*

"Another couple has reserved the suite," Connor said. "They should be here later this afternoon."

"What about my room? Is it still available?"

"Yes. Until Saturday, and then—"

"Okay, let's move Caroline's stuff to my room. I'll settle her bill, and then we'll decide what to do when she gets out of the hospital."

It seemed like a good idea to Connor; he ran my credit card through his machine, made me sign the receipt, and gave me a key to the suite. Except he was awfully busy all of a sudden. Could I pack up Caroline's belongings? Sure, I told him. He was anxious about cleaning the room before his guests arrived. Could I take my shower and change clothes *after* I made the move? Fine.

"McKenzie?" Connor said.

"Yeah?"

"I didn't do it."

"Do what?"

"I didn't shoot Caroline."

"Who said you did?"

"People in town think I stole the violin. They'll think I did this, too."

"I wouldn't worry about it."

"I do worry. I'm trying to build something here. A city this size, all of us more or less in the same business, we rely on each other's goodwill."

"Did Chief Neville or someone from the sheriff's department question you?"

"No."

"They probably won't, but if they do ask you where you were at about eleven thirty last night, what are you going to tell them?"

"I was at home. In bed."

"Can you prove it?"

"No."

"Neither can most of the people who live in Bayfield," I said. "So relax."

I didn't think he was going to take my advice, though.

I climbed the stairs to the Queen Anne Suite. The door was unlocked, which gave me pause. I swung it open cautiously and found—chaos.

"Connor," I said.

I went to the top of the stairs and called down.

"Connor."

He bounded up two steps at a time. The effort caused him to lose his breath.

"What?" he asked.

I gestured at the suite. Heavenly's belongings had been thrown about carelessly. Suitcases were opened and discarded on the floor. Every drawer of every dresser and armoire was hanging open. The bedspread and sheets had been pulled down, and the mattress and box spring were out of place as if someone had searched beneath them. Whatever the intruder had been looking for, I bet he found it.

"Oh no, oh no," Connor chanted. "Someone must have broken in. It must have been after Caroline . . . oh no, oh no." He slumped against the wall. "First the violin and now . . . What are the police going to say? Bayfield? No one will believe . . . I worked so hard."

"You act as if you've never had a messy guest before," I said.

Connor's eyes snapped onto mine as if he couldn't believe he had heard me correctly.

"The room was ransacked," he said. "After Caroline was shot."

"Not necessarily. My girlfriend's daughter, a college kid, what a slob."

"What are you saying?"

"Unless you want to charge Caroline with, I don't know, vandalism, I'd keep this to yourself."

"McKenzie—"

"I'll gather up all of Caroline's belongings as promised, and then you can get the room in order before your guests arrive."

Connor paused for what seemed like a long time before he replied.

"Thank you," he said.

I dumped the two suitcases on the bed and began filling them with Heavenly's clothes, folding each article as best I could. It gave me a strange feeling touching her things—jackets, sweaters, skirts, slacks, and shoes that I placed neatly into one suitcase; bras, panties, camisoles, pajamas, shirts, and socks that I carefully packed in the other. I tried to make it impersonal, like when I packed my own clothes, yet it made me wonder about her. It occurred to me that I knew nothing about Heavenly for sure, not even her name. Maybe Caroline Kaminsky was her real name and Heavenly Petryk was the alias.

Very little of what I found in the suite gave me clues. She had hairbrushes in the bathroom, and a handheld dryer, and all kinds of beauty aids I didn't think she needed that went into a plastic bag that I dumped on the bed. 'Course, anybody could use those. In fact, the only personal item that I found was a framed photograph, Heavenly six or seven years ago dressed in a black graduation gown and cap with a gold tassel that matched the honors stole around her shoulders. She was surrounded by three older women all hugging her simultaneously. I thought that if they were her mother and aunts, she was wrong to worry. The women in Heavenly's family looked pretty damn good after they rounded forty.

I held the photograph with one hand and reached for a small nylon carry-on bag that had been tossed carelessly across the room. It seemed heavy to me, yet when I glanced inside I discovered that the bag was empty.

Why is it so heavy? my inner voice asked.

I examined the bag carefully, pulling on this and pushing on that until I found the latch that opened the hidden compartment.

The bottom of the bag was lined with cash.

Seeing it made my ears ring.

I finished packing as quickly as I could and moved all of Heavenly's belongings into the Peacock Chamber. Once I was behind the locked door, I sat on the bed and attacked the carry-on bag again. I reopened the secret compartment and spread the contents over the bedspread.

There were ten stacks. I counted them twice—one, two, three . . .

Each stack contained a hundred bills.

All fifties.

I stared at the money for a long time.

I was hungry, so I returned the $50,000 to the carry-on's hidden compartment, undressed, brushed my teeth, shaved, took a shower, combed my hair just so, dressed, and went out. It was sunny and warm, about seventy-five degrees, and I didn't wear a jacket, but that was mostly because I didn't have a handgun to hide beneath it—which made me nervous. The streets were crowded with tourists, and any of them could have been the person or persons unknown who shot Heavenly, who might have been trying to shoot me and missed. I watched them carefully. They all seemed to be going about their business with joyfulness and vivacity. Or maybe it was just me.

The Egg-Ceptional Breakfast and Bakery was closed by 2:00 P.M., and I had had enough of both the Lakeside Tavern and Hill House, so I went to Evelyn's near Memorial Park. It was filled with customers who seemed to delight in the eccentricity of the place, what with the flamingos, old signs, antique toys, off-center photographs, and electric trains running on tracks hanging from the ceiling. The waitress dressed like she worked for a circus. She wore a garish button that read WELCOME TO EVELYN'S, and my first thought was that Evelyn was a nut job. Yet she served a decent cheeseburger and fries that made me go "Hmmm."

I was finishing up and wondering if Chief Neville and I shouldn't have another talk when Herb Voight walked in. He gave a halfhearted wave at the hostess and started toward a table for two next to the door that led to the kitchen, the worst table in the restaurant. I called his name. He pivoted toward me.

"McKenzie," he said. "Don't you lead an interesting life."

He came to my table and sat down.

"Do you enjoy being the most talked-about person in town?" Voight asked.

"I really don't."

"How's the girl, what's her name—Caroline?"

"Caroline Kaminsky."

"She okay?"

"As well as can be expected with a bullet in her shoulder."

"That's just crazy, a shooting in Bayfield. I heard that, I was shocked. So's just about everyone else that lives here. I overheard some of the chamber types talking about visiting Chief Neville or the county sheriff, see what they can do about getting you out of town. They say you're hurting the tourist trade; they say you're an undesirable."

"Yeah, I get that a lot."

"Is this all about the violin, Duclos's Stradivarius?"

"I won't know until I find the shooter. That's my guess, though."

"It's crazy. But—did you just say 'until *I* find the shooter'? What does that mean?"

"It means I'm not going anywhere."

"A lot of folks are going to be unhappy to hear that."

Voight smiled. I think he wanted me to know that "a lot of people" didn't include him. I decided to ask an ill-mannered question just to see if he really was on my side.

"Mr. Voight, someone shot my friend," I said. "When I find out who, I just might shoot them. I don't want it to be you. Please tell me that it wasn't you."

"It wasn't."

"Prove it."

Voight stared at me for about ten seconds before he replied.

"When we spoke before, I said things about my wife and Paul Duclos," he said. "I shouldn't have. I shouldn't talk at all. See, last night I was with Maggie Pilhofer. On the *Heather II*. We were together belowdecks when Chief Neville called on Jack Westlund."

"You and the Ghost Lady?"

"She wasn't doing the tours when we first started seeing each other. That was what? Fifteen years ago? I was single then, and she was married to an asshole who later ran out on her. Her and the kid. We get together four, five times a year. More often than not we'll rendezvous at a marina somewhere along the lake and go off on my boat. I wouldn't want that to get around."

"Okay."

"Okay?"

"No one will hear it from me."

"I know what you must think of me. It's just that—there are times when I look at Heather, I think to myself, I could have done better, you know?"

"She's pretty; she has wealth, position."

"It's not about that, though. Never is. More often than not—Mags and me, we actually like each other, enjoy each other's company. Heather and me, not so much."

"I understand."

"Do you, McKenzie?"

"I think so. Tell me one thing, though. It's none of my business, but . . ."

"Yes?"

"Is Heather having financial problems?"

Voight stared at me for a few beats, a pensive expression on his face that quickly turned to one of amusement.

"Are you kidding?" he asked.

"I heard that a couple of her restaurants aren't doing well."

"You mean like Superior 13 that she's selling to the Chippewa; that she built knowing she'd eventually sell it to the Chippewa. Heather's smarter than all of us, McKenzie."

I stood and threw some money next to my plate.

"Good luck to you, sir," I said.

Voight covered the bills with his hand.

"I got this," he said. "Another restaurant owned by Heather."

"Then tip the waitress."

Bayfield City Hall consisted of three rooms in a gray wooden building that had seen far too many Lake Superior winters. I went into the room marked POLICE DEPARTMENT without bothering to knock. I heard Chief Neville say, "I told the mayor you would behave after your last dust-up. Now what should I tell him?" When he saw me he stopped talking.

Officer Pilhofer was sitting in one of two wooden chairs positioned in front of the chief's desk looking remorseful, a penitent taking a scolding from the head of his order. His eyes came up when I entered the room. His expression turned to one of rage and scorn. He rose quickly from his chair.

I walked deeper into the room. The chief gestured at his officer.

"Brian says you're lying," he told me. "He says he never told you to leave town; he says he never assaulted you at the Iron Bridge Hiking and Nature Trail."

"That's okay," I said. "I don't mind. I didn't come here to file a complaint or press charges. I would never do that to a cop. I wouldn't even have mentioned what happened except you asked."

Pilhofer squeezed his fists tight.

"It's a fucking lie," he said.

I sat in the second chair without being asked.

"Let's forget about it, then," I said. "For all I know, you have the makings of a fine police officer—once you get past all that rookie crap."

Pilhofer took a step toward me.

"Brian," Chief Neville said.

Pilhofer glanced at the chief, back at me, and at the chief again. He slowly unclenched his fists and sat down. Yet his breathing suggested that he was still angry.

Good, my inner voice said.

"What rookie crap?" Pilhofer asked.

"Thinking that you know it all, losing control of your emotions, lacking respect for the job and the citizens you serve; generally believing that your badge means you're in charge and everyone else had better watch out. I was kind of a jerk myself when I was first sworn in, and look how well I turned out."

Chief Neville rolled his eyes.

"How 'bout you?" I said. "Walking those means streets in Houghton, Michigan?"

"Michigan Tech is in Houghton," the chief said. "Typical college town. Half the morons I dealt with on a daily basis when I was a rook were about my age, and I was always trying to prove that I was smarter and tougher than they were."

"Yet here you are."

"Here I am. Is this just a social call, McKenzie, or did you barge into my office for a reason?"

"I wanted to ask—three rounds were fired at Heavenly and me last night. Two missed their mark. Can you tell me if they've been recovered?"

"No. The sheriff's department forensics team scoured the area, but they were unable to find any impact craters. Why?"

"I don't know if you've heard, the docs at Memorial Medical refuse to take the bullet out of Heavenly Petryk's shoulder."

"I heard."

I turned in my chair so I was looking directly at Pilhofer when I asked the next question. "You guys carry nine-millimeter Glocks, am I right?"

"Yes," he said.

"Heavenly was shot with a small-caliber handgun, .22, .25, maybe a .32. Anything bigger would have torn her shoulder off."

"What's your point?"

"Do you own any small-caliber handguns?"

I was shocked at how quickly Pilhofer jumped to his feet, at his willingness to start beating me about the head and shoulders right there and then. Chief Neville stood, too. He shouted Pilhofer's name. Pilhofer spun toward him.

"Did you hear what this sonuvabitch said?" he asked. "I don't need to take that shit."

"No, you don't. McKenzie, what the hell?"

"Remember what I said about controlling your emotions?" I asked.

"I don't need to take this shit," Pilhofer repeated.

"Spoken like an outraged suspect."

"McKenzie, Jesus Christ," Chief Neville said.

"Did you ask him where he was last night?"

"Stand up," Pilhofer said. "Stand up, damn you."

"Someone shot my friend last night, Officer Pilhofer. Was it you?"

"McKenzie, enough," Chief Neville said.

"Were you trying to get back at me and missed?"

"Stand up," Pilhofer said. There was genuine anguish in his voice.

"Where were you last night?"

"He was with me."

We all turned to find the Ghost Lady standing in the doorway, only instead of a flowing black cloak and lantern, she was wearing cargo shorts and a tight, long-sleeve T-shirt that outlined large breasts that had been hidden before. I thought, Mr. Voight, I get it now.

She slammed the door shut.

"Brian was with me," she said.

"Mrs. Pilhofer," the chief said.

"Don't give me that Mrs. Pilhofer stuff, Jeremy."

"Maggie—"

"Are you accusing my son of shooting that girl last night? You are, aren't you?"

"Ma," Pilhofer said. "What are you doing here?"

"You think I don't know what's going on? You think I don't know what they're saying? I know."

Even though the Ghost Lady pointed at the office wall, I suspected it was someone on the other side of the wall that might have tipped her.

"Ma, please," Pilhofer said.

"You were with me last night," she said. "You were with me. Tell them."

Pilhofer looked down and away.

"I was just about to," he said.

"We were watching that Will Smith movie on HBO and eating popcorn. Tell them."

Pilhofer turned toward the chief.

"We were—"

"Yeah, yeah, yeah," the chief said.

"Don't you believe us?" the Ghost Lady asked.

Chief Neville didn't say if he did or didn't.

"Maggie," I said.

She pointed a finger in my face.

"Don't you dare speak to me," she said.

"He can't hide behind your skirts forever."

If she had been carrying her staff, there's no doubt in my mind, she would have driven it through my chest.

"We're leaving," Maggie said. "Brian?"

Pilhofer looked at the chief.

"We'll talk before your shift begins," the chief said.

Mother and son left the room, the Ghost Lady slamming the door behind her yet again. It echoed through the room.

"Chief?" I said.

"Fuck you, McKenzie. I don't want to hear it."

"Okay."

I started drifting toward the door.

"Ahh Christ," the chief said. "What?"

"I don't know where Pilhofer was last night, but he sure as hell wasn't with his mother."

"How do you know?"

"I can't say."

"What do you mean you can't say?"

"I made a promise to someone. I don't want to break it unless I have to."

"Guess what, you have to."

"The question is—is Maggie lying to protect her son, or is my source lying to protect himself? Or maybe to protect Maggie."

"That's three questions, and who exactly is he?"

"I can't say."

"Does the term obstruction of justice mean anything to you?"

"I have a friend who's a lawyer who has made it quite clear on numerous occasions exactly what obstruction means."

"Yet you're going to stand there and screw with me anyway."

"I want to talk to the Great Lady. It would be better if you came along."

Chief Neville stared at me for a few beats before speaking.

"Phil Speegle is the only person I know who calls her that," he said. "Look, I don't know what he told you about Heather, but he's been trying to fuck her over for years."

"Actually, I think he just wants to fuck her."

"That, too."

We drove up the hill in the Bayfield Police Department's only cruiser, parking in the long driveway between Heather Voight's mansion and her small carriage house. The entire trip took all of three minutes. When I asked why we drove instead of walked, Chief Neville said, "The car makes it official."

We followed the winding cobblestone sidewalk to the front door. The chief pressed the doorbell. I was as surprised when Heather answered it as I had been when Duclos answered his doorbell, and for the same reason—the house was so big and opulent, I expected servants. Only there were none.

"Jeremy," Heather said. "More questions?" Then she saw me. "McKenzie. It's going to be one of those visits, isn't it? Please, come in."

She stepped aside, and we moved past her into the house. It was as old as the Queen Anne, yet better furnished.

"To what do I owe the pleasure?" Heather asked. "Is this about the shooting last night? Honestly, Jeremy, I don't know what Bayfield is coming to."

"We've been friends for a long time," the chief said.

"Just not today."

"I have hard questions."

Heather curled her arm around the chief's and led him into her parlor.

"Hard questions to ask or hard to answer?" she said.

Walking behind them, I couldn't help but notice Heather's tight blue jeans. And her boots. And the soft pullover sweater. Her attire was very similar to the clothes Heavenly had worn the night before. There was no chance anyone could confuse the two women, though, I told myself. Except maybe in the dark.

Heather sat the chief in an overstuffed chair and moved to the chair directly across from him. They were nearly knee to knee.

"Sit anywhere you like," she told me.

I did, on a love seat where I could watch them both at the same time.

"There's a rumor that you're sleeping with my officer—Brian Pilhofer," Chief Neville said.

"This city's rife with rumors, you know that. Remember a few years ago when they said you and I were having an affair?"

"I remember."

"It wasn't true, though—was it?"

"No."

Heather patted the chief's knee.

"Pity," she said.

"Heather, are you . . . ?"

"It's more like an adolescent crush than an affair."

"Is that why Brian warned McKenzie to get out of town? Is that why he attacked him near the Iron Bridge, because of an adolescent crush?"

Heather looked at me.

"Did that really happen?" she asked.

"That's the rumor," I said.

"Heather," the chief said. "Why would Brian do that?"

"Astonishing as it sounds, he thinks I stole Paul Duclos's Stradivarius. He keeps thinking it no matter how many times I tell him that it's not true."

"So does his mother," I said.

"Good ol' Maggie. Did she tell you that we went to school together? Not many of us left from the old crowd. Me, her, Phil Speegle . . ."

"The Maestro."

"Him, too."

"Heather," the chief said, "I'm this far away from arresting Brian for attempted murder."

No kidding? my inner voice asked. *Do you mean it, or are you just messing with her?*

"If you know of any reason why I shouldn't do it, now's the time to tell me," the chief added.

Heather closed her eyes and shook her head.

"I don't," she said.

"Heather?"

"I don't."

She rose from her chair and walked to the large window overlooking the carriage house. She leaned against the sill and shook her head some more.

"It'll be easier now than later," the chief said.

"There are things," Heather said, "once you say them out loud . . ."

"Anything you tell me today remains confidential. Just between you and me. Everything you say after an arrest is made, that becomes public record."

"McKenzie . . ."

"I won't repeat a word," I told her. "You have my promise."

"Your promise? Are you an honest man, McKenzie?"

"I've always tried to be."

"How's your success rate?"

"Better than average, I think."

Heather spun away from the window to face us.

"Brian and I were together last night," she said. "We spend most of our Wednesday evenings together."

"Why?" I asked.

"It works with our schedules."

"No, I mean, a woman like you . . ."

"What do you know about a woman like me?"

"I know you're smart. I know you're ambitious, you're accomplished. I know that you're attractive—"

"For a woman my age."

"For a woman of any age."

"What do you want to know, McKenzie? Spit it out."

"Why Pilhofer?"

"Why not him?"

"His age, for one thing."

"Look around. There aren't that many options available to me up here."

"Your husband—"

"Don't. Don't, McKenzie. Don't bring him into this. He's the kindest person I've ever known."

"Then why are you cheating on him?"

"I need someone stronger. Someone . . . sometimes—you're going to think I'm a heartless bitch, both of you, but sometimes I look at Herb and I think I could have done better."

"Thank you, Heather," the chief said. "We won't trouble you any longer."

Clearly, he had heard enough, yet I hadn't.

"Heather," I said.

"You don't get to call me by my first name anymore," she said.

"We're done here," the chief said.

"Just one more thing," I said.

"What is it?" Heather asked.

"The violin case was found outside your house."

"What of it?"

"The GPS tracker placed in the case was meant to help lead us to the Countess Borromeo."

"So?"

"So, what if the case was dropped at your doorstep following the theft in order to lead us to you?"

"I don't . . . I don't know what you mean."

"You own a lot of property."

"Three restaurants in Bayfield, one in Washburn, another in Red Cliff, a motel, a full-service gas station. I'm also partners in an art gallery. What of it?"

"What happens if you're . . . incapacitated?"

"You mean if I'm arrested and sent to prison?"

"Exactly that."

"I have people . . ."

"I'm sure you do. But who takes charge?"

"My husband. No, no, no, he would never do anything like that."

"Because he's such a nice guy?"

"McKenzie, I want you to leave now. Both of you."

We were outside, the door firmly shut behind us, and walking toward the police cruiser parked in the driveway.

"What the hell was that, McKenzie?" Chief Neville wanted to know.

"Just giving Heather something to ponder when she goes to bed tonight. And you too, for that matter."

"I don't know what you're talking about."

"She's your friend, isn't she? So is Voight. So is Maggie. So is Speegle. So is Pilhofer, for that matter. You can't imagine any of them stealing the Countess Borromeo, can you? You can't imagine any of them shooting Heavenly. Can you?"

"No."

"No," I repeated.

"But you can."

"You bet."

"Uh-huh. Tell me—why do you think I've been putting up with your bullshit for the past three days? So far, though, all you've given me is bupkis."

Oh, my inner voice said. *That's why the chief all but gave you permission to investigate the theft when you first arrived. Well, I'll be . . .*

"I'm working on it," I said aloud.

"You can walk back," he said.

TWELVE

Twenty minutes later, I found Jack Westlund sitting in his boat in slip number 76 at the Bayfield Superior Marina. He was sipping Leinie's from a bottle with his feet propped up on the gunwale. Slip 77 was empty.

"Hey, hey, hey," he said when he saw me. He was quick to rise and stood next to the hull. "How is she? How's my girl?"

Your girl?

"Heavenly's all right," I said. "She wanted to leave the hospital today, but they decided to keep her overnight, make sure she's good to go."

"I was so upset when I heard what happened. In Bayfield, no less. Are you sure she's all right?"

"She's fine."

"Maybe I should run up to Ashland? Is she accepting visitors?"

"I'm sure she is."

"It's Heavenly, though, right? You introduced her to me as Heavenly. When Chief Neville came by this morning, though, he was calling her Caroline, and I'm like—is this the same girl we're talkin' about?"

"It's complicated. Just . . . her name's Heavenly."

"Who did it? Do you know? I was talking to Neville—that was like three in the A.M., the man wasting no time at all. I told him what happened on Madeline. I hope that was all right."

"We're cool."

"It wasn't them kids, though, what shot her; they never left the island. So I don't know. Do you know what happened? Who did it, I mean?"

"Not yet, Jack . . ."

"Look at me, no manners at all. Come aboard, come aboard. Can I get you anything? Want a beer?"

"Yes sir, I do."

Westlund opened a Leinie's and handed it to me. I took a long pull. It went down smoothly. I found a seat and looked out on Lake Superior. There were boats out there, and the ferry, and the island with the sun shining bright and a light breeze from the northwest.

"I could get used to this," I said.

"Nah, not you, McKenzie. Got to have the right attitude to live on a boat, right disposition. Fella like you, I take you out and three days later you're gonna wanna come back in again. You're just not the type t' sit back and let the world go by. You're one of them people gotta get out and push."

"You think so?"

"Oh, I know so. Been around people and boats my whole life. Seen plenty of 'em what buys a boat thinkin' they're gonna live on the lake. They mean it, too; they're all in. Six months later their boat's up for sale and they're lookin' for a place on shore. Just don't have the right mindset. Got to where I can pick 'em a mile off.

"I notice the *Heather II* is gone," I said.

"Herb left this afternoon; don't know where. Had hisself a late lunch and took off. He does that a lot these days. Troubles at home, I figure. I had plenty in my time, so I know the symptoms."

"Tell me something—the night of the concert, you said that Voight woke you up around one o'clock."

"Thereabouts."

"You said you looked out the window—"

"Porthole."

"You looked out the porthole and saw a woman. You said it was Heather."

"Yes."

"Did you see her face?"

"In the dark, no, but . . ."

"But what?"

"Pretty sure it was her."

"Except that it wasn't her face that you were identifying, it was her size and shape."

"I suppose . . ."

Confirmation bias, my inner voice said. *He expected to see Heather, so he did, yet it could have been anyone.*

"What you thinkin'?" Westlund asked.

"I don't know. All the puzzle pieces are spinning around in the air, and I have no idea how they fit together."

"You like it, though, don't ya?"

"Like what?"

"Puttin' them pieces t'gether. It's like me and boats. It's what makes ya happy."

"Sometimes. Friends getting shot—that takes a lot of the fun out of it. Jack, how far is it from here to Duluth?"

"Sixty-six miles. Nautical miles."

"How long does it take to get there?"

"Depends. If you're fuel conscious like me, making eight-ten knots, it takes six-seven hours. If you don't care how much time and money you spend at the fuel dock, punch it up to twenty knots and you can get there in half the time. 'Course, we're talkin' a thirty-footer like mine. Not a sailboat or runabout."

"The *Heather II* is a thirty-footer."

Westlund shielded his eyes from the sun with the flat of his hand while he answered.

"Thirty-one. So?"

"Do you know what marina Voight uses when he's in Duluth?"

"SSL Harbor Basin, I guess. Same as me. Now whaddaya thinkin'?"

"Just tossing a couple more pieces into the air."

I had a second Leinie's and a couple of brats that Westlund cooked on a small propane grill. And another Leinie's. He regaled me with tales of his life and times on Lake Superior; places he'd gone, people he'd met, storms he rode out bouncing like a bobber on the angry water. I told him he was wrong, that I would like life on a boat just fine, yet I knew it was untrue. I had a handsome lake home in northern Minnesota where I spent a grand total of twenty days a year, if that. A boat like his would have been just another colossal waste of money.

At about six thirty, he announced that I didn't need to go home, but I couldn't stay there. He was going ashore.

"Gonna scoot up to Ashland and visit my girl," he said.

I told him the next time I'd get the beers. He thought that was a good idea.

We left the marina together. He went left toward the parking lot where he kept his car. I went right toward Memorial Park. It was Thursday. A bluegrass band was setting up in the gazebo for another Concert in the Park. Zofia McLean was there, and I gave her a wave. She must not have noticed, because she didn't wave back.

I sat on a metal bench facing Lake Superior and pulled out my smartphone.

"It's about time you called," Nina said. "I would have called you, only I didn't want your cell to ring in the middle of a gunfight."

"About that."

I told her everything, starting with the shooting last night and filling in the details around it. She seemed genuinely concerned about Heavenly's health and well-being.

"What is she going to do when she gets out of the hospital?" Nina asked. "Does she have family that can take care of her?"

"I don't know."

"How come we don't know if Heavenly has family?"

"She's a secretive girl."

"I suppose she could stay with us for a while. Erica and a couple of her college friends are off to Wyoming to hike mountains; one of them has a place out there, I guess. So that leaves the guest room free."

"You're aware that Heavenly thinks you hate her, right?"

"Of course she does. Every time we meet we snipe at each other. The only reason she hits on you is to annoy me."

"I thought it was because I'm such a fine figure of a man."

"No, that's not it."

Damn.

"She makes you so angry," I said.

"That's because . . . How do I explain this? Heavenly is doing all the things I wish I had done when I was her age, at least to a point. McKenzie, I married at twenty-one, less than a month after I graduated from college, and spent the next five years being both abused and cheated on. When I was Heavenly's age— she's what, twenty-eight now?—I was busy raising a six-year-old daughter, fending off a deadbeat ex-husband, and working day and night trying to build my club into something to be proud of. I never had the chance to be irresponsible, to go off on whatever adventure appealed to me at the moment, to have . . . experiences. I'm forty-three, McKenzie, and I have no memory of being twenty-three. Please, don't get me wrong. I'm really happy the way things turned out; the way Rickie turned out. Only, every time I see Heavenly, I'm left wondering about all the stuff I missed out on."

"Like getting shot?"

"I nearly did get shot. Remember that one time—"

"I remember."

" 'Course, Heavenly's so . . . what's the word?"

"Dishonest?"

"Untrustworthy. She has the morals of a . . . Name something that has no morals."

"A United States congressman?"

"No, God, not that bad. Anyway, I guess I'm a little jealous of her even though I wish she were a better person."

"People look at my new Mustang and they think I'm the one who's having a midlife crisis. Nina, this might come as a shock, but last night while she was bleeding all over my car, Heavenly told me that she was jealous of you, jealous of your perfect life."

She paused for a ten-count and said, "That bitch."

"Nina?"

"Bring her home, McKenzie. I'll lock up the good silverware."

The bluegrass band played two tunes back-to-back before addressing their audience. They thanked everyone for coming out, praised Bayfield for its kindness and beauty, and declared that they had CDs for sale that they would be happy to autograph during intermission. The banjo player held up his instrument and announced, "Deering Goodtime banjo. I bought it for five ninety-nine at a music store in Nashville." While he liked it, he doubted that it was worth stealing, unlike the Stradivarius that disappeared last week, although there were plenty who would be happy to smash it over his head once they heard him play. Zofia cringed, half the audience laughed, and the rest glanced at one another and said, "Huh?"

The band launched into a robust cover of the old Doyle Lawson tune "Rosine."

Maryanne Altavilla sat on the bench next to me.

"I hate bluegrass," she said.

"There isn't any music that I hate," I said. "There's stuff I don't particularly care for, don't listen to, but there's nothing I hate."

"How very mature of you."

"I like to think so."

We listened to a couple of choruses while I waited for Altavilla to get to the point. She finally did at the same moment the banjo player launched into an extended solo.

"It occurs to me, Mr. McKenzie, that you're no closer to finding the Countess Borromeo now than when you started."

"I thought you didn't want me to find the Countess."

"Midwest Farmers Insurance Group doesn't want it found. I, on the other hand, would be delighted if you came up with it."

"Excuse me?"

"I had thought that Heavenly Petryk might have it, or at least knew where it was. The shooting last night left me confused. Are you confused, McKenzie?"

"Thoroughly."

"When she's discharged from the hospital tomorrow, are you going to take Heavenly back to St. Paul?"

"I don't live in St. Paul anymore. I moved to Minneapolis in January."

"I didn't know that."

"Sonuvabitch. It was you."

"What was me?"

"You're the one who sent the invitation."

"What invitation?"

"The one enticing me to search for the Stradivarius by telling me not to."

"Are you susceptible to that sort of artifice? I would never have guessed."

"Maryanne—it seems that there's a great deal more to you than meets the eye."

"There's a great deal more to everyone than meets the eye."

"Does Midwest know you're in Bayfield?"

"I wouldn't think so."

"Vincent Donatucci knows."

"How?"

"I told him."

"That's unfortunate."

"Why?"

"I haven't spoken to Mr. Donatucci since he left the company; since they escorted him from the building. It broke my heart when they did that."

"Why did they?"

"He became . . . violent when they told him they were going to make him a part-time consultant."

"Consultant?"

"As far as he was concerned, it was the same thing as being let go, as being . . . marginalized. I assured him that it was untrue. I told him how much I required his expertise." Tears formed in Maryanne's eyes, yet she refused to let them fall, brushing them away with a knuckle instead. For a moment, I actually liked her. "He had done so much for me; recognized my abilities, allowed me to utilize them—I studied his work for the past ten-twelve years. Read every one of his files, including those about you."

"Now you want to recover the Stradivarius," I said. "Just to prove to one and all that you can do it. Meanwhile, Donatucci wants to do the same thing just to prove that he can do it. Both of you decided to use me. How wonderful. Yet Midwest Farmers doesn't want either of you to find the violin. Why is that, Maryanne?"

"McKenzie, there's a man about your age, height, and coloring wearing a dark blue sportcoat. He's standing across the street next to the Coca-Cola machine by the rear entrance to the Pier Plaza Restaurant. He's eating a double-scoop ice cream cone. The top scoop of ice cream slipped off the cone, but he caught it with his bare hand and placed it back on top. He would like to wipe the ice cream off his bare hand. Unfortunately, the only napkin he has is wrapped around the bottom of the cone. When he's not worrying about his ice cream, he's watching you. He's been watching you for the past forty-five minutes."

The band finished a song, and the audience offered a polite ovation. I turned my head while they applauded as if I were looking over the crowd. That's when I saw him, exactly where Maryanne said I would. I slowly directed my gaze back toward the gazebo.

"You impress me, young lady," I said.

"Do I? That wasn't my intention."

"No. Your intention was to change the subject. Who is he?"

"I was going to ask you."

"He's been following me since I arrived in Bayfield."

"Why?"

"I think it's about time I asked him."

"Forgive me if I sound like an alarmist, Mr. McKenzie. However, it is certainly possible that he's the one who shot Ms. Petryk."

"The thought had occurred to me as well. Maryanne, the local constable has confiscated my gun. Tell me—are you carrying?"

She shifted her large black bag so that it was between us and opened the top flap. I could see the butt of a handgun inside.

"May I?" I asked.

"Nine-millimeter Ruger, seven rounds in the magazine and one in the throat. I want it back."

I pulled the shirt out of my jeans and waited. The band finished its set and promised to return following a short break—and don't forget those CDs. People around me stood and stretched. I reached in the bag, secured Maryanne's Ruger, and quickly tucked it into the waistband of my jeans beneath the shirt. I stood and strolled swiftly in the opposite direction of Pier Plaza. I didn't look back to see if the man in the sports coat was watching or not.

I walked along the sidewalk to Manypenny, hung a right and then another on South First Street, moving with purpose. I reached Rittenhouse Avenue and slowed. My hand went to my stomach. I patted the handgun beneath my shirt and turned right again. I took a dozen steps toward the Pier Plaza before I realized that the man in the sports coat had disappeared. I stopped and searched the avenue for him.

There, my inner voice said.

The man in the sports coat was still on Rittenhouse, but he was heading away from the lake, moving at a brisk pace. He was no longer holding his ice cream cone. I followed.

He took us past Greunke's First Street Inn, Big Water Coffee Roasters, and Brownstone Centre Gallery and Gift Shops before heading east on Second Street. I matched his speed while remaining at a discreet distance. Not once did he look behind him.

We soon left the downtown area and became surrounded by residential housing. My first thought was that he didn't know I was following and would soon lead me to where he was staying. That changed, though, when he angled north on Washington Avenue and headed toward the Iron Bridge Hiking and Nature Trail.

In the back of my mind I could hear my father telling stories about fighting in bitter cold with the 1st Marines at the Chosin Reservoir in Korea. He had been outraged that the newspapers back home called it a "retreat."

We weren't retreating, he said. *We were finding a better place to fight.*

I pulled the Ruger out from beneath my shirt and thumbed off the safety.

"Wait," I said.

The man reached under his sports coat and brought out his own handgun. I was desperate for him to turn and shoot at me so I could shoot back. He didn't. Instead, he started running.

I gave chase, carrying the Ruger with both hands. It was lighter than I was used to; I doubt it weighed much more than a can of chunky chicken noodle soup—not that I eat that stuff.

The man in the sports coat turned into the parking lot, dashed across it, scrambled over the hardpack, rocks, and brush, and disappeared into the ravine. I closed the distance between us, yet deliberately slowed when I reached the edge.

I could no longer see him.

There were rocks and brush where the creek flowed and thick forest on both sides—plenty of places to spring from ambush. A narrow trail cut through and around it all. I followed it, advancing cautiously.

The trail took me beneath the iron bridge. I was no longer able to see the street or any structures. I might as well have been in the Amazon rain forest for all the landmarks I could identify.

I kept moving.

There was still a half hour of sunlight left, yet inside the ravine it could have been midnight. I nearly stumbled on a wooden staircase leading to a wooden deck perched on the wall of the ravine that gave tourists a pleasant view of the hiking trail and creek. I climbed the steps, staying low.

From the deck I examined the creek beneath me and the

trail twisting above me as best I could in the dim light. Nothing stirred. I heard nothing, not even the sound of leaves rustling in the wind.

A thought came to me then that was like a slap across the face. *What the hell are you doing chasing this guy through the forest?*

What do you hope to accomplish?

You don't know who he is. You don't know why he's here, what he's doing. And if he did shoot Heavenly, what the hell is keeping him from shooting you? Fear of being seen?

Wise up.

I eased myself off the platform and cautiously backed down the trail, all the time aware of just how vulnerable I was.

Finally, I reached the parking lot.

I wanted to shout something—"Hey, pal, better luck next time" or "I'll catch ya later"—so the man in the sports coat would know that I wasn't afraid of him. Really, though, how silly was that?

Instead, I tucked the Ruger under my shirt and slowly retraced my steps along Washington to Second Street. I looked over my shoulder only a half-dozen times.

The bluegrass band had just completed its second set and was receiving a hearty ovation by the time I returned to Memorial Park. I searched for Maryanne Altavilla, yet could not find her in the departing crowd. I knew she was staying at the Bayfield Inn, though, so I headed in that direction with the idea of returning her handgun.

My smartphone played "West End Blues" before I reached the entrance. The caller ID read SCHROEDER PRIVATE INVESTIGATIONS.

"McKenzie," I said.

"McKenzie, Greg Schroeder."

I nearly said, "I forgot all about you," but caught myself. "It's about time," I said instead. "How long does it take to check out a lousy fifty-nine names, anyway?"

"Hey, man, you owe me big for this one."

"I thought it was understood that I was only paying your going rate."

"Ha, ha."

"What do you have for me, Greg?"

"Are you sitting down?"

"Why? Is this going to be a long story?"

"A little bit."

"Do me a favor. Just skip to the ending."

"I not only know the name of the man who stole the Countess Borromeo, I know where he lives."

THIRTEEN

The door to Heavenly's hospital room was propped open. I knocked anyway as I stepped past it. Heavenly was sitting up in bed and talking on a cell phone. She was dressed in a hospital gown identical to the one she wore the day before. The sling was different, however. It was a very pale blue and seemed to hold her left arm closer to her body.

"Someone just came in," she said. "I need to go . . . Yes, I'll call you soon."

Heavenly dropped the cell on the bed and swung her legs over the side. She stood gingerly, although if she was experiencing any discomfort, her face didn't show it.

"Ordering a pizza?" I asked.

"My mom. What did you bring me?"

I set a shopping bag on the bed.

"Your mother?" I asked.

"You don't think I have a mother?"

"I've often wondered."

Heavenly opened the bag, dumped the contents on top of the bedspread, and began sorting through them: dress shirt, jeans, socks, boots, and underwear.

"Her name's Patricia, Patricia Petryk," Heavenly said. "She lives in Denver with my aunts Monica and Florence. In my family, they're known as 'the Sisters,' as in *you don't want to mess with the Sisters*. They're the ones who raised me after my father dumped Mom for a younger woman when I was in the eighth grade. I've only seen him twice since then, once at his wedding, the second time at his funeral."

"I lost my mother when I was in the sixth grade," I said. "Cancer."

"It's not the same thing."

"It's not?"

"I bet she didn't want to leave you."

No, my inner voice reminded me. *She didn't.*

"Did you tell your mother that you were shot?" I asked.

"Lord, no. Only that I fell and broke my collarbone. My mother thinks I work as a freelance security consultant. I try to keep it vague. I've practiced conversations in my head where I tell her what I really do, but it always sounds like I'm explaining a joke." Heavenly held up the lavender bra and panties I had brought; there wasn't much to them. "Really, McKenzie? This is what you picked?"

"It was what was on top," I said.

Heavenly smiled. It was one of her favorite things to do—embarrass me.

"I'll step outside," I said.

"No, that's okay."

Heavenly gathered up her clothes and moved into the bathroom, closing the door behind her. I gave her a slow twenty count before retrieving her cell phone. It was a flip phone, the kind you can buy at Target for $19.99—not the expensive smartphone I saw her use earlier. I felt a little guilty when I examined her call log, but then she had given me reason to be suspicious of her, hadn't she?

At least fifty thousand reasons, my inner voice reminded me.

I discovered that several calls had been made in the past week, one incoming, four outgoing, all to a single number with a 215 prefix. No other telephone numbers appeared.

I heard a noise from the bathroom, a cross between a moan and a curse. I dropped the phone back on the bed and went to the window. The fields outside hadn't changed since the last time I looked at them. I pretended to gaze at them anyway while I pulled out my own smartphone and inputted the 215 number into a reverse phone directory that I had an account with. The information the Web site returned:

Phone Type—cell phone
Company—Unknown
Name—Unknown
Location—Philadelphia, Pennsylvania

Heavenly called to me a few minutes later. "McKenzie."

I don't know why, but I knocked on the bathroom door even as I opened it just far enough to poke my head in. Her back was to me, and she was clutching her shirt to her chest. She stared straight ahead.

"Help me," she said.

"What?"

Heavenly was wearing jeans and boots; her sling was draped over the sink. Her bra straps were hanging on her shoulders, but the clasp was undone.

"I can't move my arm behind my back," she said. She refused to turn her head to look at me and for the first time since I had known her, she was the one who was embarrassed. "I tried hooking it in front and then turning it around, but I can't slide my arm through the strap. Could you . . ."

I hooked the bra ends together.

"I have a couple of bras that snap in front," Heavenly said.

"I should have asked you to bring one of those, but I didn't think."

I left without a word, closing the door behind me.

A couple of minutes later, Heavenly left the bathroom, the sling holding her damaged arm against her torso. I was surprised when she wrapped her good arm around my waist and rested her head against my chest.

"I've teased you so often for so long, and when you had the perfect chance to tease me back, you didn't take it," she said.

"I'm a helluva guy."

"One of the very few."

"Has it really been as bad as all that, Heavenly?"

"One of these days I'll tell you about my father."

"You already told me enough."

"No, not even close."

"Let's go."

Heavenly gathered her few belongings into the wicker bag, including her cell. She took her time.

"I need to be careful," Heavenly said. "Dr. Sauer warned me about sudden movements."

"I have to say, even shot up you look like a million bucks."

"Yeah, green and wrinkled."

"No, I mean it. You look like money."

"Any woman under the age of forty who stays out of the sun and doesn't have a weight problem looks like money. Are we going back to Bayfield?"

"To start with."

"What does that mean?"

"I have a plan."

"Would you like to share?"

"Nope."

I helped Heavenly into the Mustang, tilting the passenger seat forward so that her back was straight. A few minutes later, we were on Highway 13 and approaching Washburn. The windows were down, and the warm summer wind was blowing through her hair. She didn't seem to mind, even though several times she had to brush it out of her face.

"Hungry?" I asked. "Thirsty? Do you want to stop?"

"No, I'm okay."

"Just let me know."

Heavenly rummaged through her wicker bag with her right hand while trying mightily to keep her left side immobile. She found a small orange medicine canister and popped the white cap off with her thumb. She shook out two pills and swallowed them. The remaining pills she dumped out the window; they scattered like snowflakes on the pavement behind us.

"Aren't you going to need those?" I asked.

"They make me light-headed. Besides, pain doesn't hurt."

"Who told you that?"

"Patrick Swayze in *Road House*."

"And you believed him?"

By then we were through Washburn and on the fast track to Bayfield.

"What's that smell?" Heavenly asked.

"Disinfectant."

"Oh, yeah. Sorry about the blood."

"That's okay. She cleaned up real nice."

"This is a fabulous car. I like it much better than your old Audi."

"Nina gave it to me. For my birthday."

"That's too bad."

"It is?"

"Too bad that she feels she needs to buy your affection with expensive gifts."

"I'm going to tell her you said that."

"Do you tell Nina everything?"

"Pretty much."

"I wish I had someone I could tell all my secrets to."

"You could tell me."

"Hardly."

"How 'bout the Sisters?"

"Them least of all."

"By the way, Nina said you're welcome to stay with us while you recover from your wounds."

Heavenly's head snapped toward me. She stared for a good ten seconds before she replied.

"That bitch," she said.

Bayfield came up in a hurry. I slowed and cautiously maneuvered the Mustang along the highway as it angled through town. It was midmorning on a Friday, and the number of tourists on the streets appeared to have doubled; some of them seemed to think that the traffic laws only applied when they were at home. I surprised Heavenly when I didn't take the turn for the Queen Anne, but instead remained on 13 until it led us out of town.

"Where are we going?" she asked.

"Duluth."

"What about my stuff?"

"Packed up and stored in the trunk."

"And my car?"

"I called the rental company. They're sending someone over to pick it up, although they said they're going to charge Caroline's credit card extra for the service. By the way, someone broke into your room at the Queen Anne sometime after you were shot, searched it pretty thoroughly. I don't suppose you know what the burglar was looking for?"

Heavenly gave me a hard look. I pretended that I didn't know why.

"I don't know," she said.

"You'll want to go through your stuff when we reach Duluth to see if anything is missing."

Eventually, she settled back against the seat.

"You were right," she said. "I shouldn't have thrown away the pain pills."

I pulled into the parking lot of the same hotel where I usually stayed during the Bayfront Blues Festival. When I opened the trunk of the Mustang to retrieve the luggage, Heavenly reached in, pulled out the nylon carry-on bag, and stepped back as if she expected me to take it from her. I pretended not to notice. Instead, I heaved out her two suitcases and my own satchel, which I was able to carry by a strap hanging from my shoulder. I set one of the suitcases down in order to close the trunk and carried all three bags into the hotel. Both of Heavenly's suitcases were heavier than mine.

"If you weren't hurt, I'd make you carry your own luggage," I told her.

Heavenly didn't answer, probably because she knew that even if she hadn't been shot, the way my father raised me, yeah, I'd probably carry her bags anyway. Hell, I still carried Nina's bags, and I've known her for over six years; still opened car doors for her, too.

Although we were clearly together, neither the desk clerk nor Heavenly batted so much as an eyelash when I rented two rooms adjacent to each other—one of them under the name Caroline Kaminsky.

"That wasn't necessary," Heavenly told me. By then we were alone on the elevator and heading up; I could see her reflection in the polished door as I faced forward.

"I didn't want to presume," I said. "In Bayfield I introduced you as Heavenly. That might have been a mistake."

"What do you mean?"

"The person who shot you, sweetie—was it because he thought you were Heavenly or because he thought you were Caroline? I don't know. Do you?"

"I still believe whoever it was was actually trying to kill you, and I just happened to get in the way."

No you don't, my inner voice said.

"Besides," she added, "the only person who knew me as Heavenly was Jack Westlund, and he was with us, or at least me, from the time you introduced us at the marina until right before the shooting."

"Maryanne Altavilla knew."

"Only after Jack introduced me. And that's not what I meant."

"What did you mean?"

"It wasn't necessary to get two rooms."

I let the innuendo slide.

A few moments later, I opened Heavenly's door and tossed the suitcases on the bed. It took some effort. I spoke to her over my shoulder as I headed for the exit.

"When you're finished, knock on the wall and I'll buy you lunch."

"McKenzie, why are we here?"

"To see a man."

"What man?"

"Good question," I said.

And yet I didn't answer it.

It didn't take long to unpack. I had only a few clean things left, and the rest of my belongings I left in the satchel, including the nine-millimeter Ruger that Maryanne Altavilla had lent me—I never did return it after I received Greg Schroeder's phone call.

My smartphone played "West End Blues," and my first

thought was that Heavenly was calling, although, in retrospect, no woman unpacks that fast. Besides, she would have wanted to make sure the $50,000 was still intact.

"McKenzie," I said.

"Where are you?" Vincent Donatucci asked.

"In Duluth. Why do you ask?"

"What are you doing in Duluth?"

"The same thing I was doing in Bayfield, chasing the Countess Borromeo. Again, why do you ask?"

"I just heard that Maryanne had returned to the office; I still have friends over there. I tried to reach you at the Queen Anne, but the man said you had checked out after breakfast this morning along with Caroline Kaminsky. So she's not dead?"

"Of course not."

"Of course not," Donatucci repeated. "Only the good die young. Which means Heavenly Petryk should live forever."

"Her and all the rest of us."

"Is she with you?"

"Yes."

"No, no, no, McKenzie. She's there to steal the Countess."

"I know."

"That's why she was in Bayfield, to steal the Countess."

"I know."

"Then what are you doing?"

"Keeping my enemies close—think of it that way. Look, if Heavenly gets her hands on the Countess before we do, I'll buy it from her for the $250,000—which is what we intended to do all along."

"How do we know she doesn't already have it?"

"If she did, she would have taken the deal the first time I offered."

"Unless there's someone else who's offering more."

"In which case, she'd be long gone by now."

"I don't like this. I don't like you being in Duluth, either. Mc-Kenzie, the violin is in Bayfield. It must be."

"Not necessarily."

"What do you know that I don't?"

"I'm here to speak to Trevor Ruland."

There was a long pause before Donatucci spoke again.

"How do I know that name?"

"You helped put him in jail about ten years ago."

"I did?"

"He stole a $70,000 vase from an art gallery in Omaha."

"That's right—Trevor Ruland. Very grandiose, thought he was Cary Grant in *To Catch a Thief*. He stole the vase and tried to sell it back to the gallery for $25,000. Midwest Farmers insured the vase; I played the go-between. He arranged to meet me in the most expensive restaurant in town—the man wore a tuxedo, I'm not joking you. I gave him the cash, he gave me the vase, and the Omaha Police Department arrived to take him away. He did five years for receiving stolen property."

"Ruland said at trial that you behaved unprofessionally by calling the police. He said that was against the rules."

"I remember that."

"The Duluth cops suspect that Ruland has been involved in some petty thefts since he was released from prison, but he hasn't been busted yet—a wannabe gangster pretending he's living in an *Ocean's Eleven* world."

"That sounds right."

"However—he did stay at the Queen Anne three days before the Stradivarius was taken; actually had the same room as Paul Duclos."

"Are you sure?"

"I had a detective I know do a background check on everyone who stayed at the B&B up to two weeks before the theft. His name popped up; my guy gave me the details last night."

"Ruland used his real name?"

"You sound surprised."

Again Donatucci paused before responding.

"The quality of criminals we get these days," he said.

"Let me guess—when you were young, they always walked five miles through blinding blizzards to reach their victims, and always uphill."

"You're not funny, McKenzie."

I thought it was funny, my inner voice said.

"McKenzie, he's just as liable to try to steal the Countess from you as Petryk is," Donatucci said.

"We'll see."

"We'll see, we'll see—you're awfully cavalier about all this."

"No. I stopped being cavalier when someone put a round in Heavenly's shoulder."

"What's your play?"

"I'm going to buy him drinks, talk it over. I called him last night to set it up."

"Why would he agree to meet with you?"

"I told Ruland that I'm representing the Midwest Farmers Insurance Group and I'm interested in hearing his theories concerning the theft of the Stradivarius. He said he'd be happy to discuss the matter—hypothetically, of course."

"When?"

"He'll contact me in a few hours."

"It couldn't possibly be this easy."

"Oh, I agree. I absolutely agree with that."

Minnesota Point was a narrow, seven-mile-long sand spit that separated Lake Superior from both Superior Bay and St. Louis Bay, as well as the Duluth Harbor Basin, where all the great ships and freighters were loaded and unloaded. To allow the substantial shipping traffic to move easily from one side to the other, a huge canal, called Superior Entry, was dug through the spit. Technically, this turned it into an island that was connected to the mainland only by the Aerial Lift Bridge.

The bridge was up when we arrived, and we had to wait nearly fifteen minutes as a giant freighter negotiated the canal. We weren't alone. Canal Park, on the Duluth side of the bridge, was the city's answer to Bayfield multiplied by about twenty. It was easily the most-visited tourist attraction in the area, what with its shops, restaurants, inns, and motels, plus an aquarium, marine museum, movie theaters, and a convention center where both the Duluth Superior Orchestra and the University of Minnesota–Duluth hockey team played.

"Where are we going?" Heavenly asked.

"You'll see."

"What does that mean? You haven't answered a single question I've asked since we left the hospital. If you don't start coming clean . . ."

"You first."

"I should just get out of the car and walk back to the hotel. Make my own arrangements."

"You can do that. By the way, you owe me money from both the hospital and the Queen Anne."

"You'll get it. Dammit, McKenzie, where are we going?"

By then the lift bridge had settled back into place, and I was able to proceed across the canal and up the point. I drove less than a mile before I reached the parking lot of SSL Harbor Basin Marina. I found an empty space for the Mustang and shut her down.

"Coming?" I asked.

"To do what?"

"Talk to a man about a boat."

"Seriously? Is that why we're in Duluth?"

"One of the reasons."

"I'll stay here, if it's all the same to you."

"Good idea. Call your mom. Tell her what a wonderful time you're having."

A couple of minutes later, I was standing on the fuel dock. A young man wearing a T-shirt and ball cap with the name of the marina imprinted on them had just finished topping off the tanks of a sleek runabout. He gave it a wave and shoved the nozzle back into the gas pump as the owner motored away.

"Can I help you, sir?" he asked.

"I hope so. It's a small matter of expenses. Me and a guy share a boat, the *Heavenly II*. I don't want to make a big deal about it . . ."

"I know the *Heavenly II*."

"Do you know Herb Voight? Did he gas up here last weekend?"

"He did. Twice."

"Twice?"

"Kinda unusual, I know. I hope I'm not causing problems between you two."

"No, no, no—that's what he told me. I was just checking. The partnership isn't what it should be, guys and boats, I don't know, and the man is lousy about receipts. When did he . . ."

"The first time was at about seven Thursday evening, right before we knocked off for the day. I think he was our last customer. Yeah, yeah, he was. I remember because we gave him nearly ninety gallons, which wasn't unusual; his thirty-footer had a one-hundred-gallon tank, but it took a while, you know. The second time—it was way early Friday morning, right after we opened, and he asked us to top him off, and I'm like, didn't we see you here yesterday? Twenty-three gallons I gave him. Twenty-three—are you kidding? Made me wonder where he'd been all night."

"Makes me wonder, too. Thanks, man."

I returned to the Mustang. Heavenly was staring out the passenger window at nothing in particular. Her cheap flip phone was in her hand resting on her lap.

"Miss me?" I asked.

"I'm hungry."

I told Heavenly I knew plenty of Italian restaurants that served better pasta than Grandma's Saloon & Grill, located on the Canal Park side of the Aerial Lift Bridge, including Bellisio's just down the street.

"Her Marathon spaghetti and meatballs, though—the absolute best I've ever had," I said.

She gave a small lunch plate a try and agreed that I might be onto something, which led to a conversation about finding iconic food in the most unlikely places.

"Best pizza?" Heavenly asked.

"Deep dish or thin crust?"

"Deep dish."

"Little Star in San Francisco."

"Not Chicago? Wow."

"Best thin crust?"

"La Briciola, in Paris."

"That surprises me. Paris of all places."

"Surprised me, too. Best barbecue?"

"Rudy's in San Antonio."

"That doesn't surprise me at all."

"Best fried chicken?" I asked.

"Pies 'n' Thighs in Brooklyn. Best steak?"

"There's a place, I don't even know if it exists anymore. When I was a kid, my dad took me to hunt pheasant near Jackson, Minnesota, right along the Iowa border, he and some buddies of his. It was the year after my mother died, and it made me feel very grown up, like I was one of the guys; they let me drink blackberry brandy from the bottle. After a day walking the cornfields, we went to this place—I don't know its actual name. I call it the Farm because it was located on an actual farm. The restaurant slaughtered its own beef and hogs and chicken; grew its own potatoes, carrots, beans, whatever. I ordered a New York strip. I never even heard of a New York strip until that day. It was . . . I've never eaten anything like it before or since. So tender; so flavorful. The fixings on the side . . . best meal I've ever had."

"Is it the best meal because of the food or because you were with your father?" Heavenly asked.

"Probably both."

"I never had a . . . happy meal with my father, not even at McDonald's. I was never man enough for him."

How incredibly awful, I thought but didn't say.

"Do you think that might have influenced some of my life choices?" Heavenly asked.

I didn't respond to that either.

"Best French," she said.

"Le Papillon in Toronto near the Hockey Hall of Fame."

"Is that why you went there, because it was near the Hall of Fame?"

"I was in the neighborhood, what can I say? Best Mexican?"

Before Heavenly could answer, though, my smartphone pinged. I read a text sent by a cell with a Duluth phone number.

Go to Wade Stadium and wait.

"We're on," I said.

FOURTEEN

It was a ten-minute drive from Canal Park to Wade Stadium, where the Duluth-Superior Dukes minor league baseball team used to play. I parked in the deserted lot. To kill time, I told Heavenly about watching Ila Borders pitch for the Dukes against the St. Paul Saints when both teams were in the Northern League.

"Second woman to start an NCAA men's college baseball game and the first to play pro ball since Jackie Robinson broke the color barrier," I said. "She was very good at locating her pitches, but you're not going to make it to the Show with an eighty-mile-an-hour fastball."

"This is silly."

"A woman playing professional baseball? I don't know. Someday."

"I mean moving us around like this. What does Ruland hope to accomplish?"

"Probably wants to see if we're being followed."

"The man's never heard of GPS? Cell phones? You could be making a call right now on the car's system without taking your hands off the steering wheel. Who is this guy anyway?"

"I told you; thinks of himself as a master criminal. Are you sure you never heard of him?"

"Why would I?"

"Well, you are competitors."

"I am not a criminal, McKenzie. I wish people would stop calling me that. Especially insurance companies."

"What are you, then?"

"I'm a salvage specialist."

My smartphone pinged again.

Miller Hill Mall. Walk the concourse. Don't look for me. I'll see you.

Much of Duluth is built on the side of a steep hill facing Lake Superior, not quite as bad as San Francisco, but close. The Miller Hill Mall, as the name suggests, is located at the top of the hill. It has over a hundred stores, a food court, and several chain restaurants; it resembles for the most part every shopping mall you've ever been in. We wandered the concourse as instructed. I thought there would be more kids hanging around. The fact that there weren't actually made me feel better.

Instead of a ping, my cell played "West End Blues" just as we passed Pink, a store owned by Victoria's Secret that Nina wouldn't have been caught dead in but Erica seemed to like, judging by the sweatshirt she sometimes wore.

"I'm here," I said.

"Who's the girl?"

"What girl?"

"Are you trying to be funny?"

"My friend."

"Doesn't mean she's mine."

"On the contrary, she hates Vincent Donatucci almost as much as you do."

Ruland—I assumed it was Ruland—thought it over for a moment before chuckling.

"The enemy of my enemy is my friend," he said.

"Exactly right."

"Fitger's Brewhouse—ever hear of it?"

"I'm familiar."

"That's your next stop."

"You know, Trevor"—I deliberately used his first name—"I'm not trying to jam you up."

"Others might. Donatucci comes to mind."

"Okay."

"Don't lollygag, McKenzie."

Ruland hung up. I slipped the smartphone into my pocket. Heavenly had a what-now expression on her face.

"Mustn't lollygag," I told her.

"Wouldn't think of it."

We found Fitger's Brewhouse attached to the upscale Fitger's Inn at the bottom of the hill on the north side of downtown Duluth. I knew from experience that it served pretty good pub food and craft beers, but the PortLand Malt Shoppe next door—I liked it better.

I parked in an empty space in the lot between the two businesses and was debating which direction to go—toward a Bourbon Barrel Aged Stout or Black Raspberry Truffle Shake—when my cell rang again.

"McKenzie," I said.

"You're doing fine."

"Good to know."

"Now I want you to take the Lakewalk."

"Take it where?"

"To the Old Standby Lighthouse. You can see it from where you're standing."

The canal I told you about, the one that separated Minnesota Point and Canal Park and allowed freighters to sail from Lake Superior into the Duluth Harbor Basin? The lighthouse was located at the far tip of the north pier, giving the ships a dependable landmark to steer by. It wasn't more than a couple hundred yards from the restaurant where we started.

"I see it," I said.

"On your way."

I hung up the cell phone.

"We're walking," I said.

"Walking where?" Heavenly asked.

"Back to Canal Park."

"Okay, now I'm starting to get miffed."

"It's only a mile and a half."

We took a concrete and iron staircase from the parking lot down to the Lakewalk, a pedestrian and bike path that closely followed the shoreline of Lake Superior for pretty much the entire length of Duluth. We caught it at about the midpoint and followed it south.

I noticed Heavenly wince a few times, adjust her sling, and roll her shoulder as if seeking relief.

"Does it hurt to walk?" I asked.

"It doesn't help."

"Could be worse. You could be wearing heels."

"Shut up, McKenzie."

We kept walking, first along the edge of downtown and, after we angled east, past a couple of hotels with expensive views of the lake. There were plenty of benches to sit on, most of them occupied by tourists, and huge rocks to crawl over. I asked Heavenly if she wanted to rest, but she declined.

The north pier, which completed one side of the canal, was built of concrete and steel and was very long. Tourists strolled the length of it to the lighthouse, took turns snapping photographs and selfies with the Old Standby and the big water behind them, and walked back to Canal Park. We joined the parade. I tried not to stare at the visitors sitting on benches or lingering at the concrete railing as we passed, yet couldn't help wondering if any of them were staring at me.

Once we reached the lighthouse, I asked Heavenly if she wanted me to take her photo.

"You can send it to your mom," I said.

"Very funny."

"I'm serious."

She didn't believe me, though. I don't know why.

We hung around for a few minutes. My smartphone neither rang nor pinged. We drifted to the railing. I leaned against it; Heavenly stood as straight as possible. I knew she was in pain yet trying hard not to show it. Pride, I guess. We gazed across the water toward the city. And waited.

"Maybe he changed his mind," Heavenly said.

"Maybe."

I was watching with my peripheral vision a man sitting alone on a bench just a few yards from us. People tended to dress casually Up North. Probably that's true of people everywhere who live outside the big city, or in our case, the Cities, what people who don't live there call Minneapolis and St. Paul. Yet this gentleman was wearing a silk suit, silk shirt and tie, and black brogues. He looked like he was waiting for a limo to take him to the Concert Hall at the Ordway to listen to Paul Duclos and the St. Paul Chamber Orchestra play.

I kept watching while he slowly ate mini-donuts from a bag and wiped the sugar on a linen napkin that was draped across his knee. Eventually, he noticed me noticing him and grinned like a celebrity who didn't mind being recognized by his fans. He tipped the open bag toward me while looking straight ahead. I closed the distance between us and helped myself to a mini-donut.

"One of my many vices," he said.

"Mine, too. I actually own a machine."

"Do you?"

"Belshaw Donut Robot Mark I, capable of making one hundred dozen mini-donuts per hour, although I seldom eat that many."

"I'm Trevor Ruland." He spoke his name like he enjoyed saying it.

"McKenzie."

Ruland wiped his fingers on the napkin before shaking my hand.

"A pleasure," he said.

"This is Heavenly Petryk."

Ruland handed both the mini-donuts and the napkin to me as he stood. He took Heavenly's hand and kissed her knuckle.

"A very great pleasure," he said. "But you're injured. Please, Ms. Heavenly, take a seat."

Ruland ushered her to the bench and helped her sit. Afterward he sat, angling his body so that he was facing her. There was little space left on the bench for me. I sat anyway, working my butt until Ruland gave me room. I cleared my throat, but his attention was solely on Heavenly—big surprise.

"Whatever happened?" he asked.

"I was shot," she answered.

"Surely you're joking."

"I am not joking, and please don't call me Shirley."

"I am so impressed that you're able to make light of such a traumatic event. You are incredibly brave. At the risk of seeming sexist, may I also say, Ms. Heavenly, that you are the most extraordinarily attractive woman?"

Heavenly smiled through the pain in her shoulder.

"You're very kind," she said.

I cleared my throat again. Ruland still didn't seem to notice.

"May I inquire . . . does your wound have anything to do with the theft of the Countess Borromeo?" he asked.

"We believe so," Heavenly said.

I spoke loudly.

"I am willing to pay $250,000 for the violin's safe return, no questions asked."

That caught Ruland's attention.

"Yes, yes, I understand," he said. "Publicly the insurance company announced it will not negotiate with criminals, yet privately we all know that it is more than willing to do so."

Given Ruland's previous experience with the company, I was convinced I would receive more cooperation from the man if I explained that I was *not* working for Midwest Farmers, despite what I told him yesterday on the phone.

"I represent Paul Duclos, not the Peyroux Foundation and certainly not the insurance company," I said. "In fact, the less they know of what we're doing, the better."

That caused Ruland to smile. Actually, he never stopped smiling; the wattage just went up and down depending on his reaction to what was spoken.

"Still, I'm not surprised that you have come to me with this matter, given my reputation," he said.

"What reputation?" Heavenly asked.

The intensity of Ruland's smile dipped, although not by much. Donatucci was correct; he was grandiose if not downright pompous, and I thought it would be better if I did nothing to contradict his inflated opinion of himself. After all, I was convinced the only reason he agreed to meet with us in the first place was so he could share his exploits, such as they were, with an appreciative audience. Instead of calling him out, I attempted to feed his ego.

"Mr. Ruland is a highly regarded professional thief," I said. "Do you mind if I call you a thief?"

"Not at all."

"If I'm not mistaken, he specializes in objets d'art and antiquities."

Ruland bowed his head in my direction.

"Among other things," he said.

Heavenly must have caught on to what I was doing, because she reached out a hand and rested it on his forearm.

"How exciting," she said.

"It can be," Ruland told her.

"However, sir," I said, "I am not here because of your reputation."

"No?"

"I'm here because you stayed at the New Queen Anne Victorian Mansion Bed and Breakfast in Bayfield, Wisconsin, three days before the theft of a four-million-dollar Stradivarius violin from the New Queen Anne Victorian Mansion Bed and Breakfast in Bayfield, Wisconsin."

"Ahh."

"And because of your reputation."

Ruland grinned broadly. He was having a wonderful time.

"I assure you, Mr. McKenzie, my presence in Bayfield was merely a coincidence," he said.

"I don't believe in coincidences."

"Yet they occur every day."

Heavenly squeezed his arm.

"Trevor," she said. "How did you do it?"

"But I assure you, Ms. Heavenly, I did not."

"My offer for the safe return of the Countess still stands," I said. "I can have the money delivered in three hours."

"My friends, my friends." Ruland glanced upward and spread his arms as if seeking divine guidance. "How can I make you believe me?"

Heavenly took hold of his arm again and squeezed.

"If you didn't do it," she said, "can you tell us how it might have been done?"

Ruland rested his hand on top of Heavenly's hand.

"This is all speculation, of course," he said.

"Of course," she told him.

"I suppose an enterprising young man, upon hearing that the great Maestro Paul Duclos was bringing a priceless musical instrument to Bayfield, might book a room in the same bed-and-breakfast where he was expected to stay in order to . . . get the lay of the land, you might say. I suppose he might also have made copies of the keys for said bed and breakfast."

"Yes, he might have," I said.

Ruland sighed deeply.

"However, upon closer examination the enterprising young man might have decided that making his move in the Queen Anne would have been ill advised," he said.

"How so?"

"There was no way to predict the movements of either the staff or the guests. He could easily have been seen and perhaps identified. There was the possibility that he might also have been trapped in there, as well."

"That would have been awful," Heavenly said.

Ruland smiled in agreement.

"Would the enterprising young man have had a Plan B?" I asked.

"Most certainly."

"That would have been . . . ?"

"Snatch and dash," Ruland said. "Not terribly elegant, I know, although it does have the virtue of simplicity. Duclos was very casual with his treatment of the Countess, no guards, no safety precautions of any kind. It was possible for the young man to approach him on the street, hit him with a Taser, retrieve the item, and make good his getaway. If executed correctly, he would be thirty miles away before the authorities even knew what happened."

"Except when fired, a Taser would litter the street with

dozens of confetti-size identification tags that could be used to track the weapon back to the owner of record."

"Yes, most certainly—to the owner of record, but not necessarily to the individual who, shall we say, liberated the device."

"Yet that's not what happened."

"No. I couldn't get near him."

I, my inner voice said. *He's telling his own story now.*

"The Maestro was usually surrounded by his many adoring fans," Ruland said. "When he wasn't, he was always—always accompanied by a woman; I discovered her name was Zofia McLean, and she worked for the Tourism Bureau. That's when I switched to Plan C."

"Plan C?" Heavenly said. "You're prepared for anything."

Ruland squeezed her hand even as she squeezed his arm. I tried not to laugh.

"Plan C," he said. "I simply staked out the Maestro's hotel here in Duluth."

"How did you know which was his hotel?" I asked.

"It was relatively easy to discover where the St. Paul Chamber Orchestra was staying. If that wasn't enough, while I was loitering in the parking lot I saw the Maestro's wife drive off alone in her BMW 530i. Renée Marie Peyroux—I recognized her from a photograph on the Peyroux Foundation's Web site."

"When was this?"

"Eight o'clock Thursday evening. My plan had remained essentially the same. I knew Duclos would remain in Bayfield the night of the concert. No doubt he would enjoy the Queen Anne's bountiful breakfast Friday morning before departing to Duluth. That made his estimated time of arrival somewhere between ten thirty A.M. and noon. I worked out where I would be waiting in the parking lot, a blind spot invisible to the security cameras. When he parked his car I would have approached, an appreciative fan greeting the great musician, Tasered him, acquired the violin, made my escape along prearranged routes, and immediately contacted the go-between. With luck, I would have had my money and been on my way, with no evidence connecting me to the theft, before the authorities had time to react. Unfortunately, the Countess Borromeo was stolen in Bayfield, apparently by someone utilizing my original scheme. It's all quite frustrating."

"You were working with a go-between?"

"McKenzie, only a fool would steal a priceless work of art without first having a plan for disposing of it, although I must admit"—he turned his attention back to Heavenly—"that I was negligent in that regard early in my career. Serving two-thirds of a sixty-month sentence at the Nebraska Correctional Center in Omaha taught me the error of my ways. I understand you also have reason to dislike Vincent Donatucci."

"He wants to put me in prison, too," Heavenly said.

"I can think of no greater crime."

"Neither can I."

"Donatucci seemed like such a harmless old man when I met him, too."

"Tell me more about the go-between," I said.

"Nothing to tell," Ruland said. "My instructions were to make a call immediately after taking possession of the Stradivarius. I would have been told where to take it and whom to pass it to. Since I did not take possession . . ."

"You're saying you never met the go-between and don't know who it is."

"Whoever planned the heist broke it down into components. My part was to acquire the merchandise and hand it off. The go-between was charged with spiriting it away."

"Who planned it?"

"Someone else who knew my reputation. I was contacted . . . let's see, it would have been nine days before the Maestro was scheduled to perform."

Five days after the concert was announced, my inner voice reminded me.

"How was this accomplished?" I asked aloud.

"By cell phone."

"Someone called you?"

"Not exactly. I received a cheap flip phone in the mail with instructions to call the number that was stored in its memory. I did. A voice—it was electronically altered—offered me $50,000 to steal the violin, payable in cash when I passed it on."

"Do you still have the phone?"

"No, I . . . burned it, as they say. After I made my call."

"Your call?"

"I soon as I heard the news about the Countess on the radio, I dialed the number and told the man who answered that I didn't have the item; that someone had beaten me to it. I then destroyed the phone and tossed it into the lake. Why wouldn't I? We no longer had anything to talk about unless it was expenses. He was out a lousy flip phone, but I had spent considerably more scouting Bayfield and the Queen Anne. Oh, well. Best-laid plans."

"Do you recall the phone number?"

"Only the first three digits—215."

Heavenly removed her hand from Ruland's forearm; he was clearly disappointed by the gesture.

"I am sorry I could not be more of a service to you, Ms. Heavenly," he said.

"Me, too," she said.

I returned Ruland's bag of mini-donuts and linen napkin; he held them both as if they were part of a single package.

"Now what?" Heavenly asked.

"May I interest you in—" Ruland said.

"I was talking to him." Heavenly leaned forward on the bench, even though it caused her discomfort, and looked at me. "McKenzie, now what?"

"I'm thinking."

"Perhaps you would—" Ruland said.

"Shhh."

Apparently, Ruland knew when he was no longer wanted. He stood and pivoted toward us. He was still smiling.

"It was a pleasure meeting you both," he said. "Should you ever return to Duluth, I insist that you look me up."

Neither of us answered. We just stared ahead, both lost in our own thoughts.

Ruland turned again and started walking along the pier back to Canal Park, swinging his linen napkin and bag of mini-donuts as if he didn't have a care in the world. I stood and watched him go. Heavenly grunted slightly as she forced herself to stand. We began moving in the same direction as the thief.

"Some people have a highly inflated opinion of themselves," Heavenly said.

"You mean besides us?"

"Seriously, McKenzie. Now what?"

"I know you've heard me say this before, but—*the time has come to talk of many things . . .* "

Ahead of us, Ruland had just reached the end of the pier where it emptied out onto the park.

I never heard the shots that caused his body to twist unnaturally; that caused his arms to flail upward and out, the bag of mini-donuts flying from his grasp; that caused him to fall backward onto the concrete.

Heavenly and I paused as our brains made sense of what we had just seen.

The tourists nearest Ruland must not have heard the shots either, because some of them, obviously concerned for the well-being of a complete stranger, moved toward his body, while others simply stood by and watched.

There was a scream.

Followed by another.

I began to run forward. To this day I don't know why. There was nothing I could do to help Ruland. I didn't even have a gun; Chief Neville had confiscated my SIG Sauer, and Maryanne Altavilla's Ruger was still packed in my satchel at the hotel. I guess the mechanism in my head that controlled fight or flight was locked on fight.

Tourists began to run, too—away from the body. Two people—a man and a woman who didn't run—stood over Ruland while they glanced this way and that; searching for something that would explain the blood that was pooling beneath him. At the same time, men materialized from strategic locations throughout the park. Four of them. No, six. All armed, all carrying their guns with both hands as they closed on Ruland. The man and woman saw them coming and stepped away, fear etched on their faces.

I was frightened, too, yet I kept moving forward until he loomed up in front of me—a large man carrying a large gun.

I was fifteen yards away from Ruland's body when I stopped running.

The six men didn't stop, though.

My fight-or-flight mechanism swung abruptly to flight.

I quickly looked for an escape route. There was none unless I wanted to fling myself over the side of the pier. And then what? Swim for it? To Canada?

The large man reached into his pocket as he approached. He pulled out a thin black wallet.

Heavenly appeared at my side.

She slipped her Colt .380 auto out from under her sling and steadied it on her target with her good hand, standing sideways, sighting as if she were fighting a duel and someone was shouting, "Ready, aim . . ."

I reached out, covered her hand with mine, and pushed the gun down until it was pointed at the concrete.

The large man halted on the far side of Ruland's body and held up his ID.

"FBI," he said.

Special Agent in Charge Reid Beatty was not happy. I knew because he kept telling everyone, "I am not happy, I am not happy, I am not goddamn happy." My only consolation was that he appeared to be less happy with his associates than he was with me. Specifically, he wanted to know how a half-dozen FBI agents assigned to conduct around-the-clock surveillance on Trevor Ruland could, one, let him get killed and, two, allow the killer to escape unseen.

One of his agents had an explanation.

"We were assigned to observe Ruland to see if he'd lead us to the violin," the agent said. "We weren't tasked with guarding him. That's a completely different procedure."

I believe he was transferred to Camden, New Jersey, the very next morning.

Heavenly and I were taken into custody immediately following the shooting and handed over to the Violent Crimes Unit of the Major Crimes Bureau of the Investigative Division of the Duluth Police Department. The cops weren't happy either, but they seemed to be directing their annoyance at the FBI for conducting an operation in their city without even the courtesy of a consultation.

It was the Duluth cops that scoured Canal Park for witnesses—inexplicably, there were none—and confiscated the footage from various security cameras, which also left them without suspects. And it was the Duluth PD's Crime Scene Unit that determined that Ruland had been shot twice; they recovered a perfectly intact .243 Winchester slug weighing 100 grains, originally designed as "a varmint round."

"How is it possible for someone to shoot a hunting rifle in Canal Park in the middle of the afternoon during tourist season without anyone noticing?" the special agent in charge also wanted to know.

A second agent suggested that the shooter might have hidden himself inside the trunk of a vehicle like the Beltway Snipers had done way back in '02. I think he ended up in Camden as well.

Meanwhile, Heavenly and I were ensconced in separate interrogation rooms at the St. Louis County Jail, a building located so deep in the forest on the far side of the city that I wondered if the locals were deliberately trying to keep it hidden. The Duluth cops didn't ask any questions about the shooting, though. I was under the impression that they were waiting to learn if the Justice Department was going to make a federal case out of it.

I sat quietly in a metal chair at a metal table. I had not been shackled; my wrist hadn't been cuffed to the steel ring welded to the table, so I folded my arms and rested my chin against my chest. I deliberately avoided looking at my reflection in the mirror because I didn't care for the face of the man who looked back.

Are you responsible for Ruland's death? my inner voice asked.

I didn't think so, but what had I told him earlier? I don't believe in coincidences?

Eventually, Special Agent Beatty entered the room. He paced back and forth while telling me that he was a member of the FBI's Art Crime Team and worked out of the bureau's Milwaukee Field Division.

"I know all about you, McKenzie," he said. "I know you're attempting to buy back the Stradivarius violin for $250,000. We had both you and Ruland under surveillance. If you had given him the money and he had given you the Countess Borromeo, we would have arrested you both."

"What put you onto him?" I asked.

"We knew Ruland had a record. We knew he stayed at the Queen Anne prior to the theft. His credit card records indicated that he had paid to have two keys copied while he was staying there. Tell me, did Ruland contact you or did you contact him?"

"I contacted him."

"Why?"

"I knew he had a record and that he stayed at the Queen Anne prior to the theft. I didn't know about the keys, though. Charging them to his credit card was kinda dumb."

"Ruland was kinda dumb."

"I wish I had been nicer to him, though."

"Talk to me, McKenzie."

"First, I'd like to make a deal."

Beatty stopped pacing and stared at me for a few beats.

"What kind of deal?"

"I'll tell you everything I know from beginning to end."

"In exchange for what? We know that you didn't shoot Ruland."

"My associate—"

"Heavenly Petryk aka Caroline Kaminsky—"

"Who pointed a handgun at a federal officer—"

"Who could be charged with assaulting a federal officer—"

"No charges. Not from you, the city, county, or state. She walks away clean. Seriously, Agent Beatty, you'd play hell getting a conviction anyway."

"That's *special* agent to you. You're acting a little prematurely, aren't you, McKenzie? No one's been charged with a crime yet."

"I'd like to get home sometime tonight. I have a girlfriend."

"Don't we all? Mine's in Milwaukee. I haven't seen her in seven days. All right, you have a deal. Talk to me."

I spoke for over a half hour, leaving nothing out—except the number on Heavenly's cell phone and the $50,000 hidden in her carry-on bag, which, apparently, were about the only things that Special Agent Beatty *didn't* already know. Hell, he even knew our room numbers at the hotel. Which might have explained why he didn't take notes. Either that or the conversation was being recorded without my knowledge.

"For the record," I said, "Ruland didn't steal the Countess."

"You know this—how?"

"He told me. He said he had planned to tag Duclos with a Taser at Duclos's hotel here in Duluth, grab the violin, and make a run for it, but someone else stole the violin before he could make his move."

"You think he was telling the truth?"

"Yes, sir."

"Did you offer him the money?"

"Yes, sir."

"But he didn't take it."

"No, sir."

"What would you have done if he had?"

"Why, I would have called the FBI and had him arrested. After all, it's a felony to knowingly purchase stolen property."

"I believe you. Know why? Because you have a history of being an upstanding, law-abiding citizen going all the way back to the day you retired from the St. Paul Police Department."

I shouldn't have been surprised that he knew all about me, yet I was.

"Your agent in Bayfield," I said. "The one with a penchant for sports coats; he isn't very good at one-on-one surveillance. I spotted him right away."

"No you didn't. My people know how to blend, and none of them were wearing sports coats. C'mon, we're a little more clever than that."

"Yet none of you could identify the suspect who shot Heavenly, any more than they could ID the person or persons unknown who killed Trevor Ruland."

"I'm very unhappy about that. You and Petryk should leave before I become even more unhappy."

FIFTEEN

The desk clerk was surprised when Heavenly and I checked out of the hotel without actually using our rooms. By seven thirty we were packed, in my Mustang, and driving toward the Cities, with both of us hungry yet neither of us wanting to stay in Duluth to eat. I gave it a good half hour before I started in on her.

"The time has come to talk of many things . . ."

"Would you stop saying that," Heavenly said. "Every time you say that someone gets shot."

"Nonetheless."

"I don't know what you want me to tell you."

"Start with the $50,000 hidden in your carry-on case. If you don't like that, how 'bout the 215 number on the cheap flip phone you carry that's oh so similar to the one that Trevor Ruland said he used."

"Oh."

"Oh," I repeated.

"I have a logical explanation for both."

"Please, I'd like to hear it."

Heavenly stared out the window for a few beats.

"Oh, hell, McKenzie," she said. "I'm the go-between. Don't

give me that look, Mr. 'I'm willing to pay $250,000 for the violin's safe return, no questions asked'—you should talk."

"Unlike you, I'm on the side of the angels."

"If you're going to be condescending . . ."

"Tell me about it, Heavenly, and just this once, be honest."

"Be honest—the truth is my story isn't substantially different from Ruland's. I had just finished a job in Chicago. I received a flip phone in the mail; made the call. A voice asked if I would be interested in transporting an item from Point A to Point B for $50,000. I told him no drugs, no people; nothing that goes boom, and unlike the guy in the movies, I had every intention of looking inside the bag. He had no issue with that. So I said sure. The next day I was sent $55,000 in cash. Fifty for the thief, which turned out to be Ruland, and five for my expenses."

"You've done this sort of thing before."

"Once or twice. You pretty much know the rest. I was sent to Duluth with instructions to wait day and night by the phone from Wednesday morning on. When the time came, the Voice—what I called the man on the cell phone—he said he would tell me where to meet the thief. Once I had the package in hand, I would call him back and he would tell me where to take it. I would be paid the fifty grand once I passed it on. Simple. Except I never received a call. When I heard about the Countess and figured out what was going on, I contacted the Voice and offered to return the $50,000; I was going to keep the $5,000 for my time. He was not pleased."

"I wouldn't think so."

"He accused me of keeping the violin for myself, but seriously, what was I going to do with it? Sell it at a flea market in Iowa?"

"You do have a reputation."

"Yes, I do—a reputation for delivering the goods on schedule for the agreed-upon price. I won't stiff a client once I make a deal. It's bad for business. It's bad for a girl's health. Seriously, McKenzie. You know me. I have never made any claims to virtue. I could very well have talked myself into stealing the Countess Borromeo and selling it to you for the $250,000, except A, I didn't know the Countess was in play, and B, I didn't know that you were coming. In fact, the only thing I knew for sure about the package was its approximate size and weight and that I shouldn't drop it. If Ruland had delivered it as planned, I would have transported it—as planned."

"The Voice didn't believe you."

"Yes, he did. He just didn't want to take 'Sorry, Charlie,' for an answer. Instead, he was adamant that I keep the $50,000 as down payment on finding the violin. He said that once I had it, we would proceed with our original agreement, with a little something extra for my trouble. He left no room for negotiation."

"You went to Bayfield . . ."

"After first taking on Caroline's persona so I could hide while I worked—just in case. But then something unexpected happened. Midwest Farmers and the Peyroux Foundation announced at a press conference in Bayfield that they wouldn't negotiate for the return of the violin, that they were offering only a $250,000 reward payable upon the conviction of the thieves. I called the Voice again and told him that the Countess was no longer worth the trouble. He was as surprised by what the insurance company had done as I was; very angry, too. Again I offered to return the money. He said he'd get back to me. Then you showed up, the good guy riding to the rescue, which of course, ostensibly made me the bad guy. No way you were working for the Voice, I told myself. It had to be the insurance company."

"Actually, I'm working for Paul Duclos."

"I know that now. I informed the Voice about that, too. He said to stay close to you—just in case."

"Let me guess—if I actually did lay my hands on the violin, you were supposed to take it from me."

"I wouldn't have killed you for it; I wouldn't have harmed a hair on your head. I wouldn't have slept with you, either, not that you would have let me. Other than that, I was open to suggestions. I hope you're not angry."

"No, I figured that was your plan."

"What are we going to do, McKenzie?"

"We? We're partners now?"

"The situation has changed, hasn't it?"

"In what way?"

"People are getting shot."

"Do you think the Voice is responsible?"

"I doubt it."

"Someone shot you, then searched your room. Who knew you were in Bayfield? Who knew you had fifty grand? Who knew that Ruland was involved if not the Voice?"

"It doesn't make any sense. I told him I'd return the money on at least two occasions. And why shoot Ruland? Tidying up loose ends? What loose ends? We couldn't identify the Voice even if we wanted to, and ID him to whom? For what? You could argue that technically, no crime had been committed, at least not by us."

"You're assuming he's a professional. Could be he's a rank amateur like so many of the others we've dealt with up till now."

"If he was an amateur, he wouldn't have known me."

"There's something to that. The only alternative I can come up with—maybe he was trying to keep you two from looking for the Countess. With only $250,000 on the table . . ."

"Ruland wasn't looking for the violin."

"The shooter might have thought differently when he saw us talking to him."

"And I wanted to give it up a week ago. You know who's looking for the Countess? You are."

"Yeah."

"Which leaves us where, exactly?"

"I want to talk to the Voice."

"Lucky you. I have his phone number."

"No, I mean—"

"You want to look him in the eye."

"Something like that."

"How are you going to find him?"

"Turns out I know a guy."

"I'm not surprised."

"The question is—can I trust you?"

"McKenzie—of course you can."

Nina greeted us at the door. Heavenly was even more surprised than I was when she hugged her, being careful not to jostle her injured arm.

"Look at you, all beat up," Nina said.

"It's not as bad as it appears," Heavenly said.

"I'm sure it's much worse. Have you eaten?"

"We stopped for a bite on the way."

"Here, let me take that."

Nina took hold of Heavenly's nylon carry-on and escorted the woman deeper into the condo. I was burdened with the two heavy suitcases and my satchel, yet neither of them seemed to notice until I set the bags down, and only because the noise interrupted their conversation.

"Take Heavenly's suitcases into the guest room," Nina said.

I did. Afterward, I took my satchel into the master bedroom. When I returned, the two women were embracing. Heavenly's eyes were filled with tears, and I swear I thought Nina might have been crying, too.

What the hell happened? my inner voice said. *You were gone for two minutes.*

Yet I never asked out loud, and no one ever volunteered an answer.

Heavenly wiped her tears away with the back of her hand and spun in a small circle.

"You have a beautiful home," she said.

"Thank you," Nina said.

"The view is spectacular. The river. All those books." She stepped closer to the shelves. "Tell me the truth. How many of these are McKenzie's?"

"All the ones with pictures," Nina said.

"I don't mind you two making fun of me," I said, "but can't you at least wait until my back is turned?"

I went to the kitchen area where we kept our booze.

"Can I offer you anything?"

I was speaking to both of them, but it was Heavenly who answered.

"What are you drinking?" she asked.

"Bourbon."

"Uh-oh," Nina said. "You didn't find the Countess, did you?"

"No," Heavenly said.

"McKenzie is a craft beer man. When he drinks the hard stuff, that usually means he's perplexed."

"So he drinks a lot of bourbon, then?"

"Why is it when girls get together, they always pick on the guys?" I asked. "We never pick on you."

Their response was loud and vigorous. Examples of just how wrong I was were offered by both women. I apologized. More examples were given, ranging from income inequality to sexual abuse, many of them personal. I apologized some more. By the time calm was restored I came to realize that Nina and Heavenly were much more similar than they were different. I think they would have liked to be friends, except something kept them at a distance. My ego was big enough that I wondered if it was me.

"What happens next?" Nina asked. We were sitting at the island in the kitchen area, Nina at my side and Heavenly across from me. Heavenly and I were drinking Knob Creek; Nina was sipping hot chocolate with a smile—the smile provided by a shot of peppermint schnapps. "Neither of you are going to give up on the violin, so . . ."

"Problem is, someone else wants it," Heavenly said. "Someone wants it very badly."

"Badly enough to shoot people?"

"If he's a professional, we might be able to get a line on him," I said.

"How?"

"We're going to meet a guy tomorrow, see if he can help us out."

"Who?"

"David Wicker."

Heavenly's eyes grew wide.

"El Cid?" she said.

"That's him."

Heavenly took a long pull of her bourbon before looking at Nina.

"I thought I hung out with a bad crowd," she said.

The bar was located in the Phillips neighborhood in the center of Minneapolis. I knew it was a bar because I had been there before, although I wondered who else knew. There was no name above the door, no neon lights flashing the logos of pasteurized beers from St. Louis or Milwaukee, no sign saying it was open. Only a black-and-white notification taped to the window that read NO FIREARMS ARE ALLOWED ON THESE PREMISES, which was the owner's way of warning if you're carrying a gun, they just might shoot you as you walk through the door.

Heavenly followed me inside. It was dark; the lights were

low, and a thick curtain had been drawn across the one and only window. Frank Sinatra was singing "Summer Wind" from invisible speakers, the volume turned down. Two older men, nursing bottled beer in a wooden booth near the door, looked up when we entered and kept looking, but I suspected that was just their way of thanking Heavenly for the thin, tight blue dress that she wore, the hem about two inches above her knees.

A third man about Heavenly's age was sitting alone at a table in the center of the room, his chair situated so that he had an unobstructed view of both the front and back doors. He lifted his eyes from his tablet and stared at Heavenly, too. There was a folded *Star Tribune* on the table within easy reach. I knew the newspaper was hiding a gun; it had been the last time I was there, too. The young man's hand didn't go anywhere near it. I took that as a good sign.

"I'll be a sonuvabitch."

I followed the voice to another old-fashioned wooden booth with high backs that you can't see over. A man was sitting there, his hands folded on top of the table like a schoolboy waiting for lessons to begin, two cell phones and a laptop arrayed in front of him. He was dressed in a red polo shirt, jeans, and black cowboy boots and looked very much as if he had just dropped in for a cold one, although there wasn't a beverage of any kind on the table.

"You called, said you were on your way," he told me. "But McKenzie, I didn't think you had the balls to actually show up."

I drifted toward the booth. The young man had stopped studying Heavenly and was now watching every movement I made. Still, he kept both hands on the tablet.

"Don't tell me you're still holding a grudge after all this time," I said.

"Why would I hold a grudge? Just because you gave me up to the cops . . ."

"All I did was present you with the opportunity to return

some stolen property to its rightful owners. You didn't spend five minutes in jail."

"That's because I made a couple of deals."

"Isn't that your life? Making deals?"

"It's not the cops or the deals, McKenzie. It's the goddamn IRS I object to."

"I had nothing to do with that."

"I had to pay a fine, McKenzie. Three hundred and forty-eight fucking dollars."

"Is that all? I'll write you a check."

"It's not the money. It's the principle of the thing. That and now I'm on their radar. You don't think the IRS has been studying my returns with a goddamned magnifying glass?"

"Excuse me." Heavenly positioned herself so that I was between her and the young man sitting at the table. Her right hand was inside her sling. "I apologize for interrupting. Are you El Cid?"

Cid smiled as if it were the first time he had heard the name. He slid out of the booth and offered his hand. Heavenly removed her own hand from the sling and shook it.

"Heavenly Petryk?" Cid asked.

"Yes."

"I am most happy to make your acquaintance at last."

"Me, too."

"Please." He gestured at the bench. "Sit."

They both slid into the booth, stopping when they were comfortably facing each other. Cid hadn't asked me to sit, but since he didn't say I couldn't, I squeezed in next to Heavenly. A bartender appeared. He looked at the kid, though, and not at us. The kid shook his head, and the bartender retreated.

"This is a great pleasure for me," Cid said. "I have been watching your career with some interest."

"I am pleased to hear that," Heavenly said. "At the same time, I was hoping I had been conducting my business in such a way that no one could follow my career."

"Still, we do hear names and the exploits that accompany them, don't we?"

"Of course, everyone knows the name El Cid—the Lord."

"A nickname I picked up. Please . . ." He extended his hand again. "I am David Wicker. Call me Dave."

"Heavenly." She shook Cid's hand. "My given name. I have no idea what my parents were thinking."

"Probably they were thinking you would grow up to be just as lovely as you are."

Vanity of vanities, saith the preacher; vanity of vanities; all is vanity, my inner voice quoted. Only I knew better.

"El Cid" was an affectation that Wicker gave himself, pilfering it from Rodrigo Díaz de Vivar, the Spanish knight and mercenary credited with driving the Moors out of Spain in the eleventh century. To survive, much less flourish, in his line of work, a fence must be able to negotiate with the most dangerous thieves as well as the least scrupulous customers. The fear of betrayal, of being ripped off, of being arrested, was always present, so it was important to demonstrate a certain amount of fearlessness. "El Cid"—as well as the barely concealed muscle pretending to examine his tablet while watching us—was meant to make his associates believe that no one had better mess with Dave Wicker.

As for "Heavenly," I was beginning to wonder if the name was something the lady had given herself, not unlike Holly Golightly in *Breakfast at Tiffany's.*

"My Lord," I said, "I could use some help."

"McKenzie, I wouldn't give you the time of day."

"It involves a Stradivarius violin worth four million."

"Probably six million, maybe more if it were sold at public auction. And my answer is, go fuck yourself. I apologize for my language."

Heavenly gave him one of her patented smiles.

"He does bring out the worst in people," she said.

"Tell me about your shoulder."

"I was shot three days ago."

"While searching for the Countess Borromeo?"

"Yes."

Cid glared at me as if I were the one who pulled the trigger.

"McKenzie saved my life," Heavenly added. It wasn't entirely true, but I appreciated the gesture.

Cid's demeanor softened somewhat; Heavenly had that effect on people. Still, he was a businessman.

"What's in it for me?" he asked.

Heavenly slipped a bundle of fifty-dollar bills out of her sling and set it on the table. El Cid stared at it for a good ten-count before looking her in the eye.

"Is this your money or McKenzie's?"

"Mine."

"Keep it."

"My Lord—"

"Dave. Please. Call me Dave."

"Thank you, Dave."

"What do you want to know?"

"Who would—" I said.

Cid cut me off.

"I was talking to her," he said.

"We know the Countess was stolen on commission," Heavenly said. "The thief was hired to acquire the item and hand it over to a facilitator, like yourself."

Cid bowed his head. I think he preferred "facilitator" to "fence."

"Possibly the facilitator had a buyer lined up," Heavenly said. "Possibly he intended to place the Countess in a vault for a few years and then find a buyer. Possibly he meant to hide it until the statute of limitations expires, pretend to discover it at a garage sale, and sell it at auction. Possibly he meant to sell it back to the insurance company and now is stuck with it."

"Possibly," Cid said.

"Who? Who would have the resources for a gag like that?"

"Besides me?"

"I am willing to pay $250,000 for the violin's safe return, no questions asked," I said. "I can get the money in thirty minutes."

"Shut up, McKenzie."

"Yes, McKenzie," Heavenly said. "Adults are talking here."

Cid grinned broadly. Apparently, it pleased him no end that Heavenly was taking his side against the man who ratted him out to the cops two years ago.

"There are only a few people I can think of," Cid said. "The Martin brothers in L.A.—Bryan and Brandon; 'course they're both a couple of perverts. There's Kevin Stein in New York, Lawrence Sahulka in Toronto, Doc Young in Philly, Missy Comapt in Atlanta—"

"Tell me about Doc Young," I said.

"His real name is Tim Young. Everyone calls him Doc. He's not good-natured like me, McKenzie. Fuck with him, he'll blow your brains out."

"How do I get ahold of him?"

"You go to Philadelphia and arrange a face-to-face," Heavenly said. "He doesn't talk on the phone."

"Not since Edward Snowden did his thing," Cid said.

"Do you know him?" I asked.

"Let's say I know of him," Heavenly said.

"Does he know you?"

"In this business you keep track of talent," Cid said. "If I know Heavenly, Doc knows her. Hell, he might even have heard of you."

"Why Philadelphia?" Heavenly asked.

We were back in my Mustang and maneuvering through the Minneapolis traffic toward my condo. It occurred to me that I lived less than three miles from El Cid's place of business. I found the information very disconcerting.

"We need to start somewhere," I said.

"Yes, but why there?"

"The prefix of the phone number inputted into the cells that the Voice sent to you and Ruland—215 is Philadelphia."

"I should have checked that myself, careless. Are you sure you only scored thirty-one on your ACT?"

"Now you sound like Maryanne Altavilla."

" 'Course, that doesn't mean the Voice is from Philadelphia. Only that the burner phones were purchased and activated in the area."

"Something the old man used to say—*The race isn't always to the swift nor the battle to the strong, but that's the way to bet.*"

"Something my old man used to say—*Fuck you if you can't take a joke.*"

"Sounds like a helluva guy."

"I could tell you stories," Heavenly said.

"Anytime you're ready."

"Have you ever been there—to Philadelphia?"

"No."

"I have. I know people."

"What people?"

"The kind of people who do business with people like Doc Young. Believe me, your usual charming ways aren't going to impress them at all."

"Have you ever worked with Doc?"

"No—and I have no desire to, either. He's not a nice man."

"What we'll do—"

"I'll handle it."

"You will?"

"Like I said, I've been there before. I'll get us in, set us up, arrange to meet Doc, then get us out again, preferably in one piece."

"You can do all that?"

"Trust me."

"Okay, I will."

"All I ask is that you don't get me shot again."

"I'll do my best."

"Please."

Paul Duclos couldn't sit still—or stand still, either, for that matter. He had requested a progress report and I agreed to meet him at his home on Sunday. We moved to his luxurious kitchen because that's where the coffee was; Renée Peyroux insisted on joining us. Once there, he started pacing back and forth while his wife and I sat at the table and watched.

"You still don't know where she is," Duclos said. "No one claimed the reward, no one came forward . . . Donatucci said someone would. He said, offer a reward, he said . . . I thought it would be done by now; thought I'd have her back by now . . . It's like a bad traffic accident that doesn't end, that keeps going on and on in slow motion, until . . . Is she gone, McKenzie? Gone forever?"

"Paul, please sit down," Peyroux said.

He ignored her and kept pacing except for those moments when he halted long enough to drink his coffee. He refilled his mug three times while I was sitting there. Instead of taking it black as he had before, he now half-filled the mug with sugar. The man's condition had deteriorated some since last we spoke—his skin was pale, his eyes bloodshot, and his hands shook. He reminded me now of a junkie going through withdrawal. I attempted to give him something to hold on to.

"I'm going to Philadelphia tomorrow," I said. "Have you ever been there?"

"Many times. Kimmel Center. The Countess and I once played a charity thing on the Rocky Steps at the Philadelphia Museum of Art."

"There's a man there—I think he arranged to have the Countess stolen."

"Why doesn't he sell her back, then?" Duclos asked. "Is it the money? Does he want more money?" He turned on his wife. "This is your fault. Because you refused to pay a ransom. How could you do that? How?"

"Please," she said.

"I don't think he actually has the violin," I said. "The man in Philadelphia. I think something happened before he could take possession. I'm hoping he'll tell me what before someone else gets shot."

"People are being shot?" Peyroux asked.

"One dead, one wounded."

"Oh, no."

"I don't care," Duclos said. "I don't care if a hundred people get killed. No, no, no, listen to me. I don't mean that. I don't mean . . . Please, McKenzie. What am I going to do?"

Peyroux called his name; asked him to sit with her yet again. Duclos wouldn't even meet her eyes.

"I need her, McKenzie," he said. "Don't you understand? McKenzie . . ." He set down the coffee mug and showed me his trembling hands. "I can't play. Not a note. I don't know how. Without the Countess I'm nothing."

"Yes, you are," Peyroux said. "I was in Duluth, remember? Friday night at Symphony Hall. First row center. You were brilliant."

"It's a lie."

Peyroux turned in her chair to face me.

"When I heard about the theft, I drove up there," she said. "I brought Paul's old violin, the Jacob Stainer that he used before the foundation lent him the Countess Borromeo. He never played better."

"It doesn't have the same sound," Duclos said.

"It was beautiful."

"What do you know? You know nothing about music. You know nothing about musicians."

"I know you."

"Stop it. Stop it, stop it, stop it."

"Paul—"

"Do you know what this is about? McKenzie, do you? As long I was the Maestro, I came first. I was the world-famous violinist who married the pretty rich girl. Now she's in charge. The rich girl married to the failed musician. She likes it that way. Don't you? Don't you, sweetheart?"

"How many times do I have to say it—I didn't marry you because you could play the goddamned violin. I don't love you because you play the violin."

"That's just great, because I can't play anymore."

"You can."

"Not without the Countess."

Duclos left the kitchen. Peyroux's body convulsed with anguish; the words she spoke were barely discernible.

"I love him so much," she said. "This shouldn't be happening. What can I do? What can I do, McKenzie?"

I had a few thoughts, yet I kept them to myself.

"I should leave," I said.

Peyroux pulled herself together; dabbing her eyes with the linen napkin she had taken from the counter when she had poured her coffee, and I thought, She's as strong as she looks.

"Are you married?" she asked me.

"I'm in a committed relationship."

"That's not the same thing. It would still be easy for you to walk away."

I doubt it, my inner voice said.

"But when you're married," Peyroux said. "When you're married, everything you think, everything you do is filtered through the prism that is your partner. A good day isn't complete until you tell him about it. A bad day can't be made better without his help. When he's happy, you're happy. When he's not, you're miserable. You never make plans without consulting him first. The simple act of buying clothes—will he like this color; is the skirt too short for him, not short enough? At night, you reach across the bed to touch him, reassure yourself that he's lying next to you. If he's not, you snap awake, your heart racing, until you realize, oh, he's in New York, he's in London; you'll talk to him tomorrow—can't wait to ask how did it go, did the other musicians play up to his standards, did he receive a standing ovation like usual, did he play an encore? 'Shave and a haircut, two bits' always leaves them cheering. And you wonder—does he feel the same way you do? Sometimes the answer is no. He'll ask where are you, what are you doing, but not often; not as often as you like because he's so wrapped up in what he's doing, so devoted to his mistress the Countess Borromeo and you accept that, you live with that because that's the way he is, the way he was when you married him, and there's no changing him; you wouldn't change him even if you could, yet at the same time . . . You have no idea what I'm talking about, do you, McKenzie?"

"I think I do."

"One day you should explain it to me, then, because—I don't want you to go to Philadelphia. I don't want you to search for the Countess at all. It's not worth it. Let it go."

"It's not that easy."

"Why not?"

"There's a dead man in Duluth and a wounded girl in my condo in Minneapolis. Someone has to answer for that."

"Are you really that person?"

" 'Fraid so."

SIXTEEN

Trenton Mercer in New Jersey was the smallest airport I had ever seen. We had taken Frontier Airlines there, departing through the tail of an Airbus onto the tarmac. Baggage claim was an air-conditioned garage; the luggage was piled near the door while passengers waited against the far wall. I carried our bags to the parking lot; Heavenly held tight to her nylon carry-on. I didn't know if it still contained the $50,000. If so, the TSA agents in the Cities hadn't noticed. Perhaps they were distracted by the ounce of lead in Heavenly's shoulder. It set off first the X-ray imaging machine and then a couple of handheld metal detectors. I don't know how she explained the bullet—we had gone through security separately—yet when she finished, the agents were so solicitous, they arranged to drive her to the departure gate on a golf cart. It took me fifteen minutes to catch up.

There were more sheriff's deputies hanging outside the Trenton Mercer terminal than taxicabs. They recommended we catch a shuttle that eventually carried us to an off-site car rental agency. Heavenly signed for a blue Ford Focus under the name Caroline Kaminsky. She gave me the keys, saying she would navigate while I drove. A few minutes later, we were on Interstate 95. I didn't ask Heavenly where we were going or how we were getting there, yet it wasn't a matter of trust. I just didn't want to give her the satisfaction.

I-95 became the Delaware Expressway when we crossed the river into Pennsylvania. I followed it into Philadelphia. Heavenly told me to take the Independence Hall exit, so I did. She directed me to Callowhill to Sixth Street to Lombard to Tenth Street. The streets were very narrow, and most of them one way; cars were parked on either side, allowing room for only one lane of traffic, and I thought the Philly cops probably didn't get many high-speed chases in this part of town unless they were on bicycles.

Following Heavenly's instructions, I parked in the first empty space I found on a long block jammed with tall rowhouses that harkened back to the turn of the last century. Brothers played hoops in an asphalt park surrounded by a high cyclone fence across the street; there was a coffeehouse on the corner. I carried the bags half a block to our brownstone. I saw no other places to park.

"This part of town, parking spots are prime real estate," Heavenly said. "You see an empty space, you take it. If you try to find something closer to your destination and don't, by the time you circle the block the space will be gone. Guaranteed."

She climbed the concrete steps to the door of the brownstone and unlocked it with a six-digit code pressed into a keypad that she had apparently memorized. She held the door open for me. It locked behind us. There was a bowl of fresh fruit on a small table inside the dim entryway, positioned in front of a giant mural depicting Betsy Ross sewing the first American flag while General Washington played with a small child that I assumed was Betsy's daughter. Heavenly took an apple as if she had expected it to be there and led me past the mural to a narrow spiraling staircase. We climbed it to the top floor. There was another door with another keypad. Heavenly inputted the code—this one only four digits long. The door swung open. I stepped inside and set the bags on the floor of an ancient kitchen; at least it would have seemed ancient if not for the refrigerator, stove, microwave, coffeemaker, dishwasher, garbage disposal, pots, pans, and dishes.

"In case you're wondering, this is a bed-and-breakfast," Heavenly said. "Only we will not meet our hosts. They will not meet us. Oh, and the breakfast is continental." She opened the refrigerator door to reveal two small bottles of milk and various juices, pastry, bagels, English muffins, and fruit. She set the apple on the shelf and closed the door. "It's a far cry from the Queen Anne. On the other hand, Connor's food was far too rich. I bet I gained five pounds."

"Bet you didn't."

Heavenly stepped into the room beyond the kitchen. I followed and found a king-sized bed beneath an ornate canopy, a double bed enclosed on three sides by metalwork, a large armoire, a dresser with a marble top and mirror, a couple of tables and chairs, and a rocking chair. There was a tiny bathroom with a black-and-white tile floor and a walk-in shower. Light came from huge windows with a view of the street. Everything looked as if it had been built when the country was new.

Heavenly dropped her nylon bag on top of the king-sized bed.

"Dibs," she said.

"Okay," I said. "We're in Philly."

"Specifically, the Bella Vista neighborhood in South Philadelphia," Heavenly said. "In case you're thinking of sending Nina a postcard."

We were sitting in the tiny courtyard behind the brownstone, surrounded by well-cared-for plants and drinking merlot from a bottle provided by the unseen owners of the B&B.

"Do we have a plan?" I asked.

"I don't know. Do we?"

"You seem to know your way around. I take it you've done business here before."

"Last time, I recovered a Gibson Les Paul Black Beauty electric guitar that was stolen from Jimmy Page in 1970."

"Jimmy Page from Led Zeppelin?"

"The one and only."

"No kidding? What did you get for that and who paid you?"

"I'll start answering your questions when you start answering mine."

"We should get something to eat. How are the Philly cheesesteak sandwiches?"

"Here they just call 'em cheesesteaks, and they're about as ubiquitous as brats are in Minnesota and Wisconsin. There are a couple of joints in the neighborhood—Geno's and Pat's—that have been battling for cheesesteak supremacy since the beginning of time; Pat's King of Steaks claims to have invented them."

"Who gets your vote?"

"One uses chopped steak, the other sliced. Beyond that I couldn't tell the difference."

"Perhaps a more discerning palate is required."

"There's an Italian restaurant called Luciano's; I've already made reservations."

"Luciano like the mobster?"

"Close enough."

Luciano's was located in an old brick building constructed long before Lucky made a name for himself in the New York rackets. There was an old-world vibe to it with waitstaff dressed in white shirts, black slacks, and red vests and photographs hanging on the walls of Italian celebrities like Frank Sinatra, Tony Bennett, Rocky Marciano, Tommy Lasorda, Al Martino, and Sergio Franchi, many of them signed. Plus, inexplicably, a painting of Theodore Roosevelt that greeted visitors as they entered. I asked the waitress about it, and she told me that Teddy had been a friend of the founder's.

I had the stuffed calamari and baked lasagna, and as I ate it, I added a new name to my Best List under Italian food. When Heavenly finished her rigatoni carbonara, she waved the waitress over.

"I called ahead for a special order of ricotta cannoli with chocolate chips to go," she said.

The waitress nodded and waited while Heavenly slipped an envelope out from under her sling; apparently it had become more useful to her than a purse. The waitress took the envelope and disappeared. A few minutes later she reappeared toting a white carry-out container. She set the container in front of Heavenly.

"The check has been taken care of," she said.

"Thank you."

"Thank you," the waitress said before retreating again. Heavenly stood. She hugged the container to her ribs with her good arm.

"Leave a nice tip," she told me.

I did.

I caught up with Heavenly at the door and opened it for her. We walked the narrow street to the Ford Focus. I opened her car door; Heavenly slid inside, the carry-out container on her lap. I circled the car and settled behind the steering wheel. Heavenly looked over her shoulder, saw that there was no movement on the street, and opened the container. The summer sun was still shining, so I had no trouble seeing the two handguns.

"This comes out of what I owe you for the hospital and the Queen Anne," she said.

"Call it even."

Heavenly handed one of the guns to me—a black nine-millimeter SIG Sauer with an extra eight-round magazine.

"You're a SIG man, right?" she said.

I balanced it in my hand. I liked the weight, just shy of two pounds.

"Yes," I said.

Heavenly picked up the second gun—a two-tone .40 Smith & Wesson. She ejected the fourteen-round mag, satisfied herself that it was fully loaded, slammed it back into the butt, and racked the slide. She slid the S&W into her sling and the extra mag into her bag.

"Think you have enough ammo there, sweetie?" I asked.

"If I get shot again, it won't be because I'm not shooting back."

"On that encouraging note . . ."

"We're well-fed, heavily armed, and driving a car rented under a fictitious name. We should go clubbing."

"Clubbing?"

"Music, dancing, women in tight dresses, men who haven't shaved for three days, exotic drinks with sexually suggestive names—you must have done something similar when you were young. You were young once, weren't you, McKenzie?"

"Not that I recall."

"Tim Young doesn't have an office like El Cid. That's the plan, right? To talk to Doc Young? Only we're not going to find him. He's too paranoid. The best we can do is put the word out that we're looking and let him find us."

"Where do we start?"

"He has people. One in particular."

Heavenly pulled her oversized smartphone from her bag, drew a diagram with index finger, and started typing with her thumbs—she hated it when people talked to their phones as much as I did. A map came up. She stared at it for a moment and pointed straight ahead.

"That way."

Heavenly could have been an office wonk based on her attire—loose-fitting slacks and a simple white dress shirt beneath a striped charcoal vest, because it hurt to wear anything that she needed to pull over her head, what she wore on the plane. Yet she managed to turn heads anyway, this in a club where nearly everyone else was emulating the latest fashion magazines. I watched her do it from where I was leaning against the bar and sipping a tap beer; it was her idea that I enter first so I could cover her in case it all went sideways. It was still early in the evening, and there were plenty of tables to be had; the band hadn't even begun its first set, so I had a nearly unobstructed view of the entrance. Apparently, many of the men and some of the women in the club did, too, because they all seemed to find her when Heavenly passed through the door. She wasn't even wearing a sling to attract attention. Instead, she held her arm stiff at her side as she drifted to the bar, sitting several stools away from me. Meanwhile, I was dressed in my standard uniform of loafers, jeans, polo shirt, and sports jacket. No one noticed me at all.

The bartender appeared; he smiled brightly and set a coaster in front of her.

"What can I serve you?" he asked.

"Vodka gimlet."

"Any particular brand of vodka?"

"Surprise me."

"Right away."

The bartender turned to prepare the drink. Heavenly glanced my way. I gave her a chin nod.

"What's up?" I said.

I thought I saw the bartender grin when Heavenly dismissed me.

She spun on her stool and slowly surveyed the crowd as if she were searching for someone. I had the impression that a lot of men and more than a couple of women were hoping that her eyes steadied on them. Heads tilted; whispers were exchanged; wingmen were alerted. I knew it was only a matter of time before Heavenly would be approached. Probably just minutes.

The bartender returned and served the drink. Heavenly turned back to greet him.

"I poured our well vodka," he said. "It's just as good as the name brands, yet much less expensive."

"That's very kind of you."

Heavenly pulled a twenty from her bag and set it on the bar. The bartender hesitated before he took it.

I wonder how many free drinks Heavenly scores, I asked myself.

Helluva lot more than you do, my inner voice answered.

I don't know. In Nina's club . . .

That doesn't count.

The bartender returned with Heavenly's change. She pushed a ten spot into the gutter. The bartender was visibly surprised by the size of the tip.

"All good deeds should be both acknowledged and rewarded," Heavenly said. "We witness so few of them."

"That's a generous philosophy," the bartender replied.

"I'm a generous woman."

"Beautiful, too. Are you a model?"

"Of course not."

"You're pretty enough."

"Do you really think so?"

"Oh, yes. You might be the most beautiful woman to ever walk into this club."

"I should come here more often."

"Is this your first time?"

"I came to meet someone, but he doesn't seem to be around."

"Who's the lucky guy?"

"Marcus Camby."

The bartender flinched at the sound of the name; he literally took a step backward. He was still smiling, but suddenly it seemed forced.

"Are you a friend of Mr. Camby's?" he asked.

"Merely an acquaintance."

"I haven't seen him, and Monday night, it's usually a little slow so I don't know if I will."

"Do me a favor—do you have a pen?"

The bartender found one. Heavenly took it and wrote on the coaster.

"If you see Marcus, please give this to him."

The bartender took the coaster and stuffed it in his shirt pocket.

"If I see him," he said.

Heavenly reached out and touched his hand.

"Don't worry," she said. "Nothing bad is going to happen. For the record, he's not my boyfriend."

I don't know why that cheered him up, yet it did.

Heavenly took only a sip of the vodka gimlet before leaving the club. By the time I caught up with her she was seated inside the Ford Focus and carefully adjusting the passenger seat belt over her shoulder.

"I notice you removed your sling," I said. "Is that a good idea?"

"You don't want to show weakness to these people."

I thought she was being awfully melodramatic, but what did I know? I was new in town.

"Where to next?" I asked.

Heavenly plotted a course to a club in a West Philadelphia neighborhood called Belmont Village, and I started the car. As I pulled away from the curb, I noticed the taillights flash on a red Chevy Tahoe parked up the street, signifying that someone had just put it into gear. I watched in the rearview after I passed it. The SUV gave me a healthy head start before it also pulled away from the curb. I looked for a license plate number. Unfortunately, Pennsylvania law requires that plates be mounted only on the backs of vehicles, unlike in Minnesota.

"Do you get that a lot?" I asked.

"What?"

"People watching you."

"Depends on the circumstances. Take a right at the next corner."

I did as Heavenly directed. The SUV stayed with us.

"If I'm just walking down the street, buying groceries, shopping at Target, people tend to leave me alone," she said. "If it's a place where they meet socially, clubs, restaurants, theaters, concert halls, even ballparks—that's where I get the turning heads and the wistful gaze, I like to call it. Most people look and then look away. It's the ones who stare that make me nervous. The ones who stare and glare like I committed some kind of crime, I always try to keep track of where they are at all times. Take a left and then the first right."

I maneuvered the Focus around the two corners. The SUV kept going straight.

"That's terrible," I said.

"It's hell being a babe."

Heavenly laughed, but I noticed there wasn't much mirth in it.

"How about what the bartender said, about how you should be a model?" I asked.

"That, too—since I was little. People tell pretty girls that they should be a model the way they tell tall boys they should play basketball."

"We lost the Chevy Tahoe. Either that or the driver figured we made him and decided to peel off."

"So you are paying attention."

"Enough to know that no one else has picked up the tail. *If* we were being followed, it was by a single vehicle."

Heavenly reset our course.

"Nina must get it, too," she said. "The admiring glance as she walks by. The flirting."

"Not like you do."

We hit three more clubs without incident, following the same script each time. No one tailed us when we left.

The fifth club was located in North Philadelphia. The night was no longer young, and the joint was both crowded and loud; the band played from an elevated stage at a volume that suggested it was afraid the kids in Jersey might not hear them. Colorful lights flashed for no particular reason according to no discernible pattern.

It took a few minutes before I found a spot where I could lean against the bar and a few more before I could shout my order to the bartender. I didn't see Heavenly enter the club; didn't know she was there until she sidled up to a small, chest-high table that should have been surrounded by chairs yet wasn't—the groups gathered at nearby tables had captured them. She set her bag on top of the table; I presumed her S&W was tucked inside. A waitress approached; Heavenly spoke into her ear, and the waitress moved away. By then the bartender had set a tap beer in front of me.

Heavenly remained standing. It was clear to me that she was favoring her left arm, yet I couldn't say if anyone else noticed. The waitress reappeared and set both a napkin and a drink in the center of the table. Heavenly managed to pull a wallet from the bag, shake out a bill, and set it on the waitress's tray using just her right hand. The waitress went to serve other customers. Heavenly sipped her beverage and gazed toward the band. The floor in front of the stage was jammed with dancers. There was so little room to maneuver, most of them looked as if they were jogging in place.

A man came up behind Heavenly. He was young and blessed with the kind of good looks God gives to the extras in beer commercials. He rested his hand on Heavenly's left shoulder and squeezed as if he knew exactly how to hurt her. She spun away from him. He smiled. He said something. He smiled some more. Heavenly's response was to glare at him and shake her head. He gestured at her drink. She shook her head again. The smile left his face, and he tilted his head as if he couldn't believe what he was hearing. He motioned toward a table where two guys were sitting, and I knew what had happened—he bet his pals that he could score a cell phone number or better from Heavenly and was now embarrassed by his failure.

Heavenly picked up her drink and returned her attention to the band. The young man took hold of Heavenly's left wrist and gave it a violent tug. Heavenly dropped her drink; the glass bounced off the table and shattered on the floor. From the expression on her face, I knew that the pain from her fractured collarbone was acute. She tried to twist her wrist from the young man's grasp, yet that caused even greater hurt.

I would have intervened, except a second young man appeared, this one bigger than the first. He grabbed a fistful of hair and yanked backward. The first young man grimaced even as he arched his back and flailed his arms. He tried to turn, tried to free himself. The second young man slapped him with the back of his hand, slapped him twice. He pulled his hair back even farther and gripped his throat. The eyes of the first young man bulged as the second young man leaned in and spoke harshly into his ear. The first young man nodded. The second young man released him and stepped back, fully prepared to deal with any retaliation. The first young man pushed his way past the small crowd that had gathered; he refused to look at Heavenly or the second young man. I keep calling them young men as if I were old and they were children, which wasn't true, but you get my drift.

The second young man turned toward Heavenly. She was brushing at the alcohol that had spilled on her shirt and vest with a napkin. He looked as if he wanted to help with his empty hand, yet thought better of it. A waitress appeared to wipe the table, and another swept up the remains of the shattered glass. It took only a few seconds. The young man smiled. Heavenly smiled back. He asked a question. She answered it. He turned to leave. She set her good hand on his wrist and said something more. He nodded and left.

I was thinking about moving to Heavenly's side. Possibly she read my mind, because she glanced my way while pretending not to and shook her head just enough to warn me away. I remained at the bar. A few moments later, the young man returned with a replacement for Heavenly's drink. She made an effort to pay, but he wouldn't hear of it.

They leaned toward each other, their foreheads nearly touching. I had studied body language when I was in the police academy, and I could tell they were both relaxed, yet I knew nothing about reading lips, so I had no idea what they were talking about. I only know I had time for a second tap beer before they quit.

The band was just closing out its set when they separated. The young man pulled a smartphone from his pocket. He inputted a number as Heavenly recited it to him, and brought the phone to his ear. He was looking directly at Heavenly as he spoke into his phone. They were both smiling; there seemed to be a lot of that going on between them. Yet what surprised me most was when he gave Heavenly a gentle hug and kissed her cheek as if he were wishing his lips were touching something else. Heavenly patted his shoulder, took up her bag, and moved toward the exit. The young man watched her go.

———

By the time I reached the Ford Focus, Heavenly was already inside. She was adjusting her sling; the dome light let me see the pain it caused her.

"Are you okay?" I asked.

"Do I look okay?"

I didn't reply.

"Nothing, McKenzie? You're not going to tell me I should be modeling lingerie for Victoria's Secret?"

"Is that what your friend in the club said?"

"The one who grabbed my shoulder, adding insult to injury. McKenzie?" Heavenly brought her hand to her wound. "That really hurt. It still hurts. I wonder if he pushed the bones out of alignment."

"I would have come to your assistance except the second guy beat me to it."

"That was Marcus Camby."

I started the car and pulled away from the curb.

"Marcus is Doc Young's right-hand man," Heavenly said. "I met him when I was going after the stolen Gibson. He said the doctor would be happy to chat with us. We'll arrange a meeting tomorrow."

"Sounds promising."

"We'll see."

"Where to now?"

"Back to the B&B."

"How do I get there?"

Heavenly gave me directions. They were easy to follow. So easy that the red Chevy Tahoe had no trouble keeping up with us.

"Don't look now," I said.

Heavenly was watching through the passenger side mirror.

"I see him," she said.

She reached into her bag and found the cheap flip phone that the Voice had given her. She found the last number it had captured and called it. Someone answered.

"Dammit, Marcus," Heavenly said. "I thought we had an understanding."

I couldn't hear what he said in reply.

"We're being followed . . . Never mind who *we* are. You promised to lay off until we spoke with the doctor . . . He's not?" Heavenly continued watching the SUV through the side mirror. "Are you sure? Maybe he's one of your guys trying to score extra points . . . Red Chevrolet Tahoe . . . Promise me you're not lying, because—hang on."

Heavenly covered the cell's microphone with her hand.

"Take a left at the next light," she said. "That's Broad Street."

I did what she told me. The SUV stayed on our bumper.

"All right, Marcus, I believe you," Heavenly said into the flip phone. "Then you won't be unhappy if something nasty happens to him . . . Call me tomorrow, Marcus. Not early . . . Good night."

Heavenly hung up the phone and dropped it into her bag.

"That was Marcus," she said.

"I gathered."

"He claims the tail doesn't work for him or Doc Young."

We were idling at a red light, the Tahoe directly behind us. I couldn't make out the driver's face in the mirror, and I refused to turn my head to look.

"Yes, but can he be trusted?" I asked.

"Most men lie to me; they lie all the time." Heavenly studied the SUV some more. "They say they want to be friends, but truthfully all they really want is twenty minutes of my time. You're an exception. So is Marcus. I think."

The light changed, and we drove ahead.

"Marcus said something earlier, though, that I found very interesting; something I didn't press him on," Heavenly said. "He told me that he knew someone would be going after the Stradivarius, he just didn't know it would be me."

"How 'bout that?"

"You were right to bring us here."

"We need to get rid of this guy."

Heavenly pulled the .40 S&W out of her bag.

"That's the last resort," I said.

She slid the handgun under her sling.

"Temple University is coming up on the right," she said. "Lots of narrow streets."

I took one—and another—and another, driving at speeds that invited catastrophe. I ignored a couple of stop signs, but nothing came of it. Late Monday night in Philadelphia, traffic was sparse and only a couple of pedestrians were on the streets. An old man walking a dog—I didn't know if he raised his fist out of protest or solidarity when I flew past him.

The most important thing to remember in a high-speed pursuit—especially if you're the one being pursued—is not to crash, because even if you survive an accident in one piece, you're going to be a sitting duck. That's why high speeds are not recommended. By keeping your speedometer under sixty miles per hour, you'll have greater control of your vehicle, and evasive maneuvers will be easier to accomplish. Oh, did I tell you? One of the things they taught at the police academy besides body language—how to drive.

Unfortunately, the city streets were so narrow that I couldn't allow the Ford to drift even a couple of feet one way or the other. I needed to keep it in an absolute straight line as I accelerated, no fishtailing allowed. Plus, the corners were virtually invisible from a distance what with cars parked right to the edge of the crosswalk; I only knew they were there because of the street signs. And they were so sharp that instead of gradually slowing before making a turn, I was forced to brake hard, giving up all of my speed.

Still, the SUV was outmatched. The Focus didn't have much giddy-up. It was nimble, though, while the Tahoe was unstable, with its high center of gravity; there was a real chance that it could tip over when cornering at high speeds. Also, it had four-wheel drive, which was great for off-road excursions yet reduced its acceleration. I would easily have lost it in the Cities where I knew the ground, but driving strange streets in a strange land eliminated any advantage I might have had. It became a battle of attrition—whoever lost control of his vehicle first was screwed.

To be honest, I might have enjoyed myself, except it was obvious that the driver of the Tahoe no longer gave a damn that we knew he was following us, which meant he no longer cared where we were going, only that he was there when we arrived. The man was clearly looking for a confrontation.

I took a succession of right turns, leading the SUV in a wide circle. Heavenly was uncomfortable, her bad shoulder bouncing against the car seat, yet she tried not to show it.

"This is starting to get old, don't you think?" she said.

"Just a bit."

Heavenly slipped the S&W out from under her sling.

"Anytime you're ready," she said.

I managed to get a sizable lead on the Tahoe before hanging another sharp right down a one-way avenue with cars parked on both sides. The SUV sped up; turned sharply, nearly side-swiped the vehicle nearest the corner, straightened out, sped forward, and slammed hard on its brakes. It skidded to a halt only a few feet behind the rear bumper of the Ford Focus; the car was now parked in the middle of the street, blocking traffic, the driver and passenger doors hanging open.

Heavenly and I were no longer inside. I was on the sidewalk on one side of the street, and she was on the sidewalk on the opposite side, the parked cars providing us with cover. We moved cautiously until we were even with the Tahoe, our guns held low. It took a few beats before the driver realized what was happening. I saw him peering at me through the open window. I recognized him instantly. The man in the sports coat. He looked afraid.

Well, that's something, anyway, my inner voice said.

The driver threw the Tahoe into reverse and started backing away at great speed. We stepped into the center of the street. Heavenly brought her gun up. She fired three times. The first two bullets ricocheted off the pavement. The third shot caught the front passenger tire. It exploded. The Tahoe slid sideways into a car parked at the corner. There was a satisfying sound of crunching metal and broken glass. The SUV stopped.

I ran forward. When I reached the driver's side door I brought my SIG up and pointed it at the driver's head.

"Hands on the steering wheel," I said.

He seemed confused.

"Do it now," I said.

He rested his hands on top of the steering wheel, yet kept staring at me. I opened the car door, grabbed his shoulder, and yanked him out. Heavenly was on my right, holding her gun with one hand, aiming at the driver's core. I pushed him against the car. Apparently, he had done this sort of thing before, because he immediately assumed the position. I used my foot to kick his legs apart and back farther and farther until he was positioned as if he were doing push-ups against the SUV. He couldn't have made a move against me without first attempting to stand up, which would have given me plenty of time to retaliate. Even so, I was careful, using quick taps of my fingertips to search the areas where he might have been carrying a weapon and a few where no one goes armed. He was clean. I wondered if he had a weapon inside the vehicle, yet I didn't bother to look.

"We don't have time for this," Heavenly said.

She was right. I didn't know what the Philadelphia Police

Department's response time was, but it couldn't have been more than a couple of minutes.

I found his wallet and removed his driver's license—I saw instantly that it had been issued by the State of Minnesota. I tossed the wallet inside the SUV and stuffed the driver's license into my pocket.

"Who are you working for?" I asked.

He didn't answer.

"Why are you following us?"

He didn't answer that question, either.

"This isn't getting us anywhere," Heavenly said.

He turned his head and smirked.

"I'm going to fuck you up, bitch," he said.

Heavenly kicked him in the groin just as hard as she could from behind. He screamed. His knees buckled, and his hands came off the SUV. He fell against the asphalt. His hands cupped his balls, and he rolled into a fetal position. He moaned like a dying man.

"Happy?" I said.

I was speaking to the driver, yet it was Heavenly who smiled brightly and nodded her head.

We returned to the Focus; I walked backward, making sure the driver of the SUV didn't pop up and start shooting at us. I slid inside the car and drove away, not bothering with the seat belt until we were back on Broad Street. I did not see any police cars; I didn't hear any sirens.

"That was fun," I said.

"Who was he?"

"I call him the man in the sports coat. He was following me when we were in Bayfield. He was the guy I chased out of the bar right before you were shot."

"I should have put a bullet in him."

"Maybe."

I pulled the driver's license out of my pocket and handed it to her. Heavenly dropped the sun visor and slid the mirror open. A small light flicked on, and she read the license.

"Weldon Lamm . . ."

"Weldon?"

"Really? You're going to make fun of the man's name—Rushmore?"

"Not me—Heavenly."

"Weldon Lamm, 126 East Ninth Street, St. Paul, Minnesota, 55101."

"126 East Ninth Street?"

"Is that significant?"

"I think that's the address for the Lowell Apartments in downtown St. Paul, a kind of unofficial halfway house. A lot of convicts coming out of prison stay there. It used to be convenient because it was a block away from the St. Paul PD. The cops and probation officers had an easy time keeping track of them. Not so much since the department was moved to the Griffin Building a few years ago."

"You think he's an ex-con?"

"I'll make a call tomorrow and find out."

"How did Weldon know we were in Philadelphia? He couldn't have followed us. I would have known."

"Someone must have told him."

"Who? El Cid?"

"That's one possibility."

Heavenly said the next name like it was a curse.

"Maryanne Altavilla."

"That's another."

SEVENTEEN

It was tough going to bed fifteen feet from Heavenly, but not for the reasons you might suspect. The fractured collarbone made her a restless sleeper; it was impossible for her to roll over or sleep on her side without piercing pain.

"Can I get you anything?" I asked at one point.

"No" was her flat response.

After that, I kept quiet.

When I woke in the morning, I found that Heavenly had moved to the rocking chair. She was dressed in shiny blue pajamas; I could see the corner of a bandage peeking out from under the collar.

"Morning," I said.

"Morning."

"Did you sleep well?"

"No."

Damn, McKenzie, what a dumb thing to ask.

"I need to take a shower and get cleaned up, but I waited because I didn't want to wake you," Heavenly said.

"You're very kind."

"Helluva girl, ask anyone. Do you mind if I go first?"

"Not at all."

"I already had an apple and an English muffin, so if you're hungry don't wait on me."

It took painful effort for her to extricate herself from the rocking chair. I nearly offered my assistance as she made her way to the bathroom, but thought better of it.

One dumb question at a time.

I glanced at my watch perched on a small bedside table. Eight fifteen; seven fifteen in the Twin Cities. I made my way to the kitchen, brewed a pot of coffee, and toasted a bagel that I slathered with, yes, Philadelphia Cream Cheese. Afterward, I watched the Weather Channel.

At exactly eight-oh-one Minnesota time, I made a call on my cell phone. He answered the way he always did.

"Commander Dunston."

"Hi, Bobby. It's me."

"McKenzie? It's . . . it's eight o'clock. Since when do you get up before ten?"

"Hey, man. The sun is shining, the birds are singing—"

"What are you talking about? It's raining like hell."

"It is?"

"Where are you?"

"Philadelphia."

"Are you in trouble?"

"Of course not."

"Of course not—so why are you calling me at eight o'clock?"

"Because I knew you'd be in. You're the most punctual person I know. You're even worse than Nina."

"What does that have to do with anything?"

"I need a favor."

"Here it comes."

"The computer sitting on the right-hand side of your desk. Can you type in a name for me, find out if he's in the system?"

"Some guy from Philadelphia?"

"No, no—he's from Minnesota."

"You want me to check him out because . . . ?"

"He's been following me for about a week."

"Why?"

"Bobby, this is starting to be an awfully long conversation, and I know how much you hate talking on the phone."

"Why, McKenzie?"

I told him. It took longer than when I explained myself to the FBI because Bobby kept asking questions. I was surprised that, like Nina, he took a keen interest in Heavenly's health and well-being, especially since he's been anxious to arrest her for one thing or another for years.

"Jeezus, McKenzie," Bobby said. "You can't get into enough trouble at home, you have to travel now? What's this guy's name?"

"Weldon Lamm, 126 East Ninth Street, St. Paul, Minnesota, 55101."

"Lowell Apartments? Just a sec."

While I waited, Heavenly stepped out of the bathroom. She looked gorgeous, which didn't surprise me. But I had to ask—how did she manage it with one arm, her makeup, her hair; the clingy shirtdress with all those snaps up the front?

"Magic," she told me. "Who are you talking to?"

"Bobby Dunston."

"Ask him why he wants to put me in jail."

"I can tell you that—you're a menace to society."

"McKenzie?" Bobby said.

I removed my hand from the cell phone's microphone.

"Yeah," I said.

"Lamm is an all-purpose asshole. He did time for receiving stolen property. Apparently an insurance investigator caught him attempting to pawn a boatload of jewelry. That was his first jolt in prison. The second, he shot a guy over a gambling debt. I have no idea who owed whom. His latest—the state kicked him after doing thirty-eight months of a five-year sentence for sexual assault. He raped a teenage girl who was living in his building. McKenzie, the man's a registered sex offender. He should not be in Philadelphia. He should not have been in Wisconsin. He should not be anywhere except at the Lowell Apartments. The minute I'm off the phone, I'll be notifying his PO that the man is off the reservation."

"Okay."

"Do you know where he is?"

"No."

"The Philadelphia PD will be receiving a bulletin directly."

"Tell them that Lamm is driving a red Chevy Tahoe, probably a rental. Sorry, I don't have a license plate number."

"By the way. Barbecue. My place. Saturday. No excuse will be accepted. From you or Nina."

"I'll be there."

Heavenly waved to attract my attention.

"Tell the commander I said hi," she said.

"What was that?" Bobby asked.

"Heavenly Petryk says hi."

There was a long pause. When Bobby spoke again I could hear the grin in his voice.

"She's welcome to come to the barbecue, too," he said. "Provided she's not under arrest."

I hung up the phone. There must have been a smile on my face, because of the way Heavenly looked at me and said, "What?"

I took a lot less time in the bathroom than Heavenly had, but then I had two hands to work with and I didn't need to take time to clean and rebandage a gunshot wound. When I emerged, I found her sitting on the rocking chair, the flip phone in her hand. She was wearing her sling again. I mentioned it to her.

"I'm a glutton for punishment," she said. "But not that much punishment."

"Dr. Candy said it would take a few weeks."

"I've been counting the days, trust me." Heavenly held up the flip phone. "Marcus called. We're on for tonight."

"Where?"

"What is your favorite spot in Philadelphia?"

"I haven't been here long enough to have a favorite spot."

"Let me rephrase—what is your favorite spot in any decent-size city in America?"

I gave it a few moments thought. I like to travel, and when I travel . . .

"The ballpark," I said.

"Citizens Bank Park, where the Phillies play, because . . . ?"

Really, Petryk, you're quizzing me?

"Security," I said. "Metal detectors and pat-downs at the door make it harder to smuggle a weapon inside. Plus there are guards and cameras and twenty thousand potential witnesses depending on how the Phillies are drawing this year. Whose idea was it?"

"Mine."

"You really did get thirty-two on your ACT, didn't you?"

"Actually, I lied about that. I only scored a thirty."

"Well, you'll always be a thirty-two in my book. How do you want to spend the rest of the day?"

"Would it bore you to visit the Philadelphia Museum of Art?"

"Not at all. Although, in retrospect, that might have been an even more secure location."

"Except it closes at five P.M. on Tuesdays, and the doctor refused to meet until this evening."

"I wonder why."

"Yeah. It's not like he has a daytime job."

———

Third row center in the left field seats, I was eating a sandwich with sauce that dripped over my fingers onto the wax paper on my lap.

"Eww," Heavenly said. "What is that?"

"Called a Schmitter. Really good. Thinly sliced steak, cooked salami, fried onions, tomatoes, cheese. It's the sauce that makes it tasty, though—mayo, relish, ketchup, and Worchestershire."

"God, you're brave."

"I thought it was named after the Hall of Fame third baseman Mike Schmidt, the greatest Phillie of them all, but the woman at the food stand told me it was actually named after a beer that was brewed on Chestnut Hill, wherever that is."

Heavenly glanced at her watch. She had been doing that every few minutes since we arrived at Citizens Bank Park. I told her to stop.

"One of the great things about baseball, it doesn't have a clock," I said.

She kept looking anyway. It wasn't going to make the bottom of the third inning come any sooner, though, when we were scheduled to meet Dr. Tim Young. I wondered if his nickname had anything to do with Hall of Fame basketball player Dr. J—Julius Erving—the greatest 76er of them all. Heavenly picked the ballpark, yet it was Doc who selected the exact location, the condiment island in the open area behind section 141 and to the left of Harry the K's Broadcast Bar & Grille. I had already examined the ground, taking careful note of the restrooms, escalator, and food stands; it's where I found the Schmitter. I was particularly interested in the nearest exit—the left field gate behind the Schmitter, where a man in a hurry could dash, hiding himself in the huge, crowded parking lot beyond.

I finished the sandwich and licked the sauce off my fingers, disgusting Heavenly even more. I wiped my hands with a couple of napkins and deposited them and the remains of the meal beneath my seat. I lifted my beer out of the cup holder,

took a long pull, leaned back in the seat, and sighed content-
edly.

Heavenly looked at her watch.

"Would you relax," I said.

"Did it ever occur to you that Doc Young might shoot us on
sight?"

"The man's a professional. He's here to conduct business.
He's not going to take the risk of killing us in front of twenty-
five thousand baseball fans—I'm surprised the Phillies are
drawing so well, being ten games back in the middle of July.
Anyway, if he shoots us, it'll be after we leave the ballpark."

"So we have that to look forward to."

"You're awfully jumpy given what you do for a living."

Heavenly adjusted her sling.

"I've been reviewing the situation," she said.

"Isn't there a song . . . ?"

"McKenzie . . ."

"You're just upset because you set off the alarm when we entered the ballpark."

"Do you know how many places have metal detectors at the
door? Every time I walk through one I'll need to explain myself."

"The rent-a-cops supervising the detectors—they seemed
happy to talk it over with you."

"I see my future. It's already old."

Heavenly made a production out of looking at her watch
again, tugging at her sling, folding her good arm over it, and
staring out at the field. It was the top of the second, two outs,
with the Marlins trying to get something going. She smiled
slightly when she caught me looking at my own watch out of the
corner of my eye.

Bottom of the third inning, the Phillies coming to bat. The con-
cession stands were as quiet as they were ever going to be—

most fans were in their seats, many of them finishing up whatever food or beverages they had purchased before the game began. They wouldn't be queuing up to get more until after the Phillies recorded their third out. Given their offensive output lately, I figured that might come in a hurry.

Only one man was standing at the condiment island. I recognized him as we approached—Marcus Camby. He had a pleased expression on his face that quickly turned to concern when he saw Heavenly's sling.

"What happened?" he asked. "Are you all right?"

"I zigged when I should have zagged," Heavenly said.

The explanation didn't seem to please him at all.

"The man who followed you last night."

The way Camby spoke—it was a promise of retribution. Heavenly heard it, too. She rested her hand on his wrist.

"It happened before I came to Philadelphia," she said. "I didn't wear the sling last night because I didn't want you to worry."

She's the best, my inner voice told me. *She lies even better than you do.*

Camby flung a nod in my direction.

"Who's your friend?"

"Just that—a friend."

A small, frail-looking old man approached the island; he was dressed as if he were playing golf. Two men who looked like bouncers at the kind of joint that uses velvet ropes to keep the unfashionably attired at bay stood on each side of him.

"Where's my $50,000, Petryk?" he asked. "Where's my violin? I should have one or the other from you."

Heavenly's response was to study him for a few beats.

"Are you staring at me?" the man asked. "Why are you staring at me? Stop it. I said stop it. Marcus, she's staring at me."

"Heavenly," Marcus said. "You know better."

She moved her gaze to me.

"It's not him," she said. "He's not the Voice."

"No. He's just a cog in the machine."

"Machine?" the old man said. "Do you know who you're talking to?"

"Doc," Camby said.

"That's right. I'm Tim Young. Cog in a machine? I could have you fucking killed where you stand."

He spoke loudly enough that the home plate umpire could probably hear him, but being used to such language allowed the game to continue.

"Where's my goddamn money?" Doc wanted to know.

"Shhh, Doc." Camby rested his hand on Young's arm the way Heavenly had rested hers on his. "We're here to talk."

"Then somebody had better start talking pretty goddamn fast."

"You've already told me everything I need to know," I said.

Young pointed at me.

"Who is this asshole?" he asked. "Why is he staring at me?"

"Friend of Heavenly's," Camby said.

"Yeah, yeah, yeah—McKenzie."

There's no doubt now, my inner voice said.

"You're being played, Doc," I said.

"You fucking talk to me like that? You come to my town and talk like that?"

His fists were clenched, and he bounced up and down on the balls of his feet; his face was red with exertion. He looked to me as if he were having an aneurysm. There's dangerous and then there's nuts. I decided Doc Young was both. I wondered how he ever managed to secure a position of responsibility.

"Stealing the Countess Borromeo, I thought that you might have been the one who commissioned it, Doc," I said. "I was hoping it was you. It wasn't, though. The question you just asked proves that it wasn't."

"What do you know about it?"

"Heavenly had volunteered to return the $50,000 when she realized the Countess wasn't to be had. Instead, someone shot her and stole the money from her room. You would have known that if you were the Voice, what Heavenly calls him."

"Wait," Camby said. "He shot you?"

Heavenly nodded; the lie I told did not register on her face.

"Sonuvabitch," Camby said.

At least he believed me, I thought. But Doc . . .

"Bullshit," he said.

"Real shit," I told him. "Trevor Ruland and Heavenly were hired over the phone. Ruland was supposed to acquire the Countess; Heavenly was supposed to pay him off and deliver it to . . . well, to you, apparently. You know all this, though. They didn't know who their employer was, but you—you don't like conducting business on the phone."

"Fucking NSA, fucking FBI, ain't no privacy anymore."

"Uh-huh. This Voice came to you personally with his offer. He was going to drop a four-million-dollar Stradivarius in your lap, *negotiate* with you to sell it back to the rightful owners for half of its insured value, and split the proceeds. I bet the two of you did the exact same thing sometime in the past."

"You can't prove that."

"All the Voice required to put the plan into motion was fifty large in seed money."

"Fifty-five."

"Only the plan went to hell when someone beat him to the violin and the insurance company announced that it wouldn't pay a ransom. It should have ended there. The Voice should have returned your money. Oh, well—better luck next time. Except he really wanted that violin. So he convinced some dumb schnook to pony up a $250,000 reward and convinced another dumb schnook to go after the real thieves. Problem was—what to do about you? You have a volatile personality, Doc, if you don't mind me saying so."

"Fuck you."

"If the Voice had recovered the Stradivarius and sold it back for a paltry quarter mil—without sharing—I bet you'd be offended. And he wasn't going to share. He killed Ruland and tried to kill Heavenly partly to keep them from kibitzing; he knew they both would have snatched the violin if they could. But mostly it was to convince you that it was someone else who ruined your day."

"That's not the way I heard it."

"The Voice suckered us both, Doc. I was supposed to find the violin and return it for the reward so you'd think I was the one who fucked you over and not him, and if that didn't work, guess what—he would have had you killed, too."

Doc shook his head as if I had fumbled the punchline of a good joke.

"You believe this?" he asked.

Camby didn't answer. Doc gestured with his head at one of his thugs.

"Get 'im," he said.

The thug left the island. The crowd cheered. I glanced at the scoreboard. The Phillies had scored two runs and had two on base with nobody out. Funny what you miss when you're not paying attention.

A moment later, the thug returned, Vincent Donatucci following closely behind. The old man moved easily. Apparently, he was in better shape than I had thought.

"Hello, Vince," I said.

"You don't look surprised to see me," Donatucci said.

"I knew you were here last night when you sent your punk to kill Heavenly—"

"He did what?" Camby asked.

"Let me guess—Paul Duclos told you I was coming to Philadelphia," I said.

"The man's been calling me twice a day; wants his violin back," Donatucci said.

"You disappoint me, Vince. But then, I always hate to see a good man go bad."

"Vince? What happened to Mr. Donatucci?"

"You don't deserve a mister."

"They owe me, McKenzie."

"No, they don't."

"Enough," Doc said.

"What did he tell you?" Donatucci asked.

"Exactly what you said he'd tell me."

"He knew the story because it's the truth," I said.

"McKenzie, McKenzie, McKenzie—where's the violin?" Donatucci said. "And don't you dare tell me that you don't know."

"If I did, I would have turned it in by now just like I promised."

"Hell you woulda," Doc said.

"Why not? What do I have to gain besides the $250,000?"

"We could hold out for more. Find a foreign buyer. Lots of possibilities. You tellin' me stories? I'll tell you a story. You stole the Countess from Vince—"

"Is that what he said?"

"You killed the asshole in Duluth after he did his part, then you and Petryk here, you went into business for yourselves. Together, you came to my town to see if I'd make the same deal with you that I made with Vince; half of whatever we get for the Strad. But McKenzie, I don't fuck over my friends."

Wow.

"I suppose it would be useless to try and convince you otherwise," I said.

"Convince me," Camby said. "Why did you come here?"

I pointed at Donatucci.

"I came for him." To play off Camby's obvious affection for

her, I added, "And to protect Heavenly in case the good doctor thought she was the one playing him."

"He's lying," Donatucci said. "He didn't know I was the one on the flip phones."

"I guessed a long time ago. I wanted Doc to confirm it. He did."

"I promise you, McKenzie and Petryk have the Countess. They're just trying to shake you down."

"I'll make it easy for you." Doc was still bouncing on the balls of his feet when he spoke; his face was still flushed. "You deliver the violin, I'll not only let you both live, I'll let you keep the fifty."

"Fifty-five," I said.

I had to give Heavenly credit. Throughout the entire episode, she didn't bat so much as an eyelash. She nudged me with her good arm.

"Hungry?" she asked.

I nearly reminded her of the Schmitter. Instead, I said, "I could eat."

"Let's get a cheesesteak."

"Pat's or Geno's?"

"We'll decide on the way."

"You think you can just walk away?" Doc pounded his chest. "From me?"

"We don't have your violin, Doc." I pointed at Donatucci. "He does. You don't believe us—there's nothing we can say."

I directed Heavenly toward the left field gate.

"What are we going to do?" she whispered.

"Get as far away from these guys as possible."

I glanced over my shoulder.

"Don't do this, McKenzie," Donatucci said. "Don't you do this."

"How far do you think you'll get?" Doc said. "How far? This is my town."

The inning had ended, and many more fans were moving to the food stands and restrooms, which might have been why Doc's thugs didn't attempt to stop us. We weaved around them, walking briskly. When we reached the gate, I threw another glance over my shoulder. The two thugs were standing next to Doc Young, who was talking to Camby; Camby was nodding his head. Donatucci was on his cell phone.

I was about to say, "Run," but Heavenly broke into a sprint before I could.

I hadn't parked in the stadium's lot. Instead, I rented a spot at the Holiday Inn at Tenth and Packer just across from the stadium, partly because it was cheaper, but mostly because it allowed us to get out on the street quicker. Unfortunately, it was also much farther away. We had to cut through the stadium lot to reach it.

Running wasn't doing Heavenly's shoulder any good; she braced it with her right hand, but I knew it was hurting. I kept glancing over my shoulder; I couldn't see anyone following us, couldn't see anyone in the parking lot at all, and thought maybe we could slow down. It was because I was looking behind me that I didn't see Weldon Lamm until he was ten feet away and standing between us and where we wanted to go.

That's who Donatucci was calling on his cell, my inner voice told me—long after the information would have been useful.

Lamm was carrying a rifle.

I stopped when I saw it; I would have bet the ranch it fired a .243 Winchester slug.

Heavenly and I were trapped between parked cars with nowhere to go, Heavenly in front of me. I wanted to get past her, put myself between her and Lamm. She wouldn't move. Instead, she straightened up, almost as if she were accepting the situation, and slid her right hand into her sling.

Lamm brought the rifle up.

"I said I'd fuck you up," he said.

Heavenly shot him three times.

The bullets tore through her sling.

They lifted Lamm up and threw him onto the asphalt.

She pulled the Smith & Wesson out from under her sling and centered the sights on his unmoving chest.

At the same time, she shook her left arm; empty shell casings fell out of the sling.

"That hurt," she said. "Hot."

I thought, Heavenly couldn't fool the metal detectors at the entrance to the ballpark, but she had no trouble at all fooling the rent-a-cops that supervised them; they'd hovered around her, convinced that it was the bullet in her shoulder that set off the alarm, the poor woman.

"Don't move."

The order came from behind me.

I turned toward it.

Donatucci was standing there; he was breathing hard, and his face was flushed.

He was holding a handgun as if he knew how to use it.

C'mon, my inner voice said. *You're supposed to be too old to run.*

"Drop the gun, Petryk," he said. "Drop it now."

Heavenly let the S&W slip from her hand onto the pavement.

"Goddamnit, McKenzie—if you had just done what I asked," he said.

I was hoping to buy time with conversation, maybe convince him to let us go.

"We can still make this work," I said.

"You made your choice."

I gestured at his handgun and said, "Times have changed."

"Where's the violin?"

"In Bayfield."

"Where in Bayfield?"

"Give it up, Mr. Donatucci. If your wife knew what you were doing—"

Marcus Camby shot Donatucci in the back of the head.

He didn't say a word, just walked up to the old man from behind, pointed his own gun, and squeezed the trigger.

Donatucci's body lurched forward.

He fell at my feet.

I was surprised by the lack of blood.

Heavenly dove for her S&W.

"No, no," Camby chanted. "Leave it."

Heavenly straightened and moved away.

Camby brushed past me, bent at the waist, and picked up the gun.

"Are you all right?" he asked.

"Yes," Heavenly told him.

"I got this."

"Marcus—"

"You and McKenzie, get out of here. Get out of Philadelphia. I'll smooth it over with Doc, tell 'im Donatucci confessed before I shot him, so you won't need to be looking over your shoulder for the rest of your life."

Heavenly hugged him as best she could with her damaged arm.

"Thank you, Marcus," she said.

"Call me in a couple of months. We'll go dancing."

We walked to the Holiday Inn as casually as we could manage, found the Ford Focus, and fired it up. I drove randomly for half an hour to make sure we weren't being followed; drove longer than was necessary. It gave me a sense of control that I badly needed.

Heavenly suggested we stop at a tavern she knew near Logan

Square. We ordered drinks, yet barely sipped them while we watched the rest of the Phillies game on the TV above the bar. The home team won; good for them.

"You knew Donatucci was the Voice all along," Heavenly said.

"I suspected."

"Why didn't you tell me?"

"I was hoping I was wrong."

"How did you figure it out?"

"Donatucci was in Philadelphia a week or so before the Countess was stolen; I saw the receipt from a tour he took to see the Liberty Bell. The flip phones that were sent to you and Ruland were activated in Philadelphia. Doc Young was in Philadelphia."

"Intuitive thinking," Heavenly said.

"Also, you and Ruland were involved with Donatucci in the past. Lamm, who was busted by an insurance investigator while trying to unload stolen jewelry—I bet he was, too. Donatucci knew we were speaking to Ruland in Duluth because I told him several hours before the meeting; Lamm must have followed Ruland instead of us. He knew you were in Bayfield, but I didn't tell him that you were going under the name Caroline Kaminsky. Did you tell him, tell the Voice, I mean?"

"No."

"And yet he knew that, too. I thought Maryanne Altavilla was behind it all; at least I was hoping it was her, the way she behaved. I'll ask her about it when we get home."

"If you had it all figured out, why didn't we just stay in Minnesota?"

"What about Trevor Ruland? What about the bullet you're going to carry in your shoulder for the rest of your life? There's no hard evidence; nothing that would've held up in a courtroom, that's for sure. Donatucci would have gotten away with all of it. Lamm, too."

"You're saying we came here so you could manufacture a little justice?"

"Not really. I just wanted to know for sure if I was right. The justice part I was going to leave for later."

"Jesus, McKenzie."

"I wasn't going to kill him."

"No?"

"I was going to call Special Agent Beatty at the FBI and make him angry some more."

"Sure."

I had stashed the SIG Sauer in the glove compartment of the Ford Focus. When we returned to the car, I wrapped it in Heavenly's shredded sling; she assured me she had another at the B&B. I drove to Penn's Landing and walked along the wharf while Heavenly waited for me. When no one was looking, I let it slide into the Delaware River.

Following Heavenly's directions, I drove back to the B&B; we were forced to park two blocks away.

Once we were inside, Heavenly moved directly to the rocking chair as if that had been her destination all the while. She sat down, hugging her left arm close to her torso; she rested her right hand on the arm of the chair.

"I'm tired," she said.

"We need to think about getting out of Philly—the sooner the better."

"I'll take care of it."

"Heavenly—"

"I'm going to sleep here tonight. It's easier on my shoulder. If you want to use the big bed . . ."

"The double is fine."

She closed her eyes.

I made myself ready for bed as quickly and as quietly as I

could. When I emerged from the bathroom, I noticed that Heavenly was wearing her spare sling. She had kicked off her shoes and wrapped herself in a quilt that she had taken from the armoire. I extinguished the lights and crawled into the double.

"McKenzie?" she asked.

"Yes, sweetie?"

"I never shot anyone before. I never . . ."

"It's not an easy thing to live with," I told her.

"Goodnight, McKenzie."

"Goodnight, sweetie."

EIGHTEEN

The moment the Airbus rolled to a halt, passengers clogged the aisle and gathered their belongings from the overhead luggage compartments—and then stood quietly for several minutes while waiting for the door to be secured. It was a ritual that I did not join. I never minded being one of the last to leave a plane.

Slowly, the aisle cleared. Only a few of us remained, including Heavenly, who sat staring out the window at the Minneapolis–St. Paul International Airport terminal named after Charles A. Lindbergh. She had been the one to arrange our passage out of Philadelphia. From that moment to this I don't think she spoke more than twenty words.

"I'll get your bag," I said.

"No. Thank you. I decided to go on to Phoenix."

"Why?"

"Visit my mom." Heavenly gently massaged her shoulder. "Heal."

"I thought your mother lived in Denver."

"How naïve you are, McKenzie, believing a liar like me."

I yanked my bag out of the storage compartment and stood

staring at Heavenly's nylon carry-on for a couple of beats. I had to ask about the $50,000.

"I once told you," she said. "As long as I came out ahead—that's the main thing."

"You're welcome to stay with Nina and me."

"I know."

"Bobby Dunston has a rack of baby backs with your name on it."

"Tell him he was sweet to offer."

"Heavenly . . ."

"McKenzie . . ."

I leaned in, cupped her chin, and tilted her head toward mine. I came *this*close to kissing her on the lips. Instead, I kissed her forehead.

"Take care of yourself, sweetie," I said.

"You, too."

"Don't be a stranger."

I turned to leave. Heavenly called my name.

"Will you tell Nina something for me?" she asked.

"Sure."

"Tell her—we all have to be who we are in this world. Anything else is just pretending. It might be pleasant, but it never lasts."

"I'm not sure what that means."

"You're not supposed to. McKenzie, before you go, just out of curiosity, tell me—do you know who stole the violin?"

"What makes you think it was stolen?"

Nina was double-parked near the Frontier Airlines sign outside the entrance to the terminal. She was driving my Mustang, which annoyed me, I don't know why. She offered me the keys, but I told her to drive.

"Where's Heavenly?" Nina asked.

"She's going home."

"Where's that?"

"Damned if I know. Nina, when we get back to the condo, I'm going to ask you to take my bag upstairs while I take off. There's something I need to do, and now's as good a time as any."

"What exactly, if I may ask."

"I'm either going to save a marriage or shatter it into so many pieces it can never be saved."

"My experience, no outside force can help or hurt a marriage. Only the two people who are married can do that."

The first words out of the Maestro's mouth when I entered his house—"Do you know where the Countess is?"

Renée Peyroux, on the other hand, wondered if I was all right.

"You look tired," she said.

I asked for coffee, but that was just to get them sitting down. I positioned myself at the head of the kitchen table. Paul Duclos was on my left. Peyroux sat across from him on my right.

"Do you know where the Countess is?" Duclos repeated.

"I think so."

"Where?"

"Do you have the money?"

"Upstairs."

"Go get it."

Duclos left the room in a hurry. I turned to his wife.

"You never filed an insurance claim, did you?" I said. "That's why Midwest Farmers wasn't all that concerned about getting back the violin."

"What are you saying?"

"You were in Duluth on Thursday evening—with the Jacob Stainer violin. You knew that the Maestro wouldn't have the

Countess for Friday night's concert with the chamber orchestra; you knew at least one full day before it was taken. Didn't you?"

Peyroux refused to answer. I could hear the Maestro's footsteps drawing near.

"I need to know right now," I said. "Do you love your husband?"

"Yes."

"Do you love him so much that nothing else matters?"

"Yes."

"We'll see."

Duclos entered the room carrying a small suitcase. He set it on the table and opened it. The money was inside.

"Put it on the table," I said.

He did what I told him without asking why. It made for an impressive pile, sixty stacks of a hundred twenty-dollar bills and twenty-six stacks of a hundred fifty-dollar bills heaped on top of each other.

"Just for the record," I said, "the money came from Heather Voight, didn't it?"

The Maestro's eyes found Peyroux's. He quickly looked away.

His voice was soft. I had trouble hearing it.

"She's my friend," he said.

"More than a friend, I think, going all the way back to high school."

"Renée wouldn't help . . ."

"Yeah."

I put both hands on the bottom of the pile so the stacks wouldn't spill and pushed it toward Peyroux.

"What are you doing?" Duclos asked.

"Here—$250,000 for the safe return of the Countess Borromeo," I said. "No. Questions. Asked."

Peyroux stared at the money.

"Renée?" Duclos asked.

Peyroux rose from the table and left the kitchen.

"McKenzie, what's going on?" Duclos asked.

Even as I answered, I remembered what Chief Neville told me in Bayfield—was it already nine days ago? *You can't discount the nitwit factor.*

"Payback, you dumb sonuvabitch," I said. "You cheated on her, cheated on your wife with your high school sweetheart. You didn't think she knew?"

"It wasn't like that," Duclos said.

"What was it like? Tell me before she comes back."

He didn't. This time it was Peyroux's footsteps I heard nearing the kitchen.

"Do you love your wife?" I asked.

"Of course I do. This thing with Heather . . ."

"Do you love her so much that nothing else matters?"

"McKenzie . . ."

"It's a simple question."

"Yes."

"Then you might have a chance."

Peyroux returned to the kitchen. She was carrying a violin case. She set it on the table in front of Duclos and moved behind her chair. He hopped to his feet and actually stepped backward away from the table.

"It's not . . ." he said.

The Maestro slowly returned to the table and opened the case. He sucked in his breath; it seemed to take a long time before he exhaled. From where I was sitting I could see Harry Potter's lightning bolt scratched into the maple between the F-hole and the corner. Duclos reached out his hand. It was as if he wanted to touch the violin but was afraid.

"It's all right," Peyroux said. "You can keep it. Consider it part of the divorce settlement."

The word forced his head up.

"Divorce?" the Maestro repeated.

"I'm done, Paul."

"Divorce—you can't mean that."

"I was willing to share you with one mistress, but not two. I went to Bayfield to tell you that."

"You were in Bayfield?"

"No questions asked, remember?"

"Please, Renée. Please . . ."

"I knew about you and Heather in Chicago; knew that you drove up to Wisconsin when she opened her new restaurant that time I was in New York. I knew about Bayfield, too. You didn't tell me you were giving the concert until right before it happened because you didn't want me to go, but I knew. Herb Voight told me, Heather's husband. He had had enough just like me. I drove to Duluth, and he met me there; took me to Bayfield on his boat. I brought the Jacob Stainer with me because—I wasn't going to steal the Countess, that wasn't my intention—I was going to . . ."

Peyroux stopped speaking as if she was confused by her own story. She took a deep breath and started again.

"It was my intention to confront you and Heather in flagrante delicto so there could be no denials, no lies. It was my intention to force you to choose between her and me, and if you chose her, I was determined to take the Countess Borromeo home with me—it was mine, after all. I only lent it to you. But I didn't want to hurt you, either. I did, but I didn't want to hurt your music, the SPCO, so I brought your old violin, the Jacob Stainer, with me. I couldn't leave you without a violin. I couldn't do that to you.

"Only when I was about to knock on Heather's door—I became sick, Paul. Physically ill. I thought it was from seasickness, from bouncing around on that damn boat; why we even had to come by boat, I don't know. It made Herb comfortable, I guess;

gave him the sense of being in control. Yet once we reached land it became worse. And standing outside Heather's door—I was terrified, Paul. Terrified that you would pick her over me. I could barely stand, I felt so ill.

"I convinced Herb that we should leave, that what we were doing was crazy. I stumbled down the driveway; I had to stop and lean against a car because I felt so dizzy. That's when I saw it. The violin. In its case. I couldn't believe it. You left the Countess Borromeo on the front seat of your rental? The door wasn't even locked. I was so angry. I was angry at you. Angry at me. Angry at the damn violin. I grabbed it. I took it out of the case because—I know you told me about the GPS thing, but I didn't think of that. I thought—I don't know what I thought. That I was going to smash it. That I was going to throw it into the lake. I don't know. I didn't, though. I didn't do any of those things. All I wanted to do—I wanted to punish you.

"I'm sorry, Paul. I didn't fully appreciate how much you loved her. I didn't appreciate how much you needed her. I didn't know that you would react to her loss the way you did; that it would hurt you so much. I would have returned the Countess right away, except I was afraid if you found out what I had done, you would have left me. And because I was still angry—you told people the Stradivarius was stolen from the B&B instead of admitting where you really were."

"I did that because I was afraid you would leave me," Duclos said. "I was more afraid of that than I was of losing the Strad."

"It's too late. What I did to you . . ."

"What I did to you . . . It's not too late. It can't be too late. You taking away the Countess—I deserved that and more, but please, oh God, please, Renée, don't leave me."

"We can't go on like this. I can't. Heather . . ."

Peyroux brought her hands up and covered her face. She

began to weep; her cries were loud and filled with anguish. Duclos pushed the violin away and rounded the table. He took his wife in his arms.

"I'm sorry, I'm sorry, I'm sorry," he chanted.

He began to cry, too.

The Maestro and his wife embraced each other and slowly sank to their knees as one. The sound of their weeping blended into harmony.

"I'm sorry," he said.

"I'm sorry," she said.

Over and over again.

I don't know if they could hear me, but I told them anyway— "Whatever happens between you kids, please, at least keep the money."

I left my seat at the table and crossed the kitchen.

"I'll let myself out," I said.

An hour later, I set the nine-millimeter Ruger I had borrowed in the center of Maryanne Altavilla's desk. She stared at it for a long time.

"He's dead," she said. "I read it in the paper. Three paragraphs on page two; no explanation."

"I'm sorry."

"Is this what killed him?"

"No."

"Did you . . ."

"No."

She opened a drawer, placed the gun inside, and closed the drawer.

"I suspected it was him," she said. "I suspected Mr. Donatucci from the very beginning. I just didn't want to be the one . . ."

"When did you know he was involved?"

"I suspected him on Friday, the day the violin was stolen. You think I'm lying."

"I didn't say a word."

"Your expression."

"How did you know?"

"I didn't know. I suspected. I went to Bayfield as soon as I heard about the theft. I ingratiated myself with the FBI, Special Agent Beatty. You might not believe me, but when I want to, I can be awfully charming."

"I don't doubt that for a moment."

"I meant what I told you, though—if you had recovered the Stradivarius violin, paid off the thieves, I would have had you arrested for receiving stolen property and aiding and abetting an offender."

"I don't doubt that, either."

"I read the Queen Anne's ledger. I recognized Trevor Ruland's name. He had attempted an art theft in Omaha several years ago, one of Mr. Donatucci's old cases—I told you I studied his files at some length."

"Did you tell the FBI about Ruland?"

"Yes, although I didn't offer anything else, my early suspicions. I kept those to myself. After all, it was an improbable leap from Ruland's name to Mr. Donatucci's."

"Intuitive thinking is difficult to explain to those linear types."

"What happened next, though—I received a phone call after Midwest Farmers and the Peyroux Foundation announced in Bayfield, at the scene of the crime as it were, that they would pay only a nominal reward for the return of the violin and only upon the conviction of the thieves. It came within the hour, the call, Mr. Donatucci telling me what a catastrophic mistake it was."

Heavenly told him about the announcement; told the Voice, my inner voice reminded me.

"His outrage was shocking," Altavilla said. "His demeanor, his language, echoed his behavior the day he learned he had lost his job. It was—disheartening. It also convinced me that my earlier conclusion had been correct—Mr. Donatucci had stolen the Countess Borromeo and was now angry that he would not receive the payday he had anticipated. Soon afterward, however, I discovered that Ms. Petryk had also arrived in Bayfield. I knew of her from Mr. Donatucci's files as well, of course, the ones concerning the Jade Lily. It caused me to take a step back and reevaluate my position. If Mr. Donatucci had already acquired the Countess and Petryk was working with him, what was she doing in Bayfield? I became confused, a state in which I am not at all comfortable."

"That's when you sent the invitation."

"Yes."

"You wanted me to point the finger at Mr. Donatucci?"

"I wanted you to discover what happened to the Countess Borromeo. You knew Mr. Donatucci. You knew Heavenly Petryk. You enjoy tilting at windmills. The fact that he convinced you to undertake the identical task would seem to support my decision."

"The scene you played in the parlor of the Queen Anne . . ."

"I wished merely to introduce myself."

"Sure, and keep me motivated. What about the suggestion that Midwest Farmers didn't want me or anyone else to actually recover the violin?"

"Ms. Peyroux—I contacted her, informed her that I was investigating her claim personally. I must admit I found her cool and calm deportment during this affair quite impressive. I told her it was necessary to complete a certain amount of paperwork before we could process her claim, and yet she seemed almost indifferent to my request. As far as I am aware, she never officially filed a claim."

"There's a reason for that, but put it aside for now."

"Then tell me—why? Why did he do it, Mr. Donatucci? Why did he kill Trevor Ruland, have him killed? Why did he try to kill Petryk? Why continue working with Doc Young even after his original plan failed and the reward was taken off the table?"

"He did it for the money he thought he might make."

"I don't believe that."

"Pride, then."

"Is that so important?"

"He lost his wife; he had no family, just his job. Something he was extremely good at. They took that away from him. Pride was all he had left."

"You're suggesting it was all to prove that even at his age he was still smarter than everyone else?"

"It's as close as I can get."

"Where's the violin, McKenzie? You know, don't you?"

"Yes, but do you really want to know?"

"Of course I do."

"With no one going to jail? With no money changing hands?"

"What are you telling me, McKenzie?"

"Without charges for filing false police reports, without even a whiff of insurance fraud?"

Altavilla stared at me. Her eyes became large and bright with surprise, then narrowed considerably as she thought it through. She was one of those rare people—you could actually see her think.

"The violin was never actually stolen," she said. "That's why Peyroux didn't file a claim. How did I miss it?"

Wow, she really does think intuitively, my inner voice said.

"Apparently, I'm not nearly as smart as I think I am," Altavilla said.

"None of us are."

Altavilla stared some more.

"Favors." She spoke the word as if it were the answer to a question. "Favors for favors—that's the coin of your realm."

"I only do favors for my friends. Are you my friend, Mary-anne?"

"What exactly do you want from me, McKenzie?"

I gave Altavilla a rough idea.

"You're asking a lot," she said.

"Not so much when you consider the big picture."

"No one will ever know why Mr. Donatucci was killed. Or Weldon Lamm and Trevor Ruland either, for that matter."

"That's what I mean by big picture."

"What favor will you do for me in return?"

"You mean besides keeping quiet about Mr. Donatucci and never ever divulging to anyone that you *knew* exactly what he was doing long before people started getting shot, yet neglected to tell a soul including your employers? Or that you engaged an ex-cop of dubious reputation to do your dirty work?"

"I admit that would make my next performance review go more smoothly."

"Well, then, I suppose if you were to do a little of this for me, I could do a little of that for you."

"You make it sound less like a favor and more like extortion."

"That's certainly one way to look at it."

JUST SO YOU KNOW

It was a miracle.

A University of Wisconsin–Madison undergrad named Ellis was minding her own business, walking the Iron Bridge
Hiking and Nature Trail in Bayfield, when she came across a
suitcase that had been carelessly tossed into the creek bed. She
opened the suitcase and—holy moley Rocky—discovered a
four-million-dollar Stradivarius violin called the Countess Borromeo wrapped in towels and tucked inside. The authorities
speculated that the thieves who stole the violin must have
dumped it there as soon as they had learned that both the Midwest Farmers Insurance Group and the Georges and Adrienne
Peyroux Foundation for the Arts had publicly refused to negotiate with them for its safe return. The violin became, the authorities said, too hot to handle.

World-renowned concert violinist Paul Duclos was so thrilled
to regain his prized instrument that he gave Ellis the $250,000
reward, more than enough to pay off her student loans and give
her a head start when she graduated. He also agreed to play
another free concert in his hometown, this one thoroughly covered by the media. It was reported that the concert had attracted

a crowd that was even larger than those that regularly attend the city's annual Apple Festival. They all cheered when he played "shave and a haircut, two bits."

The Maestro's wife, the beautiful and spectacularly wealthy Renée Peyroux, had attended the concert with her husband. The happy couple stayed together at the New Queen Anne Victorian Mansion Bed and Breakfast. They were seen holding hands almost constantly on those rare occasions when they actually left their room. Photographs of the two, along with owner Connor Rasmussen, appeared in the *Ashland Daily Press*, on the B&B's Web site, and in its promotional literature.

A raucous party was held following the concert at the Bayfield Inn. Everyone who was anyone in Bayfield was there, including Zofia McLean, whose contract as the city's marketing and events manager had been renewed for another three years.

Heather Voight had volunteered one of her restaurants for the party. However, the offer was declined. And she was not invited to the party. No one seemed to know why. Sometime later, she and her husband of ten years separated pending divorce; Herb was last seen cruising in his boat somewhere on Lake Superior—without Maggie Pilhofer.

I wasn't in Bayfield for any of this; Jack Westlund gave me the heads-up. Instead, I stayed home with Nina.

I told her what Heavenly had said before I left her on the plane.

"I can't worry about her," Nina said. "I have my own daughter to worry about. But McKenzie, the way she lives, the things she does—she might get . . . Something terrible might happen to her."

"Oh, I don't know. Like the man said, only the good die young."